**From Award-winning author
Denise Domning**

THE FINAL TOLL

PRAISE FOR THE
SERVANT OF THE CROWN MYSTERIES

"Domning brings the English country-side alive with all the rich detail of a Bosch painting. CSI 12th century style."
— Christina Skye, *New York Times* best-selling author of *A Highlander for Christmas*

"Pure and unapologetically Medieval ... Five solid stars."
— Kathryn LeVeque, *USA Today* best-selling author of *The Wolfe*

"Fascinating details of Medieval life"
— Catherine Kean, author of *Dance of Desire*

RING FOR THE ANGELS!

Sir Robert of Offord dies mysteriously just after accusing his new wife of adultery and his son-by-marriage wants the shire's new Crowner to prove the knight was murdered. Instead, Sir Faucon de Ramis discovers that a bell owned by the dead man is missing. But who could have taken it— the daughter who loved it as a child, the knight who wants it as collateral, or the prior who wishes to restore it to its holy purpose of calling the angels? Follow Warwick-shire's new Servant of the Crown as Sir Faucon embarks on his most unusual and convoluted hunt yet.

Other books

For Children
Moosie and Bear

Historical Romance
Winter's Heat
Summer's Storm
Spring's Fury
Autumn's Flame
A Love for All Seasons
The Warrior's Wife
The Warrior's Maiden
The Warrior's Game
Lady in White
Almost Perfect
Awaken the Sleeping Heart

Novellas
An Impetuous Season (Kansas, 1870s)
Perfect Poison, A Children of Graistan novella

Servant of the Crown Medieval Mystery
Season of the Raven
Season of the Fox
Lost Innocents
The Final Toll

Co-written
Men-ipulation

Epigraph

Laudo Deum verum, plebem voco, congrego clerum; Defunctos ploro, nimbum fugo, festa decoro.

I praise the true God, I call the people, I assemble the clergy; I bewail the dead, I dispense storm clouds, I do honor to feasts.

My Apologies

Mea culpa to everyone who waited far too long for this book. 2018 turned out to be a year full of twists, turns, overwhelming failures, and unbelievable successes. That included my inability to prove whodunnit to Faucon, who persisted (for more than two months over my objections) until he got it right.

As always, I offer my apologies to the people of Warwickshire for absconding with your county, adding places that don't exist and parsing your history to suit my needs. Beyond that, I've done my best to recreate the 12th Century as accurately as possible.

The Final
Toll

DENISE
DOMNING

THE FINAL TOLL

Copyright © Denise Domning 2018

ISBN: 978-1790354399

EDITED BY: Martha Stites and Kimberly Spina

COVER ART DESIGN: Denise Domning

Printed in the United States of America, First paperback edition: December, 2018

Horarium (The Hours)

Matins	12:00 midnight
Lauds	3:00 A.M.
Prime	6:00 A.M.
Terce	9:00 A.M.
Sext	12:00 noon
None	3:00 P.M.
Vespers	6:00 P.M.
Compline	9:00 P.M.

Martinmas

I jerk into consciousness. Pain wracks my body, and my soul. Frantically, I reach deep within me, seeking His holy presence.

There is nothing.

My heart breaks. The punishment of the scourge wasn't enough. I am no longer a vessel for His will. Despair joins the fire that consumes my back.

Only then do I recognize that I lie face down on a cot. With my head resting to one side I can see a tiny tallow lamp atop the stool set near my head. Its wee flame batters valiantly at the enclosing night.

Light in the dark hours is a luxury allowed only in our infirmary. My precious privacy has been invaded! Moaning, I shift, intending escape, but I haven't the strength to move, much less walk.

"Ah, you are with us once more, Sister Cellaress." Mother Superior speaks from near my feet. Although the abbess of our house is the younger, her voice quavers like an old woman's. I am incapable of turning my head to look at her.

"You vowed not to interfere," I whisper because it hurts to draw breath. All the better that I am too weak to express my outrage.

Our prioress already dislikes me as much as I dislike her. The noblewoman who shepherds our convent is everything the men of this world expect of the daughters of Eve. Plump and sweet-natured, she rules with a gentle hand, one ignorant of the rigor necessary to forge saints from sinners. Nor will she heed me when I tell her that her gentleness cheats those under her care of our rightful seats at our Lord's table. Goodness is not enough. The path of righteousness requires mortification of the flesh and self-abnegation.

"You have gone too far this time, Sister," Mother chides with unexpected harshness for her. "It is a miracle you survived long enough for that child to find you. Sister Infirmaress says your wounds already fester. By my command, you will confine yourself to the infirmary until you are completely healed." She pauses. "And I have confiscated your scourge."

Even though I despise her for her ignorance, I forgive her. The men who control her hoard the truth, scheming to keep our Lord to themselves, believing all women undeserving of His love.

Much to my surprise with my act of forgiveness the barest hint of Life stirs within me. I breathe out as I understand His message. I have not failed. Instead, it is my time, my time to join Him and the sweet innocents I sent ahead of me.

But that cannot be. We are only eleven when there must be twelve.

With that thought peace overtakes me. I drift back into unconsciousness, certain I will not make my journey alone.

Chapter One

Leading his borrowed horse, Faucon de Ramis strode steadily toward his new home at Blacklea, eyes narrowed and jaw tight. Dressed in a tunic and chausses of hunter's green, he wore a boiled leather hauberk and an old brown cloak that the day's chill wind tossed as it howled through the fields and orchards that spread out before him. God's breath pummeled the rise of earth on which the villagers had built their homes, tearing at thatched roofs and slamming unattended shutters.

All of Blacklea's folk were in the orchard for the day. The adults, dusky homespun blankets cloaking their jewel-bright attire, manned ladders and baskets as their children scampered like squirrels along knobby branches, claiming the last of this year's fruit.

His villagers. Although Faucon hadn't lived in Blacklea a full two months, it already felt more like home to him than had either his father's hall or his foster father's keep. Then again, he had never expected to have a home of his own. He was a second son, the son traditionally given to the Church.

And, priest he would have been if not for his brother's accident. Faucon glanced at Will, or rather not-Will, for the man who had awakened days after taking a severe blow to his head wasn't the brother Faucon remembered. Will was also afoot, walking between their mounts, whistling a bawdy tune. Like everything else he'd done since appearing unexpectedly almost two weeks ago, even Will's choice of song rang false. Although Faucon was grateful that his brother wasn't screaming like a madman or hunkering in a corner, rocking and clutching at his head, almost two weeks spent in constant contact with his sibling had introduced him to a man he wasn't much sure he cared to know.

"Sir Faucon?"

Faucon looked over his shoulder at Alf. Tall and fair-haired, the former miller and soldier, now Faucon's man-at-arms, lagged a polite distance behind the two better-born knights. Lashed to the saddle of Alf's piebald nag was the skinned and gutted roebuck that Faucon and Will had taken in Lord Graistan's chase just after Prime this morning.

As Alf caught his master's gaze the soldier gave a jerk of his head in the direction of the well-traveled road behind them. Four mounted men had appeared in the distance, making their way along that thoroughfare at an easy walk. Despite that they wore only unmarked leather hauberks with no helmets on their heads, Faucon knew them. Sir Alain's men had appeared here and there on the road over the past week, always following at a discreet if ominous distance.

What little joy Faucon had managed to wring from this day dissipated. He turned his gaze back to the village ahead of him. Not only had they taken their roebuck far too quickly, now the sheriff was once again reminding him that he also hunted, his prey being this shire's new Coronarius. Faucon's mouth twisted. As if Sir Alain hadn't made his threat clear enough by way of the assassins he'd sent not long ago.

Will's whistle faltered. That brought Faucon's attention back to his brother. They favored their mother, their faces wearing the stamp of the de Vere family: black hair, broad brow, lean cheeks, and long nose. As did Faucon, Will wore a closely-trimmed beard, choosing that style to hide a chin they agreed was too pointed. With Will wearing the same style hauberk and green and brown attire, they looked almost like twins. The only difference was that the hair at Will's temples was already silver, he being Faucon's elder by two years.

No expression filled his brother's dark gaze. "What is it?" Will asked.

"Naught," Faucon replied with a shake of his head and a casual shrug.

His brows lifted, Will studied the settlement before them. "I vow, Pery," he said with a laugh, using Faucon's pet name. Pery was short for Peregrine and a play on the meaning of Faucon. "I look upon this place and am once again awed by your incredible good fortune. Our uncle must truly love you. Not only has he arranged for you to have your own village, he's given you an income! Why, twenty pounds a year is more than I will inherit when our father passes."

Rather than joy for a beloved brother, subtle rancor soured Will's words. It was a reminder that Will understood just how damaged his accident had left him. So too did he understand why their father had diverted Faucon from his monastery school— and the potential of celibacy— to make a knight of him.

"Hardly a gift, Will," Faucon replied, once again scanning the fields and orchards that lay between them and Blacklea. "Not only must I pay rent to Lord Rannulf, but I also support both my clerk and Alf. You've seen how much of my time is consumed by the tasks delegated to this new position of mine. Is this not the first day since your arrival that I've been free to please myself?"

"True enough," Will agreed, rancor giving way to a hint of satisfaction. "Better you than me, Brother. Not only do I question if your new duties befit a knight, but

I know I'd find your doings boring."

Faucon couldn't disagree with his brother over uninteresting work. There hadn't been an intriguing death since that of Jessimond of Wike. Of the six corpses he'd examined since then, only one had been a murder. But the murderer— an almost penniless cottager— had killed for food and had been caught in the act.

Pity for the man shot through Faucon. The wretch owned little more than his knife, his cup, and the clothes on his back. With no one in his village willing to vow they'd bring him before the justices when called, he'd been imprisoned in the sheriff's keep at Killing-worth. Without the coin to buy himself free or kin to feed him, he would surely starve unless some charitable townsman chose to save him.

"Sir Faucon!" a boy shouted from the field at Fau-con's right. It was the lad who tended the village geese. Today, his feathered charges grazed among the stub-bled remains of autumn wheat, seeking what seeds might be left after the humans, cows, hogs, and sheep had done their gleaning.

As Faucon lifted his hand in acknowledgment, the goose boy started toward him at a trot. The blanket tied around his shoulders flapped as he ran, startling his birds. They honked the alarm and scattered.

"Sir, Lady Marian said I should warn you that a foreign knight came looking for our new Crowner," the lad called as he came, using the title the English -speak-ing folk had given Faucon's new position. "He waits for you at your house."

Although Faucon understood the commoners' guttural tongue well enough, he frowned at the word *foreign* until he realized the boy meant only that the stranger wasn't from Blacklea. "Many thanks for the warning and for delivering the message," he called back.

"By chance do you know if men came from Graistan with our horses?"

"Aye, sir. Walked past me not long ago, they did," the boy replied with a grin and a wave, pleased at having won his new master's notice and gratitude.

The boy's cheery enthusiasm teased a scornful laugh out of Will. "Yokels," he said with a shake of his head, then went back to whistling his tune.

Faucon's jaw tightened until he thought bone might shatter. More than anything he wanted to ask his brother when he intended to depart. He couldn't. He was trapped in the role of gracious host, and there he would stay until Will either chose to leave or lost himself in one of his mad fits.

To the warble of his brother's lilt they made their way past the orchard, Faucon exchanging greetings with his folk. Once through the flimsy gateway that stood in the weathered and even flimsier wooden wall encircling the mound, the track became little more than a narrow and deeply-cut footpath. That forced them to walk single-file up the face of the mound. The higher they climbed, the closer the cottages stood to the path until Faucon could have stretched out either arm and touched a door.

The top of the mound had been flattened by men from some long-forgotten age who had then used the local reddish stone to build a structure upon it. That building was naught but tumbled ruins that grew now ever more sparse. Not even fear of the dead prevented the villagers from plundering the past to create their future. The stones had been used throughout the village, including for their tiny church. That chapel with its newer, square tower stood among the homes of Blacklea's wealthiest inhabitants, among them the erstwhile steward.

The remainder of the mound top belonged to Blacklea's landlord, much to Faucon's benefit. Enclosed by low stone walls were the gardens that fed him, several paddocks, and a pasture for his horse, as well as a stable and a kitchen shed. As with the church, the house that presently belonged to Faucon had also risen from that ancient ruin. Three times the size of the largest cottage and also capped with slate, his new home had thick defensive walls, but no keep tower for a final refuge.

Faucon's gaze flickered across its front wall to linger longingly on the three closely-spaced arrow slits cut into the stone. Those defensive openings marked what was a private bedchamber, fitted out with a comfortable curtained bed, his to use as long as he lived here. That was, unless he had a visitor. Will presently slept in that bed while Faucon bore Alf company in the hall, both of them taking their rest on straw-stuffed pallets.

Sighing, his gaze shifted to the wooden stairway that clung to the exterior wall, leading to a doorway raised a storey above the earth. Beneath the steps, their backs to the house as they sheltered from the wind, were four men and a lad. The men were Graistan's grooms, or so said their pale blue tunics, come to reclaim their lord's hunting horses. The lad, dressed in vibrant yellow and green, was Robert, son of Blacklea's steward Sir John and his wife Lady Marian. Not yet old enough to be squired, Robert played a string game with one of the younger grooms while the other three men diced.

As Alf turned his horse to take the carcass it bore to the kitchen shed, Faucon and Will brought their borrowed mounts to a halt at the foot of the stairs. The grooms rose and Robert tangled his string around his fingers, then skipped and hopped his way to join Blacklea's new master.

"Sir Faucon! Maman is fetching food and drink for your visitor. Look at what he gave me," Robert finished, wiggling his string-bound fingers at his benefactor, the same groom who had just claimed the reins of Faucon's borrowed mount. "Now I know how to play my own game without Mimi." Robert pined for his older sister Marianne, who had just begun her fostering with the sisters at Nuneaton.

"That was kind of him," Faucon replied with a smile.

It was easy to like the lad. Not only was he a handsome, fair-haired boy, he'd inherited his mother's cheerful disposition. For that reason Faucon was considering Marian's request that he take her son as his squire for as long as he lived at Blacklea and acted as the shire's Coronarius.

It was the thought of becoming the boy's teacher that made him ask, "Did you thank the man? A knight always offers thanks when he receives a gift."

Robert grinned. "I did, because I was very glad to have this gift."

Just then Robert's dam rounded the corner of the house. Lady Marian moved at her usual bold pace with her head raised to a proud angle. Braced on her arms was a tray on which sat a pitcher, a half loaf of bread, and a wedge of cheese. The woman who had once claimed Faucon's new home as her own and who still served as its lady wore a fine green mantle atop her blue work-a-day attire. Her plain face was framed by a clean white headcloth.

As usual, her lips were lifted in a smile and her blue eyes sparkled. That was, until she saw Will. Instantly, Marian's pace slowed. She bowed her head until her face was shielded in the folds of her head covering.

Halting well out of reach of either Faucon or his brother, she gave a quick bend of her knees. "Well come home, Sir Faucon, Sir William," she said, her voice lowered to the soft tones expected of a well-bred woman. "Sir Faucon, Sir Adam of Bagot arrived a short while ago. He insisted on waiting for you even though

I couldn't say when you might return. Thus did I suggest he take his ease in your hall. He has enjoyed our fresh cider, but with the hour growing late, I invited him to partake of our midday meal. This I did with the warning that our meal is simple and the only thing I could offer him for drink better than cider was ale."

Irritation stirred sharply in Faucon. Although Marian had made no complaint against Will, her unnatural reticence in his presence said she didn't trust his brother. Truth be told, neither did Faucon, but then he knew how unpredictable Will could be. Marian didn't.

"Many thanks, Lady Marian. I can bear your tray into the hall for my guest if you do not mind returning to the kitchen a second time on my behalf, so my brother and I might also eat." As he spoke, he stretched out his arms to take her burden, his irritation with Will growing. It cut him to the quick that he had to speak with such awkward formality to a woman he thought of as a friend.

"But of course, sir," Marian replied, her gaze still downcast as she transferred the tray into his care.

Without lifting her head, she extended a hand to her son. The instant Robert's fingers curled around hers she swiftly retreated around the house, dragging her child with her. Faucon watched her go, knowing he'd see no more of her or Robert this day. She'd send another servant with their meal rather than enter the hall whilst Will was in it.

"I make her nervous," his brother said flatly, also watching Marian's swift retreat.

"Not at all," Faucon lied. Having to tell polite lies was yet another thing he disliked about playing host to Will. He started up the steps with the tray. "She's but modest."

Just in case, he added, "And devoted to her husband."

Will snorted at the mention of Blacklea's steward as he followed Faucon. "I don't understand why you keep a crippled man to do a job that requires mobility, any more than I understand why you keep that rude clerk of yours. I'll play Father's role and ask you what good either of them does you."

Faucon's eyes narrowed. This wasn't the first time Will had said this. He stopped on the landing before the thick oaken door with its metal bossing. Many an old scar marked that arched wooden panel, suggesting it had held back at least one wave of intruders. The door stood slightly ajar, and so it would remain as long as a fire burned on the hearth.

Shifting to face Will on the steps, he touched his shoulder to the oaken door. "As I have already said, I keep Brother Edmund at our Uncle Hereford's request just as Sir John remains at Blacklea because Lord Rannulf asked it of me. But know this. Even if neither bishop nor baron had made their requests, I would still keep them both. Brother Edmund's knowledge of the law serves me well, and Sir John knows this place, all its folk and all its history, when I do not."

Then, with little hope that Will would cease his subtle jabs, Faucon pushed with his shoulder to open the door.

Chapter Two

This hall hardly warranted the name. A short table made of wooden planks set on braces with a pair of benches for seats took up most of the space. The hearth, a low stone pedestal, stood opposite the door beyond the far end of the table. It was so small its fire was more useful for light than heat. Although it could hold but a little wood, it still produced smoke enough to paint the ceiling and the upper reaches of the once-white walls the color of charcoal.

Sir Adam of Bagot sat at the table, a wooden cup cradled in his hands. If a warrior's habit put him on the bench facing the door, he'd shifted on the seat to watch the flames of the small fire. Behind him was the wall that divided Faucon's home into this public chamber and the bedchamber Will presently used.

As Faucon set the tray on the table, his visitor came to his feet. The middle-aged knight was a little taller than both Faucon and Will, who were of average height. Rather than chain mail, Sir Adam wore his sword belted over a vest of boiled leather atop a knee-length blue tunic that had been gusseted more than once to accommodate his increasing girth. Thick brown chausses covered his legs, while soft leather boots were cross-gartered to his calves. Wind-torn hair the color of rust streamed out from under a simple brown woolen cap. His thick beard and faint brows were a lighter, golden-red color, his eyes a startling shade of blue.

"I am Sir Faucon de Ramis, newly-elected Keeper of the Pleas for this shire," Faucon said in introduction, extending his hand, "and this is my brother Sir William de Ramis, presently visiting me from Essex. Sir Adam, is it?"

"It is, and well met, Sir Faucon," Sir Adam replied, his voice deep and rough-edged. His grin was easy. He wrapped his hand around Faucon's fingers, then Will's, as they met man-to-man.

With introductions complete, the older knight returned to his seat as Faucon pulled out the opposite bench and slid to its far end. That left Will sitting near the open door, in the path of the draft. It was a calculated and inhospitable choice on his part. A good host was expected to offer the warmest seats in his home to his guests.

His gaze locked on Faucon, Sir Adam said, "I'm told by Father Otto of Haselor that you, and not our sheriff, are now responsible for inspecting the bodies of those who die under suspicious circumstances. He named you our new 'Crowner.'"

Faucon smiled at that. His position had only been created at the Michaelmas court just past, and had been given the Latin title of *Coronarius*, which more or less meant 'a servant of the crown.' "That is what the commoners prefer to call me, but the title that best fits my duties is Keeper of the Pleas, as it is mine to see that all appeals for royal justice are scribed onto parchment and collected for that time when the Justices in Eyre arrive to hear the pleas," he said. "My clerk also makes note of my appraisals of the estates of those who murder, rape, or burgle, so our king can better determine what fine to collect from these wrongdoers.

"But to your point, Father Otto is correct," Faucon continued. "It is now my duty to view the dead and call the inquest jury to confirm murder when I deem it was done."

Sir Adam nodded, his expression considering. "Well

that will be quite the change for Sir Alain, won't it?"

So it had been, and not a happy one for the shire's sheriff. As with many sheriffs across the land, Alain had been accustomed to skimming a portion of the king's rightful fines as part of his own pay, sometimes legitimately, sometimes not. Faucon, who was allowed no compensation for his duty, knew for a fact that the sheriff had also accepted coins to ignore certain crimes.

Faucon crossed his arms on the table. "Now I have a question for you, Sir Adam. How is it you came to speak with Father Otto about me? He hardly seems the sort of man a knight seeks out to ask who now investigates suspicious deaths in our shire." Haselor was a tiny hamlet, and Father Otto as English as those he served.

"Ah that," the knight replied as he pushed his cup in suggestion toward the tray and the pitcher upon it.

Before Faucon could unwind his arms, Will took the man's cup. He shot his younger brother a quick smile. "I'll pour." It was the first time since Will's unexpected arrival that Faucon caught a glimpse of the sibling he'd once adored.

Will looked at Sir Adam. "It's freshly brewed ale if you'll have it."

"Happily so," the older knight replied with a grateful nod. To Faucon he said, "Father Otto came in the night to give to Sir Robert of Offord, my father-by-marriage, his last rites. Although Offord is in Wootton Wawen's parish, Saint Mary's at Haselor is just as close. I sent for Father Otto because he is— shall we say, more likeable?— than the prior from Saint Peter ad Vincula."

That Offord was near Haselor was news to Faucon. Although he would one day inherit a piece of land in Warwickshire, the same bit of forest land from his mother's dowry that had been intended to buy him a position in the Church, he was a newcomer to this shire.

"After Sir Robert's passing," Sir Adam continued,

"both the priest and Offord's bailiff, whose wife has kin in Haselor, told me of you. They also mentioned how you directed the search for a missing girl some days ago, and that the lass was found alive."

"Aye, so she was, God be praised. A miracle indeed," Faucon said, as Will handed the knight his cup.

Sir Adam lifted it to his host in salute, took a sip, then lowered it to the table and curled his hands around the base. "I'm hoping you yet have some sway with our Lord, Sir Faucon. As I said, my father-by-marriage died last night. Although there's no mark or wound on him, I'm certain he was murdered."

"If there's no wound, what convinces you it was murder?" Faucon asked in surprise.

Sir Adam made a harsh sound. "Because I watched him die just hours after he confronted the common whore he wed, rightfully accusing her of cuckolding him," he said, glancing from Faucon to Will, his voice rising with every word. "She killed him, even if I don't know how she did it. By God, I won't stand by while her bastard steals what is my son's rightful inheritance!" he finished at a roar.

Faucon fought a smile. Well, that explained why the knight had raced to find his new Crowner. The sooner the widow could be accused of murder and her babe proven a bastard, the sooner Sir Adam secured Offord for his own line. Regardless of the knight's twisted intent, Faucon was content to let the man use him. Anything was better than being trapped in here for the rest of the day with not-Will.

"So you can prove the babe the widow carries isn't Sir Robert's child?" Faucon asked.

"I know as sure as the sun rises in the morning," Sir Adam said, his expression hard, "as would be any man who had watched his wife swell with child. Hasn't my lady wife given me three living babes and two who didn't survive their first year? I know well enough that no woman's belly distends less than two months after her wedding night, not unless someone breached her gate before her rightful husband."

With his elbows braced on the table, he glanced between the brothers. "Mark my words, sirs. Even if Sir Alain witnesses that babe's birth and declares it Robert's heir, the little bastard won't survive a day at Offord." Having stated this bold threat before witnesses, Sir Adam drained the contents of his cup and pushed it again toward Will.

Honest exasperation filled the man's face. "I cannot comprehend what came over Robert. Since the birth of my son, his only grandson, Robert has been content with Young Robert as his heir. Then, right after celebrating his saint day last winter, Robert started fretting about needing a son of his own. Didn't he make a complete fool of himself by going a-wooing among our neighbors? God be praised that every knight in this shire had more sense than to give his daughter to Robert," Sir Adam finished, nodding his thanks to Will as Faucon's brother returned his cup.

"They refused him because your father-by-marriage was elderly?" Faucon asked, thinking that more than a few of those men should have considered the union. A young girl wed to an aging man nigh on guaranteed that she'd make an even better second marriage, having added the value of her first dower to her existing dowry.

"Robert wasn't elderly," Sir Adam retorted, startled. "He was but two score and five, only a year older than I. Nay, they refused him because everyone knows Robert is cursed. He can't seed a son."

Leaning back on the bench, Sir Adam threw his hands wide. "Two wives he's had, and nothing but girls from either of them. And of all the babes he made, only his first daughter, Joia, my lady wife, survived. When no well-born man would give Robert his daughter, I thought that would be the end of it. Then two months ago, Robert went to Rochester to attend the Michaelmas court.

The corner of the knight's mouth lifted. "Robert's been arguing for years with the king's clerks about a parcel of Offord's wasteland," he offered in aside. "Robert says it's inland, but they insist he owes tax on it because of some agreement made four score years ago. He went one more time, determined to finally put the argument to rest."

Then, closing his fists, Sir Adam leaned toward his host. Outrage darkened his blue eyes. "Or so I thought! I couldn't believe it when Robert returned from Rochester already wedded and bedded to some cloth merchant's daughter. Without so much as a word to me or his own daughter about his intentions!

"Tell me, sirs," he demanded. "Do either of you know any man— knight, baron, greedy merchant, or even a simple plowman— who weds off a daughter that quickly?" Sir Adam didn't wait for them to answer. "No, you do not! That is, unless the man knows his daughter's maidenhead has already been broken. Thus did I think the moment I saw that sly little blouze, and so she proved a month later when her belly started swelling."

"He wed a tradesman's daughter?" Will said, his words thick with disgust.

"Didn't I think the same?" Adam agreed, courting Will's reaction. "Where Robert was proud of how much fabric and silver she brought with her as her dowry, I told him that such riches were a sop, proof that her father knew she was damaged goods. I told Robert that greed had blinded him and turned him into a dolt. By God, he promised her the profit from Offord as dower if she bore him a son!" He shared this at a bellow, so his listeners understood just how wrong the dead man had been to do so.

"Wed to a commoner," Will sneered again, this time shaking his head.

Having recruited the support of his Crowner's brother, Sir Adam turned the full force of his persuasion on Faucon. "But Robert wouldn't hear me no matter what I said. Instead, he went on and on about how Prior Thierry had prayed on his behalf and how God had answered the prior, promising that Robert's seed would find fertile ground this time."

The knight's lip curled. "It wasn't our Lord doing the promising. It was all Prior Thierry. That's because the prior wishes to plunder Robert's treasury so he can add a new chancel to that ancient church of his. Expensive nonsense! Only the prior and one monk live in that holy house.

"But on and on Robert went, not caring that all this talk of sons was like a knife to his daughter's heart. Then, yesterday, Robert finally saw the truth. He at last heard me and demanded his wife admit the babe wasn't his, that some other man had plowed her field before they were wed. When she refused to name her babe's true father, he took his fists to her." Sir Adam paused to take another sip of his ale.

"No better than she deserved," Will remarked.

Nodding, Sir Adam set down the cup. "So it is."

"Did Lady Offord surrender the name of her lover?" Faucon asked, using the widow's title to needle the two of them. It was her title after all. Just as Marian, who was also a merchant's daughter, was now Lady Marian, so too had Lady Offord become a gentlewoman the moment she wed Sir Robert.

That teased a grimace out of Sir Adam. "She did not, but she might well have done if not for my brother Luc. May God take that boy! He intervened where he had no right to meddle. He said he couldn't bear to see a pregnant woman beaten, no matter whose babe she carried. He restrained Robert as the little whore made her escape. It wasn't until many hours later, just as Robert was breathing his last, that the servants finally found her hiding in Offord's dairy."

"Wait," Faucon cried, holding up a hand as if he meant to stop the man's words in his fingers. "The woman you accuse of killing her husband wasn't in his presence for his last hours?"

Concern flashed across Sir Adam's expression. "Why does that matter?"

"I don't know that it does," Faucon replied. "It's just strange. Tell me this. Was Sir Robert hale and hearty prior to last night?"

"Save for a few insignificant bouts of illness lately, he was," Sir Adam said, nodding emphatically, "and he has always been, at least for as long as I've known him. We met just after Robert returned from the first Irish campaign, which proved miraculous for him. Robert left as a squire and a third son with few prospects, but returned knighted with treasure enough to steal the heiress of Offord from me," he offered with a smile. "Men as full of life as Robert don't die so swiftly."

In that Sir Adam was mistaken. Brother Edmund had a growing list of names, some of them men younger than Sir Robert, who had done just that with no one assisting them toward Saint Peter's gate. One more time, Faucon sought to guide the knight where he wanted him to go. "Can you describe how death came upon Sir Robert?"

"I can, and may I say that it was horrible to watch. Hour by hour, Robert steadily lost control of his limbs until he couldn't move so much as a finger. It began just after our little celebration ended, perhaps around Vespers. He breathed his last not long after Matins this morn." Something that might have been grief twisted the man's face.

"You say you were feasting? Did anything out of the ordinary happen at that meal?" Faucon asked.

The knight frowned at him. "Do you mean other than an honorable if foolish man learning he'd been cuckolded?" he asked, a note of annoyance in his voice.

Faucon tried again. "Describe the events of yesterday for me. The more detail you can give me, the better. And I'll beg your pardon in advance, for I may interrupt to ask for further explanation."

Struggling to tame his impatience, Sir Adam leaned back on the bench and aimed his gaze at the curls of smoke writhing along the ceiling above them. "As I said, yesterday we celebrated my youngest daughter's fifth saint day."

"Who was present?" Faucon asked.

Sir Adam ticked his fingers as he spoke each name. "My lady Joia; our two daughters, Martha and Helena; my brother Sir Luc of Bagot, who acts as my steward during those seasons when my lady and I reside at Offord; Sir Robert; and, of course, that whore Idonea. As the servants cleared away the first course to bring the next, Idonea rose and started to leave the hall. Robert stopped her, demanding to know where she went. He was angry with her. He'd looked for her earlier in the day and couldn't find her. When she finally appeared, he'd demanded to know where she'd been. She told him in the latrine. But he had looked there and hadn't found her."

The knight shot them a quick, hard grin. "That's when I saw my moment. When she said she was going to the latrine, I pointed to the bulge of her belly and told Robert that it had doubled in size in only two weeks. Then I reminded Robert that only a woman far gone with child needed to visit the latrine so often during the day. After that, I demanded Idonea tell us whose child grew in her, because it surely wasn't Robert's."

As he spoke, Sir Adam again pushed his cup toward Will in suggestion. "That's when the whore started sobbing. She actually tried to tell us that she wasn't certain she was with child at all. Robert leapt to his feet in outrage. He shouted that she lied, that everyone could see a babe grew within her. Then Robert hit her, demanding she tell him whose bastard she bore, because it wasn't his babe."

Still grinning, Sir Adam continued. "As I said, my brother Luc then intervened. He held Robert while Idonea fled the hall. Once she was free of the door, Luc released Robert. Robert immediately turned on my brother, beating him before he banished Luc from Offord Hall. As he should have done," the knight added harshly, then gave a sour laugh.

"That was the end of poor Martha's happy celebration. Even though the second course included some of Robert's favorite dishes, he was more interested in keeping his cup filled than eating. For the rest of the meal he stayed in his chair at the high table and glowered at everyone. Joia and I tried to comfort him by telling him tales of how well Young Robert was doing."

Sir Adam's smile warmed. "Young Robert is but eight, and is squired with Lord Hervey of Stafford, Robert's liege. Thus far there isn't a skill my son can't master."

Having played the role of proud father, Sir Adam launched back into his tale. "But not even such talk soothed Robert last night. When the meal was done and the servants were clearing away the tables, Martha tried to cozen her grandsire into playing Hoodman Blind with us. It surprised us all when she failed at it. She can usually get Robert to do anything she asks."

Again Sir Adam paused, this time to sigh. "If only I had known," he said, regret filling his voice. "But what

31

good would that have done?" he asked, glancing between Faucon and Will.

"What do you mean?" Will asked.

"Robert didn't refuse to join Martha's game," Adam
answered. "Instead, he said he couldn't play because he
couldn't feel his feet. I put that up to drink, and said as
much. He laughed and agreed, but now I think it wasn't
the drink at all.

"So while the rest of us played the game, he watched
from his chair. When we had all taken a turn with the
hood, Joia returned to sit with her father. This time
Robert told her that his legs felt numb as far as his
knees and his thighs ached. My lady felt for a fever but
there was none. When she pressed him to retire, he
refused, insisting that whatever this strange malady
was, it would surely pass. He doesn't like"— the knight
caught himself— "didn't like his daughter to make much
ado over him.

"After that, the servants brought their instruments
and we all started to sing. Robert joined us in that. But
an hour later he yielded, admitting that the pain had
grown beyond bearing. He said he wished to retire, but
he couldn't lift himself out of the chair."

Sir Adam gave a shake of his head. "I could hardly
believe it, but it was true. Offord's bailiff and I each took
an arm. Robert couldn't so much as move his feet to
help us. His legs were useless.

"That put an end to our gaiety. My lady wife went
with him to his chamber. She sat by his side, trying to
soothe him as he shifted between fearful prayers and
raging over how his new wife's family had misused him.
By the time my girls were abed on their pallets in our
private corner of the hall and I joined my lady wife,
Robert could no longer lift his arms. That's when he
asked me to send to Wootton Wawen for the prior. As
if Prior Thierry has ever truly heard Robert's confes-

sions!" the knight added with a scornful snort.

"But there was no reasoning with Robert last night, even when I told him that Father Otto was sure to come from Haselor. Robert wanted the prior. In the end I sent men both ways, and a good thing that was. Father Otto arrived swiftly and Robert still had breath enough to respond as he received his last rites. By the time Prior Thierry reached Offord, Robert could no longer speak."

Scorn again twisted Sir Adam's features. "Not that being mute or the fact that Robert had already received his last rites stopped the prior from sending us all away! The Churchman claimed he needed privacy in which to hear Robert's last confession. I argued, but in the end, Robert managed to blink to show his agreement when Prior Thierry asked him if he wanted us to leave. My lady and I weren't allowed back into his chamber until Robert was breathing his last."

Sir Adam's tale was strange for certain. Faucon had never heard of such an illness, but then he didn't know much about ailments. It was fortunate for him that he knew a man who did.

Just then the hall door opened. Alf stepped inside, bearing a large tray. "Sirs," the soldier said, acknowledging the knights as he shifted to one side, allowing the lad responsible for cleaning the cooking pots to enter around him.

The boy carried two pitchers, one in each hand, and a cup under each arm. After he'd set these onto the table, he emptied Alf's tray. Each knight got a spoon and a wooden plate upon which the boy placed a half-loaf of stale bread. Then, taking up the good-sized iron pot and making sounds that suggested his fingers burned, the lad placed it at the center of the table.

Faucon wasn't surprised to smell mutton. Marion had culled the old ewes from Blacklea's flock last week.

Since then they'd eaten nothing but mutton stewed with turnips and parsley. She'd promised fish on the morrow, now that Advent had begun.

Rather than serve his betters, the lad set the ladle beside the pot and made a swift escape from the hall. As it wasn't Alf's duty to serve, the soldier turned to follow.

"Hold a moment, Alf," Faucon said, rising swiftly to his feet as he looked at Will. "Let me pass, Will."

His brother grinned, once again giving Faucon a glimpse of the sibling he missed. "Leave, and your place is mine, Pery," he threatened, as he rose to let Faucon exit.

That made Faucon laugh. "I yield it to you," he replied, as he eased his way to the door.

Before following Alf out onto the landing, Faucon nodded to Sir Adam. "Please begin without me. I must direct my man." Then pulling the door nearly closed behind him, he followed Alf to the base of the stairs, stopping on the final step, which brought him eye-to-eye with the taller soldier.

"Do you recall Brother Colin, that monk from the mill, the one who showed me how Halbert died?"

Interest flared in Alf's pale eyes. "I do indeed, sir."

"It seems I again have need of him. Ride to Stanrudde and the Abbey of Saint Peter. If he's there, beg him to join me at Offord Manor."

"If the brother is not at Stanrudde, what then?" Alf asked.

"Then ask where he is and join me at Offord, so I may ride with you to find him." Faucon replied.

"And if the brother is in his abbey but isn't permitted to join you?" Alf countered.

"Then you must tell him that a man who was but two score and five has died unexpectedly, death creeping upon him over the course of less than a half day. Whatever took his life stole all the sensation and

34

mobility from his limbs, the numbness rising steadily from his toes. Ask if the brother knows of any illnesses that could cause this. If he can think of none, then he must speculate as to what might have caused this manner of death."

Nodding to show he had committed his employer's words to memory, Alf threw a glance heavenward. "I doubt I'll make Stanrudde before the monks are at their rest for the night. At best I won't make Offord before midday on the morrow."

"As I expected," Faucon replied. "Will you need coin to secure shelter for the night?"

The soldier offered his snaggle-toothed grin at that. "The abbey stables will do for me, sir. The only thing that costs is my prayers at Prime mass in the morning. Name me fortunate!"

That made Faucon laugh aloud. Although Alf never missed a holy day, not wishing to incur the fine for being absent, he wasn't a particularly religious man. "As it suits you," Faucon said. "I'll need Brother Edmund as well. Stop at Saint Radegund's on your way and warn him that I ride for Offord within the next hour or so. Or, if it's more convenient, seek him out on the morrow on your return from Stanrudde and escort him to Offord."

"I'll stop on the way to Stanrudde," Alf replied. "I don't think the brother will ride with me."

Faucon offered a shake of his head at that. "He is a creature of strict habit," he offered in apology. "In that case, warn Brother Edmund to make all haste for Blacklea. Sir Adam is over-anxious to have me at his wife's home. Travel with God, Alf." Turning, Faucon started back up the stairs.

"You as well, sir, and watch your back," the soldier called after him.

Faucon threw a quick smile over his shoulder. "I always do."

When he reentered his hall, he saw that Will had again played the role of servant. All three bread trenchers had been filled with stew. Sir Adam, his spoon already in hand, shifted to watch his host enter.

"Well, are you coming to view Robert's body this day?" the knight more demanded than asked.

Faucon wondered at the man's urgency. "I think I must," he replied as he took Will's place on their bench and picked up his spoon. "There is something strange about how your father-by-marriage died. However, I cannot leave Blacklea before my clerk, who dwells in Priors Holston, arrives to join us."

"Priors Holston is not so far. He'll be here soon," the knight replied, grinning in triumph. Then he began to eat with unseemly haste.

Chapter Three

"**I**s that your man at last?" Sir Adam asked, once again giving way to impatience as they watched the little donkey and its black-clad rider on the Stanrudde Road.

From the moment Faucon had agreed to view Sir Robert's body, Adam had become the perfect guest. Their conversation over the meal had ranged from the battles they'd fought, who they knew, and which of their ancestors had rowed for Rollo the Viking. But the moment the last crumb of the meal had been consumed there'd been no holding the knight inside Faucon's hall. He'd insisted on mounting up and meeting Brother Edmund on the road.

"It is," Faucon replied.

Even with the wind at his back, Edmund's mount moved at his usual snail's pace. His rider had his head bowed, his habit tucked around him, and his black cowl pulled as low as possible. Thrusting up above his shoulder was the top of a tubular basket. That suggested Edmund had finally found a replacement for the traveling basket that had been crushed in Wike. This one was taller and wider than the original. Although its size made it unwieldy for riding, it was a better fit for Edmund's precious writing implements and the leaves of parchment upon which he scribbled.

Sir Adam cupped his hands around his mouth. "Brother," he shouted, "put your heels to that little beast of yours! These days are short and the sun will soon seek his rest. Hie or you'll be sleeping out-of-doors this night."

As he dropped his hands, Sir Adam shot Faucon a wink and a grin. The man was in fine fettle now that he believed himself well on the way to removing the threat to his son's inheritance.

In the distance the skirt of Edmund's habit flew as the monk beat his heels into his donkey's sides. This was usually wasted effort for the stubborn beast kept to his own pace, no matter the goad. Not so today. The donkey immediately jerked into a trot, nearly unseating his rider. Both man and basket bounced as the small creature trotted toward the waiting knights.

Assured the monk would follow, Sir Adam turned his mount southward at a fast walk. Will immediately brought his horse— Legate's brother— abreast of Sir Adam. Legate would have joined them but Faucon held his courser in place, unwilling to abandon Brother Edmund to the vagaries of his unpredictable ride.

Still yards away, the monk threw up a hand. "Move on or he'll slow once again."

"As you will," Faucon called back, turning Legate.

Recognizing a now-familiar traveling companion, the little ass matched the bigger horse's gait as he came abreast. That encouraged Faucon to urge Legate to slightly more speed. Much to his surprise, the donkey followed this time.

Panting, Edmund looked up at his employer, his well-made face framed by his black cowl. As most churchmen did, Faucon's clerk shaved not only his pate but his jaw. The tip of the monk's jutting nose was chill-reddened. His brows were drawn down over his dark eyes as he aimed his gaze at the two knights ahead of them.

"Sir Faucon, are we truly traveling so far that we must sleep out-of-doors this night? The message I received from Prior Lambertus was that I was needed at

Blacklea."

"We are for Offord, which I'm told is but a few miles from here, and I doubt we'll sleep outside. That said, know that we will likely be staying at Offord Manor for the night, what with the hour so late."

Edmund's mouth twisted at that. He disliked sleeping in close proximity to anyone, male or female, who wasn't avowed to the Church. In those instances when they were too far to ride for home, he always sought out some holy house, be it even a Cistercian farmstead, in which to lay his head. Those few times he'd failed at that, he'd retreated to a shed or barn, where he could be alone and his prayers undisturbed. However, with winter almost upon them and the weather turning steadily colder, such accommodations would soon be untenable.

"And why are we for Offord?" Faucon's clerk asked.

"Sir Adam, the knight who called to you, claims his father-by-marriage was murdered last night," Faucon replied.

Edmund looked askance at him. "Claims?" Frowning, the monk considered the back of the bigger man riding ahead of them. "Either a man is murdered or he isn't."

"Just so," Faucon nodded. "All I know thus far is that no weapon was used to end Sir Robert's life. Nor, according to Sir Adam, is there any sign of violence upon the dead man's body. Something else happened, something strange enough that I decided I must work out for myself how the knight died."

The crease on Brother Edmund's brow deepened, this time in confusion. "No wounds? I suppose there was no hue and cry then? Does the knight know who did this deed, if there was actually a deed done?"

Faucon gave a quirk of his brows. "No hue and cry, but Sir Adam claims Sir Robert's wife caused her husband's death."

The monk gave a confused shake of his head. "But if he witnessed the woman do murder to her husband, why is there no wound and no hue and cry? This is all very wrong. If the knight saw her commit the act, how can he not know how the man died?"

"You mistake me," Faucon replied with a smile. "The only thing Sir Adam witnessed was Sir Robert's steady progress into death. Lady Offord left her hall before her husband began his journey to our Lord's holy house and did not return until just before Sir Robert took his final breath." As Faucon spoke these words, the huntsman within him stirred, pleased at the prospect of a second chance at sport after the day's earlier and wholly unsatisfactory chase.

"But the knight cannot accuse the lady if he saw nothing," Edmund complained, his voice rising.

Again, Faucon grinned. "Oh but he can, especially if his accusation results in securing Offord Manor for his son instead of the widow's child."

Edmund blinked rapidly at that. "I beg your pardon?"

"Sir Robert's widow— his third wife— is pregnant," Faucon told his clerk, restating his comment for the literal monk.

That cleared the confusion from Edmund's dark eyes. "Ah, so this is a matter of contested inheritance, and not murder." This time the monk shook his head with enough vigor that his donkey sidled. "Sir, this is not our purview. By the knight's own admission, there are no wounds, no witnesses to a murder, no hue and cry. We should leave this death and the lady to the sheriff."

Faucon glanced at his clerk in surprise. "We cannot know what happened to the dead man until we've examined him. I must convince myself that murder was not done before I can state that this death does not concern the Coronarius."

"Well and good, sir, but what if you prove murder—what then?" Edmund asked, his voice tight with worry. "Are you certain the Coronarius has the right to call the common men bound to Offord to confirm that the one who ruled them has been murdered by his lady wife? Did you ask Sir Adam if Sir Robert held the franchise for delivering justice to his folk? If not Sir Robert, then does his overlord hold that right? Perhaps Sir Adam should have ridden to that baron's keep to inform him of his vassal's death, and let that nobleman come to you in his stead. Do we even know what responsibility the Coronarii have when it comes to the better-born?"

Faucon bent a sharp look on the monk. Although Edmund's questions were appropriate given the yet undefined duties of his new position, the monk was missing the obvious. That wasn't like Edmund at all. Understanding came with his next breath. Like Faucon, Edmund was also a stranger here. Where Faucon saw this death as an opportunity to introduce himself to the local gentry, his clerk's frustrated ambitions made him fret over misstepping with his betters.

"Brother, you know as well as I that even if a nobleman has a royal patent to judge his own, our king collects the fines for murder. Baron or beggar, it remains my duty to discover the identity of the murderer and appraise his estate, and yours to note what fee the king can expect to collect. If our monarch chooses not to deliver justice or collect that fee from his knight or baron, well then, that is between them and no concern of ours.

"More importantly, you're putting the horse before the lance in this matter. Wait until we've seen the dead man before you begin exploring whose right it is to call the jury," he finished, glancing at his clerk.

Brother Edmund's face tightened in effort as he resisted his urge to argue. "If you say so, sir," he agreed however reluctantly, the words barely escaping through his gritted teeth.

In the next instant the monk's shoulders relaxed. "I believe you are correct, sir, in saying I'm ahead of myself. After all, if the widow is with child, Sir Alain must come claim her. When our sheriff arrives to take her into his custody, we can ask him whose traditional right it is to call the jury at this manor," he finished, neatly shifting a potential error elsewhere.

That reminded Faucon of Sir Adam's threat against Lady Offord's babe. He wondered if the lady had already sent for the sheriff, seeking his protection for herself and her child. In that case, Sir Alain might already be at Offord. Perhaps there would be a way to use this knight's strange death to strike another blow at the man who hunted him.

When they reached the Alne, Sir Adam turned his horse to follow the river. Faucon scanned the gentle roll of the landscape around him. Everywhere he looked the earth wore the familiar furrowed scars that spoke of crops. Yet it was clear these fields were no longer being worked. Instead, they'd been given over to pasture, and sheep now grazed where wheat and barley had once grown. Huddling hip-to-hip as they were wont to do, the fleecy creatures sought out what little green grass remained beneath the blanket of fallen leaves, then dined on the crisp leaves after.

With the next gust of wind Faucon caught a regular clanking and marked a water mill in the distance. Before they reached it, they splashed across the river, the water barely reaching to their horses' knees. Sir Adam then turned his horse onto a narrow track.

Before long they were riding through a clutch of some forty or so well-kept homes. The whitewashed cottages with their reed roofs were sprinkled around a sharp lift of land. Like Blacklea's mound, this one was clearly man-made but rose no more than four perches above the river. Although a wooden palisade concealed the top of the mound, there was no doubt the manor had its own dove-cote. The birds, kept for their meat and eggs, circled in the sky above the mound. There was a smithy as well or so said the clang of hammer against iron. A small gateway offered passage through the wall. Although the doors that guarded Offord at night both stood wide, no man waited to challenge their entry.

Just then, a woman's cry rent the air. "Have pity! It grows late and it's cold out here." There was a pause, then she shouted again, this time more angrily, "Idonea, open the door now! You've no right to bar me from my father's home!"

Sir Adam jerked upright in his saddle. "She's barred the door?!" he bellowed and kicked his horse into a gallop.

As the knight disappeared through the gateway, Will shot Faucon a grin and urged his horse to the same speed. Faucon saw no reason to hurry. With Edmund's donkey trotting close to Legate's heels, they entered the bailey of Offord Manor.

Like Blacklea, this place was no rich man's home. Those who ruled Offord Village lived only a little better than their own folk. And, just as at Blacklea, the land caught inside the palisade had been divided as best served its master's uses. There was a small pasture in which three horses grazed. A large paddock was fitted out with winter shelters for sheep as well as a makeshift stable, all of them made from woven withe panels.

Domed-shaped structures ran along the edge of a good-sized garden area, they were waist-high beehives, the much larger dove-cote and a line of small ovens. The three-walled smithy and what was surely the kitchen shed both had thatch for roof and plastered wooden walls. Faucon drew in a deep breath, savoring the rich aroma of roasting nuts.

Offord's manor house was almost twice the size of his new home, three times as large if he included the small square keep tower at one end of the house. But it wasn't as tall, nor was it built of stone, although both the wooden hall and keep stood atop a knee-high stone foundation. From what Faucon could see, there was only one entrance to hall and keep, a wise arrangement. That small door was at the west end of the hall, as far from the keep as possible. Raised three steps off the ground, a roofed porch protected the entryway from the elements.

Standing on that porch, her back to Faucon, was a small woman swathed in a dark green cloak. She wore a deep blue woolen scarf wrapped around her head. A pair of dark braids fell down her back, reaching almost to her waist. Two lasses, one taller than the other, clung to her, both of them wearing similar green mantles and scarves. However, their plaits were the same rusty color of Sir Adam's hair, naming them his daughters and the woman his wife.

Sir Adam threw himself from the saddle almost before he drew his horse to a halt at the porch. "Joia, what's happened?" he bellowed to his wife as he bounded up the steps.

As Will drew his horse to a halt beside Sir Adam's mount, Lady Bagot jerked around in surprise. Faucon blinked in surprise. She was beautiful, with a heart-shaped face and even features. The lady glanced across the faces of the strangers in her yard, then looked up at her husband. "Thank the Lord that you've returned! We've all been trapped out here since you left."

"But I told you not to leave the hall," her husband chided harshly.

"We needed the privy," his wife cried. "I didn't think she'd shut out the children."

Sir Adam pushed past his wife to pound his fist against the arched wooden panel that separated him from a life and a hall he had never expected to lose. "No common whore is going to keep me from my wife's home," he roared. "Idonea, open this door!"

Faucon halted Legate next to his brother. Yet mounted, Will grinned. "This is better entertainment than even hunting," he said, making no attempt to keep his words private.

On the porch, Lady Bagot again turned to look upon her unexpected guests. Beneath her dark brows, her green eyes were reddened by tears. The dark rings beneath them spoke of exhaustion. Faucon guessed she was no older than he. Again, he was struck by her beauty, even marred as it was by the signs of grief upon her face.

Her daughters also turned to look upon their visitors. If the older lass, a girl about half her mother's age, was her father's image from her rusty hair to her blue eyes, the younger girl had her father's hair but her mother's pretty features and green eyes. The little lass smiled at Faucon, the bend of her lips suggesting she was well on her way to becoming a practiced flirt. As Lady Bagot realized that her daughters were looking upon strange men and the men were watching them in return, she put her back to her visitors and pulled her girls around with her. That didn't stop the younger lass from watching the newcomers from over her shoulder.

Edmund brought his donkey in line with the bigger horses just as Sir Adam again battered at the door.

Startled by the banging, the monk's little beast brayed in distress and turned a quick circle, once again almost dislodging its rider. Sir Adam's youngest child giggled at this dance.

Dismounting, Faucon grabbed the donkey's bridle, holding him until his clerk found the safety of the earth. Once the monk straightened his habit and resettled his basket onto his back, Edmund looked at his employer. "Only on pain of arrest can the widow refuse to allow the shire's Coronarius to enter her home," he said flatly.

That made Faucon grin. "Now who's creating new law out of thin air?" he asked quietly.

For the briefest of instants, Edmund's lips lifted, his expression a poor facsimile of amusement. "It's cold out. As you have suggested, who knows better than we what a Coronarius can or cannot do?"

The knight again battered at the door with his fist. "God take you, woman. Let us in!"

Edmund glanced from the knight to his employer. "More to the point, it's certain that if we do nothing, we really will be sleeping out-of-doors this night."

Chapter Four

Still savoring Edmund's unexpected jest, Faucon released the donkey to join Sir Adam on the porch. "Allow me, sir," he said as he halted next to the taller knight.

Sir Adam shot him a surprised glance but stepped aside without comment. Faucon tapped gently on the arched oaken panel. "Lady Offord, I am Sir Faucon de Ramis, the king's servant in this shire. By royal command I must examine your husband's body. Will you open your door so I might do my duty to our monarch?"

Through the thick oaken panel he caught the sound of a man's deep voice. A woman's higher-pitched response followed. A moment later he heard the bar hit the floor with a thud, then the iron hinge pegs groaned in their loops. The heavy door shifted inward.

The man who stood in the opening was lanky and long of face. Well into his middle years, he wore a thick golden beard although his fair hair had thinned into a ragged half-circle at the back of his skull. His blue eyes were red-rimmed from mourning. Beneath a brown cloak, he wore a padded hauberk made of undyed linen over a thick yellow tunic. Faded orange chausses covered his legs, while fraying strips of cloth held wooly sheepskin to his calves above ankle-high boots.

Behind him, blocking Faucon's view of the hall, was the wooden screen that guarded the manor's public room from the full force of necessary door-drawn drafts. By the greasy yellow light of a pair of torches mounted high on the screen he could see that the panel had been painted a gentle blue. The floor in the vestibule was tiled, the small ceramic squares set in an attractive pattern of blue, red, and green.

"Eustace!" Sir Adam shouted from over Faucon's shoulder, filling the man's name with both relief and irritation. "If you were in there, why did you not open the door when my lady knocked?"

"Lady Offord forbade it," this Eustace replied humbly, bowing his head. His command of the Norman tongue wasn't as rustic as his appearance.

Sir Adam gave a wave of his hand. "Well, the door is open now. Move aside so we might enter."

"You promised only the king's man would enter, Eustace." The woman's cry came from behind the wooden screen, her voice piercing in fright and her words, English. Between her choice of language and her comment, this could only be the tradesman's daughter who had wed Sir Robert of Offord.

"Move Eustace. I and no other am the new master here," Sir Adam snapped at the same time.

Offord's bailiff instantly eased back from the doorway. As well he should. In this battle he was but a bone between two dogs.

"May I join you in the hall, Lady Offord?" Faucon called in his native French as he held his place in the doorway.

"Do not dare beg her permission, Sir Faucon," Sir Adam snarled, his lips almost at Faucon's ear. "I am the one you ask, and I say you may enter *my* home as you will.

"Do you hear me, Idonea?" the older knight added at a shout, making Faucon flinch. "You have no right to say who can or cannot pass into Offord Hall, no matter what might be scribbled on that agreement of yours."

The woman behind the screen gave vent to a mousy squeak. The uneven tap of leather soles on tile followed.

Sir Adam took a half-step forward, almost pressing against his new Keeper of the Pleas. For no reason Faucon could name, he was certain that the man wanted to prevent his Crowner from interviewing the widow. Lifting his heels, Faucon pushed past the bailiff and jogged around the screen.

Everything about this hall suggested it was ancient. Massive tree trunks, untouched by plane or saw, supported the chamber's plastered walls. The cross beam holding up the roof had also once been a tree of great size. In the corner farthest from the doorway and its persistent draft stood a large curtained bed. Piled around it were at least a half-dozen straw-stuffed pallets. Tables and benches filled the body of the chamber, the tables bearing the remains of the household's midday day meal.

When Sir Robert's widow shut the door, she'd also shut out the servant whose duty it was to tend the fire. Once the door was closed, cutting off the draft, the fire began to die. Smoke now choked the room and naught but smoldering ashes filled the central hearthstone.

As for the widow, Idonea of Offord was halfway across the chamber, limping awkwardly toward a door in the far wall. Beneath her knee-length blue mantle the widow wore rich green gowns trimmed in gold. Her hems dragged through the scattered rushes that covered the hall floor. A silken wimple covered her head.

"She's making for the tower," Sir Adam shouted from behind Faucon. "If she bars that door, she'll hold Robert's corpse and we'll never get her out of there!"

That drew another wordless cry from the escaping widow. She snatched up her skirts with one hand and limped faster. Faucon lifted his heels until he sprinted. Ahead of him, she pushed open the tower door with enough force that the wooden panel slammed into the wall behind it. Faucon followed her through the opening, blocking the doorway as he grabbed her by the upper arm. She was bone-thin through the bulk of her mantle and gowns. Her wimple was so fine that he could see she wore her dark hair cropped close to her skull.

"My lady, wait," he said in English, pulling her back from the spiraling stone stairway that circled upward ahead of them.

"Let me go," she cried, wrenching on her arm with all her puny might as he brought her around to face him.

The wife of Sir Robert of Offord was a child of no more than four-and-ten, and a gaunt, sickly-looking child at that. Her skin had the grayish cast given to those whom death consumes slowly, her eye color almost that same unhealthy shade of gray. That was, the one eye he could see. Her left eye was blackened and swollen shut and a fist-shaped bruise marked her left cheek. Her lower lip trembled, reopening a crusting cut.

"Be at ease, my lady," Faucon told her, holding her where she stood. "I am the king's servant and you are now under my protection. So you shall remain until the sheriff arrives to take you into his custody."

That drove all the fight out of her. She sagged against his hold. "I don't want the sheriff, I want to go home," she sniveled.

Footsteps rang out from behind Faucon. He shot a glance over his shoulder. Sir Adam was halfway across the hall, coming toward them at an easy and far-too-confident pace.

Releasing the widow, Faucon closed the tower door. The bar meant to defend it against invaders stood in the corner. He dropped it into its braces just as Sir Adam tried the latch. When the door didn't open the knight slammed both fists into the panel. "What are you doing?" Sir Adam demanded.

"Examining Sir Robert's corpse while I speak with his widow," Faucon called back. Then he added, "I won't be long."

A foul curse, one that included impossible acts and parts of their Lord's holy anatomy, spewed from the man on the other side of the oaken panel. Idonea gasped. Faucon sighed and bid fare-thee-well to being welcomed to the shire by this gentle family.

"Patience, Sir Adam," he called again, even though he knew the words were a waste of breath. This knight was incapable of patience. That won him a second, if less creative, curse.

Idonea grabbed her Crowner's hand and carefully lowered herself to her knees. "Please, sir. My husband is dead. Why must I go with the sheriff? Why can I not go home?" Moisture filled her undamaged left eye.

"Do you not carry your husband's heir?" Faucon replied with a startled shake of his head.

It was exactly because of Sir Adam's threat against Idonea's unborn child that England's sheriffs were law-bound to take custody of all pregnant widows. That same law also protected Lady Joia and her son from being cheated of their inheritance, as Sir Alain was required to witness the birth of Lady Offord's child to prevent her from replacing a weak or stillborn heir with some other woman's babe.

The widow's brow creased as if in confusion. "I don't know," she whispered.

Faucon lifted her to her feet, then eased back a step to put an appropriate distance between them. As he did, she lowered her free hand to her belly. Faucon's gaze followed her movement.

Sir Adam was right. Even Faucon, an unmarried man, could see Lady Offord was too swollen to be only a month and a half gone with child. Then he frowned. Did she mean she didn't know whose child she carried, or that she didn't know if she was with child?

"My lady, do you have the sheet from your wedding night in store?" Faucon asked, even though it wasn't rape he investigated here.

"Nay, my father holds it at home for safekeeping," Idonea answered without hesitation.

"Was there blood?" Faucon pressed where he again had no right to request proof that she had come a maiden to her marriage bed.

She blinked in surprise as she understood. That instinctive reaction made her gasp. She raised her hand to touch her swollen left eye as color washed over her cheeks, the stain dark enough to be seen beneath her bruises. Then, bowing her head, she folded her hands before her.

"Aye," she whispered. "My mother was very pleased the morning after my wedding. She praised me for being an obedient daughter." Her voice caught on her last words.

Once again Faucon eyed her shorn head through her fine wimple. "Does your illness often leave you fevered?"

She glanced up at him. "Not so much this year, but aye, it has in years past. Because of that, Mama always kept my hair short. This year I have ached more often than I burned."

As she spoke, she extended a hand to show him. Her knuckles were reddened and engorged. She tried to close her fists, but her fingertips never reached her palms. "It's worse here than it was at home."

"Do only your hands swell? What of your belly?" Faucon asked, again trespassing where he had no right to tread.

For a second time she cupped a hand to her distended abdomen. "Aye, and my stomach growls terribly. Do you think that might be a sign that I am with child?"

she asked him.

Disgust bolted through Faucon. What sort of parent abandoned a frail and ailing daughter to marriage without giving her the knowledge she needed to be a proper wife? She should know how to discern this for herself.

He hid his reaction behind a smile. "I think you would be wise to seek out the local midwife to assure yourself of this, Lady Offord," he told her.

Panic dashed through the widow's uninjured eye. "But if I step outside now, they'll bar me from the hall. That's why I closed the door on Lady Joia. This morn, while we were gathering what we needed to wrap her father for burial, she told me she would throw me from the hall once her sire was buried. She said I would leave Offord with nothing, not even my own chest."

A tear managed to escape Lady Offord's bruised eye. Her lips trembled. "Why would she threaten to do this to me when she knows I'll die if I'm banished outside the door? I don't know where to go," she moaned, sounding like the lost and lonely child she was.

There was no answer Faucon could give to that. "Perhaps it's better if we call the midwife to see you here," he suggested as someone knocked at the door.

Idonea started, only to cry out as her shift of expression aggravated her injuries.

"Do you need me, Sir Faucon?" Brother Edmund asked.

"I'm not certain as of yet," Faucon replied, his voice raised so he could be heard through the panel. "I'll come fetch you if I do. Until then, why not find a comfortable place where you can to do your scribbling?"

"As you will," Edmund more grumbled than replied.

Faucon turned to the spiraling stone stairway that led to the upper chamber of Offord's keep tower. The lift of his hand indicated that Idonea should climb ahead of him. "My lady, am I right to think your husband's remains are above?"

Chapter Five

The upper chamber of the square keep tower—
what had once been the manor's last refuge a-
gainst attack— was safehold no longer. Not only
had the door to the room been removed, a large window
had been cut into its south wall. Only a pair of slatted
wooden shutters could prevent besiegers or their
arrows from entering. At the moment, those shutters
were flung wide to allow in the day's cold air along with
what daylight remained.

Idonea entered ahead of him, moving to the curtained bed that commanded nearly a third of the
chamber. A long wooden chest, no doubt the one in
which Sir Robert's weapons and armor were stored,
stood against one wall. A massive lock held the chest
closed. Placed beneath the window was a brazier, a
wide, shallow brass pan that rested atop a waist-high
metal tripod. The coals in the brazier were as dead as
the former master of Offord, each gust of wind teasing
up swirls of cold ash.

Placed beside the brazier was a half-barrel chair, its
tall, rounded back meant to catch and hold heat. A red
tunic had been draped over one arm. The hem of the
garment was decorated with a thick band of yellow and
green embroidery.

The widow stopped beside the head of the bed, then
looked back at her Crowner as she waited for him to
join her. Faucon stripped off a glove to finger the rich
green-and-gold curtains in appreciation. "These are
beautiful."

"They're part of my dowry," Idonea replied as she pushed aside the fabric panels, the wooden rings scraping along their supporting pole.

The earthly remains of Sir Robert of Offord rested close to the edge of the bed atop a well-worn coverlet. Although his body had been arranged for winding, legs close together and arms crossed over his chest, he wore only a linen shirt that reached to his knees. A single narrow strip of linen had been wrapped beneath his chin and tied atop his head, meant to keep his jaw tight to his skull.

As always, death left the man's features strangely flattened. Nonetheless, Faucon could see Sir Robert's pretty daughter favored him, not only in her well-made features but also in hair color and height. The knight had been a short man, but his shoulders were broad, his waist flat, and his hips narrow. Sir Adam had not lied about his kinsman's fitness.

Idonea picked up a strip of linen from the pile near her husband's head. "We washed him this morning, but Sir Adam forbade us from dressing him in his tunic. Nor would he allow us to bind more than his jaw," she said, her voice still quavering.

Offering a quiet sound in response, Faucon lifted the hem of Sir Robert's shirt as high as the man's stiffened limbs would allow, then rolled the rigid corpse onto its side. There was nothing unusual about the knight's remains save for any warrior's share of scars and the occasional mole. As he resettled the dead man onto his back, Faucon eyed Sir Robert's widow. Idonea stared blankly at her husband. No sign of grief, or any other emotion, touched her thin, bruised face.

"My lady, I understand you hail from Rochester."

"London, actually," she replied softly and offered a trembling smile. "My father is a canny merchant and knows how good court is for trade. He rented a house in

56

Rochester during the court, hoping one of the better-born might be in need of a place to stay. He brought my mother to serve, and she brought me."

"Ah," Faucon said, nodding. A canny merchant, indeed. "How was it you came to be wed so swiftly to Sir Robert of Offord?"

Releasing a slow breath, the widow stirred herself from her thoughts and looked up at him. "It was Sir Robert who rented the bed in our borrowed house. On the day of his arrival he joined us at our table for our midday meal. Over that meal he told my father the tale of his two previous wives, and how he had only one surviving daughter from them."

Idonea's gaze drifted back to the body of her husband. "My father was at his wits' end over me. Although many among London's other tradesmen crave a union with our house, none would consider me as a wife for their sons."

She turned her gaze to her folded hands. "Why should they when they all knew how I have ailed over the years? But Sir Robert didn't know anything about me. After much discussion over the following weeks, my father finally proposed a union.

"My mother was furious. She told Papa it was dangerous to cheat his better. But Papa insisted that Sir Robert could see my shorn head. He said that if the knight didn't ask questions about me or my health, that was the man's choice. Papa said that my dowry, which is thrice what my younger sister will get when she weds, was enough to compensate the knight if I should continue to ail. He insisted this marriage was good business, then he reminded Mama no one can offer for my sister until I am wed and any child of my body would lift our line into the gentry. I think all Papa cared about was that he would be able to boast to our neighbors that he had wed me to a knight after they all rejected me."

Faucon nodded at that, wondering why Sir Robert might have been in such a panic to wed that he wouldn't even ask the usual questions. He again fingered the bed curtains. They were almost the quality of the curtains that hung in his uncle Bishop William's bed. Fabric this fine was worth its weight in gold. Perhaps that had been enough to sway the knight into taking a sickly child as his wife.

Idonea gave vent to a harsh breath. "Fearing for my life if I went to live so far from her, my mother called my father a dreamer who would bring ruin on our whole house. My father took her words ill, and beat her for her boldness."

With a trembling breath, Lady Offord opened her hands, once again placing her palms on her swollen belly. Her chin quivered. "What if I am not with child? How will Papa like it when I return barren, having lost the title he craved?"

"You have lost nothing, Lady Offord," Faucon replied swiftly. "Not only do you keep your dowry, but you now have the dower Sir Robert gave you as part of your marriage contract."

For the third time he dared to trespass where he had no right. "Sir Robert did offer dower as part of your contract, did he not?"

She gave a tiny nod at that. "If I bore him a son, I was to get half of Offord's yearly profit as well as the full value of the wool from the manor's flock for my lifetime. If I bear only daughters, I may live in the hall as lady until the eldest is of age to wed, but the profit of the manor goes to Lady Joia and her son. If I am childless, I get the bell as my dower and nothing more."

"A bell?" Faucon asked, startled.

"Aye," Idonea replied with a nod. "Sir Robert has a large handbell. It's all that remains of the treasure he

58

brought home from Ireland, the same treasure that won him Offord and Lady Joia's mother. He keeps it in a fine coffer in the storeroom below us. It is very beautiful, all decorated with images and a pretty stone in its handle."

Faucon eyed the widow, beyond surprised. And Idonea had called her father a canny merchant? Dower was meant to support a man's widow for her lifetime, then return intact to the husband's line upon her death. If it was a piece of land, the widow could gather whatever grew upon it for her table. If it was a mill, she had the right to the profit it generated. A house she could live in, or rent as she saw fit. But what she couldn't do was sell her dower, which seemed to Faucon the only way a bell could benefit Lady Offord.

"He showed it to me the day the servants took my dowry chest down there," Idonea was saying. She pointed toward the half-barrel chair.

Only then did Faucon notice the outline of a trapdoor in the floorboards beneath the chair. Not only had Sir Robert turned what should have been his home's final refuge into a bedchamber, he'd made a treasury of the space that should have housed both armament and foodstuffs. Curious, Faucon crossed to the chair and pushed it aside. The trap door had a rope handle.

Lifting the door, he peered into the lower chamber. A well-made ladder led down into the darkened storeroom, suggesting frequent visits. He breathed in the smell of garlic and tang of salty brine. He was wrong. This was still where the manor stored its foodstuffs.

Laying the door back on the floor to allow more light into the lower room, he eyed the space. It was cluttered with stacks of bags, barrels, and bundles. Two large chests stood close to the ladder. One was open, revealing that it contained garments or fabric. The other was locked. Sitting atop the closed chest was a much smaller coffer a little longer than the length of his forearm. Even in the dim light he could see it was richly carved. That made it seem more like the reliquaries in which Churchmen housed their bits and pieces of dead saints.

Idonea joined him at the edge of the opening. "Huh," she said, as she noticed the open chest. "Lady Joia must have forgotten to close that when she went down to fetch Sir Robert's best tunic. For shame! She knows well enough that rats cannot resist getting into fabric."

That made Faucon smile. For just an instant Lady Offord was no longer an ill-used child-bride, but every inch a cloth merchant's daughter. "Well, we cannot have that, can we?" he said. "If you will it, I'll go below and close it for you, my lady."

"If you please," she replied shyly.

Faucon climbed down the ladder. His foot slid as he stepped off the lower rung, for the tower's stone floor was covered in a layer of dirt and grit. The lid was heavier than he expected, what with brass fittings on all its corners and a metal binding strap wrapped around its middle. Once the chest was closed, he latched its metal tongue over the brass loop. "Is there a lock for it?" he called up to Lady Offord as he glanced around the chest.

"There is. It should be nearby," she replied as she came to kneel at the edge of the opening to better see him. "There!" she called, pointing to the little coffer. "I see it. It's on top of the bell box."

Faucon moved around the ladder to the other chest. That took him deeper into the storeroom's windowless dimness. He ran his hand across the top of coffer. It was indeed fine. Where it wasn't carved, the wood had been sanded to silky smoothness. His fingers found the metallic bulk of a large lock. As he lifted it, his knuckles brushed against something. Whatever it was slid over the edge of the coffer and clattered onto the top of the lower chest. He snatched it just as it started to tumble to the floor. It was a second, smaller lock.

He again looked up at Idonea. "There are two locks here. One is smaller."

She stared blankly down at him. "That's not possible," she told him. "Lady Joia only opened one lock this morn. Is my chest locked? It's the one beside you."

He touched the face of the chest at his knee. There was a lock threaded through the latch on its front. That brought his attention back to the bell coffer. Like both of the larger chests, it also had a metal tongue and loop. The tongue was latched over the loop, but there was no lock to hold it shut.

Once more, he looked up at Idonea, this time holding up the smaller lock so she could see it. "It seems that Lady Joia also opened the bell box this morning."

"Nay, she never touched it. I was watching." Then Idonea gasped. "The bell! Is it still inside its box?"

Setting both locks on the chest, Faucon brought the coffer into the shaft of light near the ladder. He lifted the lid. The little metal hinges made no sound as they moved. The interior of the box was lined with thick, felted fabric. Watching from above, Idonea moaned. The coffer was empty.

Faucon's eyes narrowed. Why did it not surprise him that Sir Adam might wreak his vengeance on an innocent, a woman he despised and whose child he wished to kill, by stealing what was rightfully hers? Dishonorable knight!

Then anger twisted into harsh amusement. Unfortunately for Sir Adam, in his need to prove Idonea a murderess, he'd invited into his home the very man responsible for identifying and accusing those who committed burglary.

Locking the large chest, Faucon carried the empty coffer and its lock up the ladder. Idonea had retreated to the bed to stand with her back to a bedpost, her face buried in her hands. "I want to go home," she cried into her fingers.

Faucon closed the trapdoor and replaced the chair, setting the coffer and the lock onto its seat, then joined the widow at the bed. "My lady, it's not only my duty to examine the bodies of those who died under suspicious circumstances, but I also identify those who burgle. But if I'm to discover who took this bell of yours I'll need your help. If, as you say, the coffer is always locked, then whoever took the bell must have had the key, for the lock is undamaged. Where is that key kept?" he asked.

Releasing a shaken breath, the widow dropped her hands, then slid down the post to sit at its foot, her knees drawn up to her chest. She pulled her skirts down to cover her shoes, then leaned her head back against the bed and looked up at him. Distress had only made her face seem grayer.

She pointed to the bedpost behind him. "It hangs on a peg there," she said flatly.

Faucon pushed his way behind the bed curtains. A ring of large metal keys hung from the peg driven into the post. Taking the ring, he retreated out from the curtains and showed the keys to her. "Is the key here?"

She only shook her head. "I don't know," she replied. "I was never allowed to use the keys. If a chest needed opening, Sir Robert opened it."

Faucon carried the ring to where he'd left the box and lock. Of the four keys, the smallest was the length of his palm. He fitted it into the coffer's lock. It turned with ease.

So not only had the one who took the bell known where to find the key to the coffer, he must have been

62

well known to the residents of Offord. No stranger could make his way unnoticed through the hall and into Sir Robert's bedchamber. Nor would any sane man show a stranger how to steal from him by revealing where he hid his keys.

That made Faucon frown. But why had this well-trusted man taken only the bell and left behind the valuable coffer? And why, after taking the bell, hadn't he returned the lock to its proper place and closed it? That was akin to advertising that a theft had taken place.

Taking up the coffer and lock, Faucon returned the key ring to its peg, then stood in front of the young widow. "If you please, Lady Offord. Tell me everything you recall about what happened last night."

"I don't know what happened for all of yestereven, only what happened before I ran away," she said, her voice still emotionless. She kept her gaze on the floor as she spoke. "We gathered after midday to celebrate Lady Martha. Sir Adam and Lady Joia had quibbled earlier in the day."

She paused to slant a sidelong glance at him. "But this was not unusual. They don't much like one another, but at least Sir Adam stays his hand, doing so because Sir Robert requires it," she said quietly, taking no note of the irony in what she said.

"Once we were at the table Lady Joia and Sir Adam set aside their discord to make merry for little Martha's sake. After a time I rose to go to the privy. That's when Sir Adam called out before all the household that I had sinned and carried another man's child. I cried that this wasn't true, that I didn't know if I was even with child.

"That only enraged Sir Robert. He caught me by the arm and demanded to know who my lover was. I told him no one, but he said I lied and began to beat me. That's when Sir Luc threw himself at my husband and told me to run."

Her expression was as lifeless as her voice, showing no passion, no trace of guilt or outrage. "He shouldn't have done that," she almost whispered, giving a tiny shake of her head. "What else was everyone to think save that he was the one?" Her voice trailed off into silence.

"Sir Adam tells me your husband had looked for you prior to the meal that day and couldn't find you," Faucon said. "Where were you?"

"Hiding," she said with a sigh. "It's what I do here."

"Why were you hiding earlier?" he asked, frowning.

Idonea looked up at him. She watched him for a moment as if she weighed whether to confide in him, then again lowered her gaze to the floor. "Sir Adam's brother Sir Luc was visiting. Whenever he comes, he pursues me even though I have begged him not to."

Thus did Sir Adam seek to convince his Crowner that this sickly child was a wanton temptress. Faucon wondered if the knight had purposefully set his brother after Lady Offord. After all, in instances such as this, fault only fell upon the pursuer if he were caught in the act. Otherwise, it was only the pursued who paid the price.

"And where did you go to hide?" Faucon asked.

"To the dairy," she replied, rubbing her bruised temple. "It's where I always go. I can bar the door from the inside. Cold it is, but I keep blankets in an empty barrel. I like it there. There's always cheese to nibble on and wine to drink." A tiny smile lifted the corners of her lips at that.

He smiled back at her. "A boon, indeed. Did you leave the dairy any time after you entered it and before your husband passed from this world?"

"Nay, I remained there until Eustace sought me out in the wee hours. I'd fallen asleep and he had to pound on the door to awaken me."

Surprise lifted Faucon's brows. "How did the bailiff know where you were hiding?"

The widow shrugged. "Everyone knows where I go, at least all of those who care to know. Last night when Eustace came, he said Sir Robert was dying and I needed to be in the hall when my husband passed. Eustace said if I wasn't there, nothing would prevent Sir Adam from stealing everything that should be mine."

She paused, then added at a whisper, "As if anything in this place might actually be mine, no matter who said what."

Faucon supposed it shouldn't surprise him that the English bailiff might prefer his common lady over his master's daughter. "So you returned to the hall. What followed?"

"Such was the chaos that no one paid me much heed," she said with another shrug. "Sir Adam was at the tower door, the one you barred. He was pounding on it, shouting that Prior Thierry must open it for him. Lady Joia was kneeling at his feet, weeping. They were so noisy they had awakened the little ladies. They had climbed into their parents' bed, and Martha was wailing as well. I started to go to them when that priest— Father Otto— called me to him at the high table. He had seen my face and asked after me."

"A kind man," Faucon commented.

"He is," Idonea agreed, gently pressing her fingers around her swollen eye. "He made Eustace send one of the maidservants to fetch water and a cloth so I might wash. I was surprised that she did his bidding without first asking Lady Joia's permission."

Turning her gaze in the direction of the open doorway, Idonea stared as if she could see into the hall through the separating wall. "Save for Eustace, all of Offord's servants treat me as an unwelcome foreigner.

They taunt me for my accent and pretend that they cannot understand me when I speak. This, when we have the same language and I have no trouble understanding them. I hate it here," she finished quietly.

Although her story added nothing to what Sir Adam had already told him, Faucon once more sifted through what he knew. No amount of twisting or turning led to a trail worthy of following, at least in the matter of Sir Robert's death. Now finding the missing bell was at least some sort of hunt.

"Are you ready to return to the hall, my lady?" he asked. "I think Sir Adam must be told that this bell of yours is gone."

She groaned at that. "Can I not remain here by myself?"

He shook his head and offered her his hand to aid her in rising. "Your bailiff is correct. You are Lady Offord, a widow of some consequence. It's no good for one such as you to hide like a child."

"You say that as if it were true," Idonea replied as she put her hand in his.

Once he lifted her to her feet, Faucon released her fingers and stepped back from her. "Because it is," he said.

Retrieving the empty bell box, but leaving the lock in the chair, he waited for the widow in the open doorway. Sir Robert of Offord's lady wife squared her shoulders and joined him.

"If I must," she said, "but promise me this. If they bar me outside the hall tonight, you'll come with and see to it that I don't freeze to death."

Faucon grinned at that. "I so vow."

Chapter Six

Returning down the narrow spiraling stairs, Faucon removed the bar and opened the door, then stood aside so the widow could enter the hall ahead of him. As she exited from the tower, he looked past her into the big room. Three maidservants dressed in red gowns topped with undyed linen over-gowns bustled as they cleared away the remains of the household's midday meal. Two manservants— one more boy than man, and both wearing red tunics over yellow chausses— strove to bring life back to the fire. One shoveled out the dead ash while the other plied a metal rake through the charred wood, seeking yet-glowing embers.

Lady Bagot and her daughters stood near the curtained bed in the corner. Despite the chill room, Sir Adam's womenfolk had shed their cloaks. Unlike Idonea and her fine garments, mother and daughters wore the same red gowns and plain overgowns as their maids. Faucon expected no less for the girls. Only a fool allowed children to ruin good fabric. That Lady Joia dressed so simply suggested she was like Marian, the sort of woman who expected to dirty her hands over the course of a day.

Sir Adam, Will, and Brother Edmund were all seated at the high table, the one reserved for Offord's ruling family. Although it wasn't raised on a dais as was customary, the table sat crossways in the hall while the other tables ran lengthwise. This not only allowed the servants to move easily along the inside of the tables, but Sir Robert and his kin could look upon their servants as the household dined.

A plain wooden chair with a tall back, no doubt the chair from which Sir Robert had ruled his folk, was set at the center of the table. Brother Edmund sat on the long bench to its right. The monk had created a workspace for himself. Sitting on the table in front of him was the small leather sack that contained his powdered ink and the tiny bowl in which he mixed it. His traveling basket, the lid askew, leaned against the end of the table. Faucon didn't need to see them to know that Edmund had arranged his writing implements— quills, blotting cloth, and knife— in front of him with his usual precision.

Sir Adam and Will had taken the bench to the left of Sir Robert's chair, both of them facing the tower door. The rusty-haired knight had his arms crossed. His jaw was tense. As for Will, Faucon's brother slouched against the table, his legs comfortably outstretched. A small smile curved his lips.

The instant Idonea exited, Sir Adam leapt to his feet, his arms opened and his fists clenched. "How dare you bar the hall door against me and my family!" the older knight roared at his wife's stepmother.

Brother Edmund wrenched around on his bench to see what happened. So, too, did all the servants and the ladies turn to watch. Idonea's frightened squeak sounded loud in the startled silence.

Faucon moved around Lady Offord to stand between her and the knight. Better that Sir Adam vented his bile on someone new and equally deserving. His host took the bait without hesitation.

"You're no better, Sir Faucon," he shouted, then pointed to the tower wall behind his new Crowner. "King's servant or not, you breached all courtesy when you shut yon door on me. This is now my home! You

68

had no right!"

"My pardon, sir," Faucon began, ready to offer a false apology for he didn't at all regret what he had done.

"Hey," Sir Adam interrupted, his eyes wide with surprise. "By what right do you carry Robert's bell and box? Where's the lock? You'll give that to me this instant."

"By Lady Offord's agreement and your need," Faucon replied, striding for the table. As he neared Sir Adam the knight stretched out his arms to take the box, but Faucon continued past him.

"Sir?!" the big knight cried in protest as Faucon rounded the corner of the table and set the coffer next to Edmund's roll of sheepskin.

"Brother Edmund, please note that there has been a burglary at Offord. A bell belonging to Sir Robert was stolen," he told his clerk as he opened the box and turned it so Sir Adam could see the empty interior.

"What?!" Sir Adam yelped. He leaned across the table and grabbed up the coffer, staring deep into its interior as if he thought the bell might yet be hiding somewhere within it.

"What?!" his wife echoed from across the quiet hall, her word torn with pain.

Lady Bagot trotted toward the table, her little lasses following in her wake. As she reached her husband, she rose to her toes, trying to see into the interior of the coffer. Sir Adam lowered the box and the lady gave a quiet cry as she witnessed its emptiness, then pivoted to look at the child who was her stepmother.

"Is this why you barred me from my own home? Is that what you think of me?" Lady Joia accused, her voice quivering and tears filling her eyes. "You craved time to secrete the bell, fearing I would steal it from you."

"I did not," Idonea moaned, sounding as heartsick as her stepdaughter.

"Lady Offord took nothing, but even if she had taken the bell, there's no one who could accuse her of wrongdoing," Faucon said, speaking over the widow. "The bell is her dower, meant to be hers if Sir Robert died before she had given him heirs."

"Says who?" Sir Adam snarled. As he bent an irate look on Idonea, he folded his arms around the empty coffer as if he feared the widow might wrench it from him.

"The lady herself," Faucon shot back. "If you don't know the details of Sir Robert's marriage contract, I suggest you send for Lady Offord's father. Have him bring those who witnessed their vows and the exchange of property. For the moment, it's enough for me that Lady Offord believes herself to be the rightful owner of the missing bell."

He glanced between Sir Adam and his lady. "More importantly, given where the key to this coffer is kept, who save one of you could have taken it from its box?" he accused flatly.

Much to Faucon's surprise, Lady Joia didn't protest in outrage. Instead, she gasped and grabbed her husband's arm. "The prior!" she cried as she looked up into his face. "That's why he banished us from Papa's chamber last night."

Releasing her husband, she turned a narrow-eyed look on Faucon. "That Churchman has coveted our bell from the moment my sire told him its tale. He stole it last night, I know it!"

At her charge, Sir Adam turned his head heavenward and freed a wordless raging sound. His pale skin was freckled with anger. "That sanctimonious, thieving bitch's son! I will have it back from him this very night, see if I don't!" Thrusting the empty coffer at his wife, he turned on his heel and jogged toward the hall door.

Will, who had kept to his comfortable slouch as he watched what played out around him, now came to his feet. The corners of his mouth quivered in amusement. "What say you, little brother? Do we stay here or follow our host as he confronts a churchly thief?"

Faucon shook his head. "Do as you please. I'll stay. There's no sense chasing around the shire until I'm certain who took the bell."

"I told you. Prior Thierry has it," Lady Joia insisted, her voice harsh. Anger made her all the more beautiful and in her rage she forgot all propriety. Lifting her head to a proud angle, she met the gazes of the strange knights before her. "If you think me mistaken, tell me what other reason that Churchman had for locking me out of my sire's chamber while my father was on his deathbed?"

"Perhaps your father made a gift of it to him in his last moments?" Faucon suggested gently.

"With what tongue?" Lady Joia shot back, almost sneering. "My father had lost his ability to speak before the prior arrived at Offord. Moreover, my sire had already promised the bell elsewhere," she added, glancing at Idonea and making a lie out of her husband's protest to the contrary. "My father would never have given the bell to Prior Thierry, not even to win the sons that Churchman swore he'd have if he gave up his bell.

"That man!" she continued, sputtering in her rage. "Time and again, he plied my sire with his false vows and empty promises, assuring my father he would have everything from glory here on Earth to a seat beside our Lord in trade for that bell. Yet my father steadfastly refused him. That's how I can be certain the Churchman took what he wanted last night."

As the lady paused to draw breath, Brother Edmund

cleared his throat. Faucon shot him a look. The monk's dark eyes were filled with concern.

"Sir, perhaps you should go to the priory with Sir Adam. I think that man very much provoked at the moment. He may not be in the right mind to confront an unarmed Churchman," he finished in understated warning.

Lady Bagot's eyes widened at this. Outrage drained from her expression, only to be replaced by something akin to horror. "Mary protect my husband, but the monk is right! Sir Adam rages too swiftly and is far too slow to regain his peace. There's no telling what he might do at the priory in his present state, especially if Prior Thierry refuses to return the bell. You must go with him to Wootton Wawen," she now pleaded of her Crowner and his brother.

Faucon gave a quick shake of his head. With Sir Adam gone, he was free to speak as he would with Offord's folk, especially Lady Bagot. "You fret without cause, my lady. No matter how angry, every man alive knows better than to harm a Churchman. The cost is too high. Think on the father of our king. Didn't old Henry end up walking unshod through Canterbury while the archbishop's monks flogged him, even though it wasn't he who had killed their archbishop?"

"What you say is true of sensible men," Lady Joia cried. "My husband is anything but sensible, especially just now. Are you not the king's man? Do as your oath requires. Go with him and see that he respects the king's peace," she commanded.

Will took a quick step forward and offered the pretty woman a swain's bow. As he straightened, he brought his hand to the hilt of his sword. "My lady, I may not be a royal servant, but I will ride with your husband. I vow to you that neither he nor the Churchman will come to harm over this matter."

Not waiting for her response, Will turned his back on the lady then leaned close to Faucon. "I was wrong to think your new duties boring. A bold and beautiful woman begging aid is definitely something I could learn to enjoy." Even at a whisper there was no mistaking the lust in his voice.

Guilt shot through Faucon as Will started toward the hall door at a swift jog. It was wrong to be grateful that he would be rid of both men for a time. But it was also wrong to squander the gift he'd been given.

Brother Edmund again cleared his throat. Faucon glanced at the monk. His clerk was frowning at him in open disapproval. Faucon offered Edmund a cock of his brow and a shift of his shoulders before he turned his attention back to Lady Joia, who stared toward the hall door even though Will was no longer in sight.

"Lady Bagot, are you content to have Sir William serve in my stead?" he asked.

"Yes, one man is enough," she said on a slow breath, her voice free of its cutting edge for the first time. "Sir Adam is less likely to strike out when others watch."

As she came back to herself, she glanced around the hall. A tiny crease pleated the space between her brows. "What is this?" she called to the watching servants, her words the crack of a whip. "I may no longer be your lady, but know that you stand and stare at your own peril. There is still much to be done if we're all to have a comfortable night."

To a one, Offord's servants leapt back to their tasks. As they did, Lady Joia hugged the coffer closer to her and began to sway as if she soothed a babe. "Why didn't I realize last night what the prior was about when he shut us all out?" she mourned softly to herself.

Her daughters, who had kept a fearful distance from their agitated parents, now slipped around the corner of the table. The elder girl wrapped her arm around her mother's waist. "Papa will get it back for us," Lady Helena assured her mother.

"It's Idonea's fault," the little one cried as she stood beside her sister. Lady Martha shook her finger at her step-grandmother. Her fine red brows lowered over her green eyes. "You have been very bad, Idonea. You had no right to lock us out in the cold."

Faucon eyed the child in shock. Although there could be no question from whom Martha had learned her bold and disrespectful manner, being pretty and petted was a dangerous combination. Young as she was, this child was well nigh on the way to being as spoiled as rotten meat.

Rather than scold as the child deserved, Lady Joia gave a watery sigh and stretched out an arm, offering to embrace her youngest. "Enough, Martha. What's done is done. We're inside and all is well again. Now, no more dawdling. Neither you nor Helena have worked on your stitchery today. Nor have you, Idonea," Offord's true lady said, turning her gaze on the child who was her stepmother.

Idonea's shoulders hunched. "My pardon, Joia," she said in passable French. "Martha is right to scold me. I shouldn't have barred the door on you."

Joia only shook her head. "If you want my forgiveness, help my daughters with their stools and baskets. Bring them to where you now stand. Those torches are fresh and the light is better. Wait," she said, instantly calling back her words.

Releasing her youngest child, Lady Joia glanced across the faces of the three girls. Although nothing changed in her expression, something about her eased. "What say you all? Why not use what's left of this day to finish Martha's poppet?"

Her offer drew a happy gasp from both of Sir Adam's daughters and a trembling smile from the young widow. Hems flying, Martha dashed to the commoner she'd just chided. Grabbing the older girl's hand, she pulled her step-grandmother toward the curtained bed. "Hurry, Idonea. You must show me how to give our poppet her eyes," she urged as she went.

"As you will, my little lady," Lady Offord replied, sounding almost happy as she allowed herself to be pulled along.

Helena followed them at a more sedate pace, her head carefully lowered. It was the sort of behavior expected of a girl-child who would likely rule a hall such as this one day.

Lady Bagot watched in silence as the children found what they needed near the head of the curtained bed. A moment later they placed three stools in the circle of the torchlight, then Idonea returned to the bed for a basket that spilled over with threads, yarn, and bits of fabric.

Once certain the girls were intent on their task and no longer paying heed to their elders, Joia's green eyes narrowed. "I know what my husband has told you about my sire's death," she told Faucon, "but he is wrong. My father was not murdered. He died because it was his time and there's nothing more to it than that. You waste your effort here, sir."

"Apparently not," Faucon replied evenly, pointing to the bell box in her arms. "Your bell was stolen."

As if prodded to it by his words, she set the coffer on the table, then shifted to stand between it and him. She crossed her arms and again lifted her chin to that imperious angle. "Nothing is stolen. The prior will return the bell to Sir Adam and the matter will be settled. Leave now, before night falls. Leave us to get on with preparing for my sire's funeral," she rudely commanded.

Faucon's jaw loosened in abject surprise. The words

he'd intended to speak, phrases meant to win the lady's trust and cooperation, melted from his tongue. Brother Edmund shot to his feet with such force the table went scratching through the rush-covered floor.

"You'll guard your tongue, woman," the monk scolded harshly. "Give me the name of your confessor so I may inform him of your misbehavior." His demand was the right of every Churchman when it came to the daughters of Eve.

Rather than bow to her head to a Churchman, Lady Joia glared at the monk. "Ask my husband if you want to know, for I'll not tell you," she snapped.

Outrage stained Edmund's lean cheeks. He pointed his finger at her, a certain sign that he intended to offer an even harsher scold. Faucon shifted, drawing his clerk's attention, then held up a hand in a wordless plea for restraint.

Gaze fixed on his employer, Edmund drew himself up until he stood lance-straight. His dark eyes narrowed in refusal. Faucon gave the smallest shrug, his brows lifted in pleading, then waited with little hope of success. He had no right to ask the monk to retreat, not in this instance.

Much to his surprise, Edmund took a deep breath and gave a single nod. Turning his back to the lady, he busied himself bringing bench, table, and his tools all back into their precise alignment. Beyond grateful, Faucon did his best to smile at his discourteous hostess.

"You may well be correct about your sire's passing, my lady, but it was your husband who called me here. As long as Sir Adam remains uneasy with what happened last night, I think I must also remain. As for the bell," he continued, "even if it returns to Offord this night, it and the identity of the thief must still be added to our record and the estate of the thief assessed.

"Is that not correct, Brother?" he asked of Edmund,

who had his head bowed over his little bowl as he made ink. The monk's response was a muted huff.

"Another waste of time," Lady Joia shot back, her lush mouth held in a sour line. "By royal edict the priory is free from all English service and toll."

Faucon fought to keep the corners of his mouth lifted and his voice gentle. "That may be, but assessing and recording value remains my duty. It's not on me to discern if the king can collect those fines."

Reaching down, he brought the bench next to her knees away from the table. "Humor me, my lady. Sit for a moment and tell me what you believe happened to your sire last night. Tell me why you are certain your father's death was natural and why your husband is not. If you convince me, I'll be free to release Sir Robert's corpse so you may prepare him for burial."

Chapter Seven

Lady Joia's eyes filled at his words. Her lips began to tremble. She dropped to sit on the bench, her back to the table. Her face was stained with grief. "Why can you not just go?" she cried, her voice softening with each word. "My father is up there in his chamber all alone, unwound and undressed. I cannot bear to leave him that way."

Tears began to trickle down her cheeks. She turned her gaze toward the tower wall. "Oh Papa, why did you wed again?"

Faucon, whose pricked pride had demanded he remain on his feet as he addressed this woman, changed his mind. Pulling out the chair at the table's center, he turned it toward her. "May I?" he asked before sitting.

Although his request earned him another huff from Edmund, Lady Bagot managed a quick nod. Wiping at her cheeks, she watched as her new Crowner made himself comfortable in her father's chair. Faucon leaned toward her, his elbows braced on his thighs.

"Are you saying that Sir Robert's recent marriage caused his death?"

"Yes," she replied, then shook her head. "No. Well, mayhap," she added, this time sounding as young as Martha.

Drawing a bracing breath, she tried again. "What I'm saying is that when my father remarried, my husband grew terrified for our son's inheritance, and his terror drove him mad. From the day poor Idonea arrived, Sir Adam was after my sire, belittling him, chiding him for being a fool and a cuckold."

"And was your father a fool and a cuckold?" Faucon interrupted.

A bit of the arrogant lady returned. Joia straightened and released a quick breath. "A fool, yes," she said harshly, her gaze shifting to her daughters and her youthful stepmother. The widow and her step-grandchildren chattered and giggled quietly as they worked, their heads bowed over a large patchwork poppet.

Lady Bagot sighed. "A fool, mayhap, but not a cuckold. Idonea is sickly, indolent, and useless save that she can teach Martha to sew, but she's no lightskirt," she told her Crowner, still watching her stepmother.

"So Lady Offord does not carry another man's child?" Faucon pressed, wanting Sir Adam's wife to speak the words herself.

"Of course she doesn't," retorted the true lady of Offord. "Idonea carries no child at all. Even if my father had been capable of planting a seed in her womb, something I doubt, Idonea is too weak to carry a babe. Indeed, as sickly as she is, I wonder if she'll survive the winter."

Lady Bagot's brow creased as she continued. "But no matter how many times I assured my husband there would never be a threat to our Robert, Sir Adam refused to hear me. He continued to hound my father until my sire finally snapped last night and vented his spleen on that unfortunate child.

"Then," Joia caught a shaken breath. "Then my father joined my husband in his madness. He turned on Sir Luc, my brother-by-marriage, and beat a man he claimed to love like a son out of his hall— out of my mother's home, the place I love most in the world— for daring to protect another man's wife.

"But not content to destroy but two lives, my father then proceeded to eat and drink too much even though

he knew doing so might make him ill. And so it did."
She started to say more but words failed her. Grief
again touched her face.

That she grieved for her sire despite the wrong Sir
Robert had done to both his daughter and his grandson
by remarrying soothed Faucon's injured pride. As he
waited for Lady Bagot to collect herself, the crackle of
newborn flames rose from the nearby hearth. He
breathed in the welcome fragrance of burning wood.
The girls laughed and Faucon watched as Martha held
up her now one-eyed cloth babe. Both Idonea and
Helena leaned back on their stools and clapped.

Their amusement stirred Joia from her moment of
private mourning. She wiped the tears from her face
with the backs of her hands. Her mouth yet trembled.
"Perhaps I have lost my mind as well," she offered in
subtle apology.

The lift of her chin indicated the children and their
toy. "Idonea's arrival turned me into naught but a
child's plaything just like that one, a toy torn between
the two men who both deserved my loyalty. Each of
them sought to force me to choose him over the other.
Well, I didn't choose. I refused, and they made my life
a misery for it."

"Has your sire often suffered after overeating?"
Faucon asked, guiding her back to where he wished her
to go.

"Not often," she said, fighting for composure. "Each
time it happened I drove him to his bed. I forced him to
stay there for a few days while I pressed a cleansing
tonic past his stubborn lips. He was himself again
within days."

"Did what ate at him include the same weakness in
his limbs?" Faucon wanted to know. "Did he ever lose
the use of his legs during those previous spells as he did
last night?"

Joia shook her head. "Nothing was like last night," she told him, then again looked boldly up at her Crowner. Her expression was stricken.

"God forgive me, but this is all my fault. Why didn't I realize that last night was something apart, something different from his other afflictions? Was he waiting for me to help him? Did he die thinking I could have done something for him and didn't?" she moaned softly.

Across the room, Martha slid off her stool and skipped toward her mother bearing her poppet. The plaything was half her size. Where its cloth torso was stuffed almost to bursting, its legs were less chubby. That left them flaccid enough that they flew with her as she skipped. "Maman! Look, I did the eye all by myself. Idonea and Helena only showed me where to put my needle."

"Well now, let me see what you've done," Joia said, opening her arms in invitation. Her youngest daughter snuggled into her mother's embrace. Lady Joia pressed her lips to the top of the lass's head before she took the toy from her and made a show of examining it.

"What of the events of yesterday?" Faucon asked. "Outside of what you've already said, and given what happened and the missing bell, does anything else about the day or anyone's actions now seem unusual or untoward?"

Joia frowned at him, then looked at Martha. "Not at all. How could anything be amiss when we were celebrating your saint day with a little feast?"

"I love celebrations," the child agreed with a winsome smile.

Turning in her mother's embrace, Martha aimed her cheeky gaze at Faucon. "Even though it was my day, Milla made Grand-père's favorite dish. That's because Grand-père and I like the same thing," she told the king's servant. "The dish with the little birds is our most special favorite."

She looked back at her mother. "And this year I was old enough to have my own portion. I didn't have to share a bite with anyone, did I, Maman?"

"You did not," Joia agreed.

"Are we still to have a posset tonight?" Martha then asked, her feet dancing as she wriggled in the circle of her dam's embrace.

"We shall indeed," her mother replied, setting her youngest child away from her.

"But when?" Martha whined.

"When Milla is finished making it and no sooner," Joia replied swiftly, a note of correction in her voice. "You know as well as I, Milla always does as she promises. Be patient, my sweet," she added, holding out the poppet for Martha to take.

Martha pushed the plaything back at her mother. "But Maman," she complained, "you didn't say what you think of her eye."

"I think it is very well done," her mother replied, teasing a happy smile from her child. "Now hurry back and finish the other, for she won't be a proper poppet until she has two. After that, she must have a nose and a mouth."

"And ears," her daughter added, touching a finger to her own ear as she took her cloth babe from her mother.

"Ears as well," Joia agreed. "If you finish her face this night, on the morrow you may make her a shift and gown."

Martha squealed in pleasure and whirled to look at the other girls. "Idonea, we can make clothing for her on the morrow."

"Sister!" The man's shout came from the other side of the screen at the far end of the hall.

Gasping, Lady Joia's face twisted in panic. She rose

so quickly that Martha stumbled away from her, almost falling. Idonea freed a frightened cry. Her stool toppled as she came to her feet.

Their reactions sent Faucon out of his chair, his hand on his sword. Stepping around the edge of the table, he tossed his cloak over his shoulders to free his arms, then placed himself between the women of Offord and whatever threat they believed advanced toward them.

Behind him, Edmund's bench shifted loudly. Faucon glanced at the monk as Edmund halted at his left shoulder. His clerk held the small knife he used to trim quills in his fist. Faucon nodded. No matter how unnecessary, Edmund deserved to know his courage was appreciated. Together, they would face this threat.

As the becloaked man strode into the hall, he threw back his hood. If his call to Lady Bagot named him kin, his face named him Sir Adam's brother. The two men shared the same thick nose, rusty red hair, and blue eyes. Rather than a full beard, Sir Adam's brother, younger by half, had trimmed his golden-red facial hair into the carefully sculpted line that was the fashion just now. But it was his fresh bruises that told Faucon this was Sir Luc, Idonea's tormentor.

Sir Luc faltered in his stride as he saw Faucon. "Who are you?" he asked, more confused than confrontational.

"This is Sir Faucon de Ramis, newly-elected Coronarius to our king," Brother Edmund called out before Faucon could speak. "He is here because of Sir Robert of Offord's untimely death."

"Sir Robert is dead?! That cannot be! My lady, what has happened?" Sir Luc cried, shifting to look at his hostess. It seemed the lack of subtlety afflicted more than one man from Bagot. That the knight sought to mislead, if not outright deceive, could be read plainly upon his face and heard in his voice.

Craving Lady Joia's reaction to her kinsman's ploy, Faucon glanced back at his reluctant hostess. Her panic was gone. Instead, anger now filled her face. She rounded the end of the table and stopped beside Faucon, her hands on her hips.

"Don't you play the innocent with me, Luc," she scolded her brother-by-marriage, using his given name without his title. "You wouldn't dare enter this hall if you didn't know your brother has left Offord. If you know that much, you also know my sire is no more."

"Play the innocent?" the knight cried, honest confusion in his voice. "But I thought—"

"Say no more!" Lady Bagot protested over him, an almost frantic edge to her voice. "I won't hear it! Get you gone, just as my father commanded last night. Be gone from Offord before your brother returns and finishes what my sire started." This was as much a plea as a command.

"Yes, go away," Idonea called. "You are not wanted here."

Sir Luc afforded the widow but a glancing look, then put his shoulder to Faucon as he brought his attention back to his brother's wife. "But my lady, I mean only to offer you my protection," he more pleaded than said.

"Sir Faucon, there has been too much violence and grief in my father's home these last days," Lady Bagot said to him, her face hollow. "I can bear no more. I beg you, escort my brother-by-marriage to Offord's gate. If you feel it necessary, you may continue at Sir Luc's side until he is mounted and rides across the village bounds." She spoke to her Crowner, but her words intended for the other knight in the hall.

Faucon nodded his agreement. "I am at your command, my lady," he said and started toward Sir Adam's brother.

"All I intend is your safety, Joia," Sir Luc called out, addressing his brother's wife with untoward intimacy, his arms spread wide. "Let me stay here until my brother returns."

Habit brought Faucon to a halt just out of sword's reach of the knight. He studied his opponent. Under the man's well-worn brown cloak he was dressed in a fine blue wool tunic and red chausses. A heavily-embroidered fabric belt was knotted around his waist. That flimsy piece told the tale. Sir Luc might be a worthy adversary on the field, but not at this moment. The only weapon that belt could support was an eating knife.

"Sir," Faucon said, extending his hand in greeting, "as you have heard, I am Sir Faucon de Ramis, this shire's newly elected Keeper of the Pleas. By royal decree it is no longer our sheriff who examines the bodies of the dead or identifies those who have done murder. Those duties in this shire are now mine."

"Well met," Sir Luc offered in rote response, as he briefly closed his hand around Faucon's. His gaze never left his brother's wife. A pained frown creased his brow. "Truly, Joia, I meant no harm by coming."

"Of course not," Faucon replied pleasantly, speaking for the lady. He rested his left hand on the hilt of his sword as he raised his right to indicate the screen and the door beyond it. "Come. I'll walk with you to Offord's gate."

Chapter Eight

Sir Luc frowned, but he had the good grace to give way. Offering no further word to his kinswoman, he turned for the hall door. Faucon looked at Edmund. His clerk rolled his eyes and shook his head, then turned back toward his table.

Smiling at that, Faucon drew his cloak back around him and followed Sir Adam's brother. As they went, they passed the servants, who were once again idle, enjoying the spectacle put on by their betters. The only sounds in the hall were the snap of burning wood and the crunch of dry rushes under the feet of the walking knights.

Making his way around the screen ahead of his Crowner, Sir Luc shoved the hall door wide. The wind moaned past them as they exited. After Faucon pulled the door almost closed behind him, he joined Sir Luc on the edge of the porch. Night was overtaking Offord's bailey, ragged fingers of darkness climbing the walls and creeping out of the corners. To Faucon's surprise he saw Legate and Edmund's donkey at the far end of Offord's bailey, grazing alongside Offord's horses. They had been stripped of their gear. Given the misadventures of the last hour he was grateful that someone had tended to them.

Sir Luc made a frustrated sound. "There's no need to follow any farther, sir. I accept that I am well and truly banished."

"Ah, but I follow you for my own reasons, Sir Luc," Faucon replied evenly. "I have questions about last

86

night that I pray you can answer for me. Perhaps we should speak privately, against the possibility your brother might return more quickly than expected? What say you? Shall we repair to the same place in the village where you spent last night?"

The knight jerked as if struck. "How— how," he stuttered, then caught himself. His russet brows lowered. "God take Eustace!"

That gave Faucon pause. Not only had Sir Robert's bailiff barred the dead man's daughter from her home, Eustace had also thwarted Sir Robert's command that Sir Luc be banned from Offord. He offered the knight a small smile.

"The bailiff said nothing to me. I have no need for another to tell me what I can see for myself. You wear your best on a wet day and no horse awaits you here in the yard, yet you entered Offord Hall only moments after your brother and mine left for Wootton Wawen."

Sir Luc's mouth opened, then closed. He settled for a wordless shrug.

"So, will you answer my questions?" Faucon pressed.

"If you agree to answer mine," Luc replied. He didn't wait for his Crowner to agree before continuing. "Did my brother truly ride out for Wootton Wawen?"

Faucon nodded. "Your brother and mine," he repeated.

Sir Luc's mouth stretched into a crooked smile. "Then Adam won't be returning until well after dark, if at all this night. That's a boon, for it means I have time to eat before I must leave," he said with a lift of his brows. "Eustace's wife doesn't much like my presence in her home. She punished both her husband and me by pronouncing that we were all fasting, it being the eve of the first night of Advent. So, sir, if you wish to speak with me, you'll have to follow me to the kitchen. Milla

87

won't send me away," Luc added as he started down the porch stairs, "or so both I and my stomach hope."

Faucon matched the taller man's stride as they made their way to the kitchen shed. Built of wattle-and-daub, the long rectangular building with its thatched roof was about half the size of the hall. The cooking fire hadn't been banked for the night, or so said the smoke that yet streamed from the roof vent. Faucon tested the wind and sighed in disappointment. The cook was no longer roasting nuts.

Turning the simple wooden latch on the door, Sir Luc entered without announcement, leaving Faucon to follow. The floor beneath his boots was hardened earth and the walls around him naught but woven withe panels coated with a thin layer of plaster. That meant, unlike the hall, the kitchen had no need of an open door to keep the air clear. Instead, the wind prized through every wall to gather up the noxious smoke and carry it from the shed.

By the uncertain light of the kitchen fire, Faucon saw rafters hung with great bunches of dried herbs and smoked meats. Hempen bags, no doubt filled with nuts or grains, and stoppered leather containers cluttered one wall. Near Faucon's left knee was a glistening wooden cask that suggested oil. Next to it was a large half-barrel lined with cloth to hold water and filled with writhing eels that swam in hapless circles.

A heavy iron tripod had been built into the central open hearth. From its chain hung a cauldron, the char on its base suggesting constant use. Steam twisted and tangled over the lip of that big pot, filling the chamber with a scent that reminded Faucon of home. Offord, his nose told him, also broke its nightly fast with cabbage pottage, this one was made with a salty rich ham broth that had been seasoned heavily with garlic. The aroma went far to ease his reluctance at having to spend the night in this inhospitable place.

The cook's worktable was at the far end of the chamber and stretched from wall to wall. Hanging from pegs driven into the wall above it were knives, rasps, spoons, large and small mallets, ladles, and sieves. A tall thin woman worked at the table, her back to the door. Her right arm moved as if she stirred something. Upon her head she wore a stained white kerchief, while the sleeves of her gown— the same shade of red as the attire of the other maids— were rolled up above her elbows.

Crouched at her feet cleaning a dirty pot was a lad wearing yellow chausses and a sodden red tunic that was several sizes too large for him. The boy glanced up from his task. Under his thatch of fair hair, his brown eyes widened. Mouth agape, he dropped to sit flat on the ground and tugged on the hem of the woman's gown. When she looked down at him, he pointed to her visitors. She spun to face them, still holding her bowl and spoon.

Fair hair straggled out from under her head-cloth. In her middle years she was yet a handsome woman, her features fine in a raw-boned face. One gently arching brow rose as she looked at Sir Luc. "Is it not enough that your brother is enraged with you? Now you dare to bring a stranger to Offord while Sir Adam is away from our walls?" she chided in the knight's native French, sounding more like a mother than a servant.

Sir Luc offered her his crooked smile and a quick shrug. "I didn't bring this man to Offord, Milla. Adam did." He looked at Faucon. "My pardon, but who are you again?"

"I am Sir Faucon de Ramis, our shire's newly-elected Keeper of the Pleas," Faucon told Milla the Cook. "By the king's decree, I now examine the bodies of the murdered and call inquest juries from the hundreds. Sir Adam brought me to Offord this day because the manner of Sir Robert's death concerns him."

That teased a single harsh laugh from Milla. "It's not Sir Robert's death that concerns him," she muttered in English.

She again looked at Sir Luc. "So you didn't bring the man to Offord, but why do you bring him here to disturb the peace of my humble home?"

"Because I'm hungry," Luc replied swiftly, his smirk growing into a full grin, "and Sir Faucon wished to speak with me in private. Before you ask, I am still banished from the hall," he added, "so feed me at your peril."

This time, the woman's laugh was more natural. Her fondness for the knight filled her face. "Everything I've ever done for you has been at my peril. What is one more perilous deed?"

Setting down her bowl, she crossed the room to stand in front of the red-headed knight. With a tsk, she touched a finger to his bruised jaw. "Look at you," she said with a shake of her head. "For shame. I vow you've learned nothing since I had you at my breast. Only an idiot steps between a man and his wife."

"Then I am an idiot," Luc replied as he moved his head out of her reach, still smiling. "But it's good to know that you still love me enough to chide, Milla."

"And I will always chide," she told him, scolding still, "because you will always behave foolishly."

"Prove how much you care. Feed me and give me a cup of Sir Robert's wine to wash down the meal." In that instant Luc sounded as cheeky as little Martha.

"You!" Milla retorted in amusement. "You'll get no wine from me and the only thing I can offer your empty belly is yesterday's bread and this morn's fresh cheese. However, Lady Bagot has me making a posset. It's almost finished. Should that suit, I've made more than enough for you to have a cup."

"I love your possets," Sir Luc replied happily. "With that to drink, even bread and cheese will be the grandest of meals."

His comment only made Milla laugh again. "And what of you, sir?" she asked Faucon. "Will you eat and drink as well?"

"A taste of the posset would be welcome, goodwife," Faucon replied, as pleased as Sir Luc at the invitation. There was nothing better on a blustery cold evening than a posset– milk flavored with honey and spices then seethed with wine and eggs until thickened.

Milla nodded, then looked at the lad who yet sat on the floor by her worktable. "Nobby," she said in English, "take our stools close to the fire for these knights. After that, bring me two wooden cups from my chest for their drink and prepare a tray for Sir Luc. He'll have a loaf of yestermorn's bread— the manchet, not the brown bread— and two scoops of that cheese I made."

"Aye, mistress," the boy replied as he came to his feet, brushing his hands clean of the herbed sand he'd been using to scour the pot.

Moments later, Faucon sat crammed between bags and barrels, but near enough to the hearth to warm his face. He cradled a wooden cup in his hands. For the sake of space, they'd arranged their stools on the opposite side of the fire from Milla's worktable.

Beside Faucon, Sir Luc had a wooden tray balanced on his thighs, his eating knife resting on its edge. The knight held his cup clenched between his knees. As Luc broke the stale flat bread into pieces, he looked at his Crowner. "So what is it you wish to ask me?"

Given that there was now a legitimate wrongdoing at Offord to investigate, Faucon started there. "Do you know that Sir Robert's bell went missing last night?" he said to the knight.

"The bell cannot be found?" Sir Luc replied, eyes wide, then returned his gaze to his meal as he shook his head. "Poor Joia! She's not only lost her father, but now our favorite plaything as well."

"I beg your pardon?" Faucon eyed the knight in surprise.

Luc shot him a quick look and shrugged. "Bagot and Offord. Our families have been close for all my life, and Joia's. So it has been even though Sir Robert wed Joia's mother, the woman my father had been determined to wed to Adam. Joia is but a year younger than me, and we were often playmates. On those occasions when my family visited Offord, Sir Robert would allow his daughter to bring out his bell. As children, she and I could play for hours with it, making up stories about who we were and why we needed to ring that bell, and of course, making as much noise as possible. She was forever after her father to assure her it would always be hers. Each time she'd ask, Sir Robert would give her his vow, then laugh and tell her his word was all in play, that Offord was her dowry, not the bell."

Faucon considered his fellow knight. "Then it must hurt her deeply knowing that, should we find the bell, her former toy will leave Offord for the term of Idonea's life."

"I doubt that," Luc replied. Taking up a piece of broken bread, he used it to scoop up a bit of the thick, clotted drink to his mouth. He savored before he spoke again.

"Joia is no longer that carefree child. How could she be, when she's my brother's wife? She's far too practical to dream about anything other than seeing her son in her father's place. As far as keeping that bell as her own, even if her father had decided to give it to her, she knows very well my brother intends to sell it the instant Sir Robert is buried, doing so for his own profit."

"Do you have any idea who might have taken it?" Faucon asked.

The knight only shrugged. "Anyone who was set on taking it, I suppose. However, the thief would have had no easy time getting to it. There cannot be many who could breach Sir Robert's private chamber for the storeroom without being noticed or stopped by the servants," he finished, echoing Faucon's earlier thought.

"Prior Thierry was among those few, according to your brother and his lady wife," Faucon said.

Luc gaped at him. "That is why my brother and yours rode for Wootton Wawen?! Adam believes the prior took the bell? Well, that settles it," he said to Faucon. "My brother has well and truly gone mad."

"Why do you say that?" Faucon asked, although he thought he knew the answer, having glimpsed Sir Adam's darker mood.

Luc turned his gaze back to his tray. "I say it because it's true. Adam lost Offord once when Sir Robert married Lady Joia's mother, but that only made him want Offord all the more. When Joia was born— she was Sir Robert's first child— Adam immediately offered for her. It was a good gamble on my brother's part, for she not only survived to wed him, but proved a beauty." He grinned in appreciation of his brother's wife.

"After they were wed and Joia had given Adam a son for their second child, the son Sir Robert couldn't produce, my brother was beside himself with joy. Believing Offord securely in his hands, Adam agreed to support Robert's plans to expand Offord's flocks.

"Offord has richer pastures and produces better wool than Bagot," the knight said, "but Robert hasn't the same talent or interest as Adam in finding profit from all he does. When I returned as a knight to Bagot and became its steward, I warned Adam that it was a foolish risk. What if Little Robert died? What if Joia died after him? Either Robert would have to marry again for another heir or the king would own Offord in Adam's place."

Pausing to enjoy another bite of posset and bread, he continued. "As if to prove me right, what happens?" he asked in rhetorical question, a note of irony in his voice. "Adam's dear father-by-marriage decides without warning to wed for the third time. From the moment of Lady Offord's arrival here, my brother has been crazed with the fear he'll lose all. So deep is his madness he now sees a thief in a Churchman."

"Lady Bagot suggests much the same," Faucon said, watching as Luc spread soft cheese on bread. "But tell me what could have happened last night to make your brother believe Sir Robert's death was anything but natural?"

"You're asking me that?" Sir Luc scoffed. He touched a finger to his bruised face. "I left the hall before Sir Robert grew ill, as you well know if you've spoken with my brother."

"But you didn't leave Offord after Sir Robert commanded you go," Faucon said.

The knight watched him for a long moment. Just when Faucon thought Sir Luc would say nothing, the man replied, "That is true. I did not leave."

"Why not?" Faucon wanted to know.

Sir Luc turned his gaze to his tray. "Because I feared for Lady Offord. I'll not see any woman mistreated, but especially not a woman who is with child. Someone had to protect her from my brother."

"It's odd you think of yourself as her protector. Do you know Lady Offord is frightened of you?" Faucon asked gently.

That brought Luc's attention up from his tray. He looked genuinely surprised. "Of me? What reason has she to fear me?"

Faucon watched him closely. "Then she's wrong to think you intend seduction?"

"I would never dishonor another man so," Sir Luc protested, but he lied again, or so said the way his cheeks brightened. As if he knew he betrayed himself, he looked back at his bread and cheese.

"There is no longer a husband to dishonor now that she is a widow," Faucon reminded his fellow knight.

"That changes nothing," Luc muttered to his tray.

"Because you are too closely related?" Faucon asked. Idonea was Joia's stepmother and Joia was married to Sir Adam. That put Luc within four degrees of relationship with Idonea.

Luc freed a strangled laugh. "Because I am a third son, without so much as a groat to my name. I will never marry."

Faucon recognized the longing in the man's voice. Hadn't he felt just as hopeless before the miracle of his new position? "Such is the fate of we who are extra sons," Faucon murmured, bringing his cup to his lips.

When Luc made no response, Faucon more chewed than drank a mouthful of posset. Unlike the wealthier barons and earls who could afford to support more than one or two sons, the extra sons from families with neither name nor riches were doomed to the lonely lot of a bachelor knight, a soldier for hire. If such a man dared to dream, he might try his skills on the tournament circuit, hoping to prove another William Marshal. An extra son himself, the Marshal was so skilled at arms that he won himself a place in old King Henry's household. But even he spent more than a score of years with no home or wife of his own before Henry's son Richard rewarded his loyalty with the hand of the richest heiress in all England and Normandy.

And if those knighted extra sons failed to find

employment? All too often they turned to thievery to stave off starvation. Or....

Faucon eyed Sir Luc over the rim of his cup, thinking it a boon for Sir Adam that the Church considered his brother and Idonea related. If the widow should produce a son for Sir Robert, thereby securing Offord as her dower, and Luc were to win her hand in marriage, Sir Adam's younger brother would rule Offord in his brother's place, at least for the widow's lifetime.

Stirring himself from his thoughts, Faucon said, "Things cannot be so bleak for you. Surely, the position as Bagot's steward offers some prospect for the future." That had been how Sir John, Blacklea's former steward, had won the hand of Marian, although he hadn't done so until his later years.

"I have the title and the work, but no recompense," Luc said sourly, still staring at the tray in front of him. "My brother didn't vow to my dying father that he'd pay me, only that he would keep me housed and fed for my life, or for as long as I choose to stay."

Lifting his cup in a small salute, Faucon smiled. "May God shower good fortune down upon all of us who have older brothers."

Luc glanced at him, then raised his own cup to acknowledge the toast.

"I've not much hope you can help me with this," Faucon continued, "but was there anything unusual about yesterday either before or during the meal?"

The knight thought for a moment, then offered a slow nod. "I wouldn't have considered it until you asked, but I now see that there was," he said. "Everyone save Helena and little Martha was on edge. Robert is—" he caught himself "—was usually a lively man, quick to laugh, quick to rage, and just as quick to forgive. And always kind. Not so yesterday. He spoke little, and when he did speak what he said was sharp and harsh. His only truly kind words were for Martha.

"For that I blame my brother," Luc continued as he spread cheese on another bit of bread. "The whole while I was in the hall, Adam was after Robert like a man baiting a bear, pricking him with words, drawing blood with each blow. The more Robert fought to keep his calm, the harder Adam pressed. Finally, my brother went too far and shouted for all to hear that Lady Offord carried another man's child."

"And does the lady carry another man's child?" Faucon asked, doing his own baiting.

Anger flared in Sir Luc's blue eyes. He sat straighter on his stool, his right hand now clenched around the handle of his eating knife. "My brother is an ass, but not even he believes that. King's servant you may be, I'll not tolerate you insulting the lady in my hearing." His outrage was mummery, behind which hid a soul who knew he had sinned.

"I beg your pardon, sir. My duty often requires me to ask objectionable questions. I'll guard my tongue more carefully as we proceed," Faucon said.

Luc released a slow breath and let the heat drain from him. He looked back at the tray in his lap. "And I shall do my best to remember you don't speak for yourself but for our laws."

"Is there anything else you can tell me about the meal?" Faucon asked.

Luc finished the last of his cheese before he looked up at his Crowner. "What else is there to say? Adam made us all miserable, then drove Robert mad. Then, in his madness, Robert drove me from the hall."

Faucon shrugged. "Not much more than that, I suppose. Was there anything else you'd like to ask me?"

The knight looked at him in blank confusion, then gave a nervous laugh as he remembered himself. "Oh, that. No, you've answered where I needed it."

Swallowing the last of his posset, Luc set his cup and tray on the floor. When he came to his feet, he made a show of straightening his cloak around him. "I'd best be on my way home to Bagot. Although we're only over the fourth rise, I'd rather not ride in full dark." Despite his words, everything about the knight said he had no intention of leaving Offord.

Faucon considered honoring Lady Bagot's request to accompany her brother-by-marriage to the village bounds. He discarded the notion as a waste of his time. This was a man who lied too easily. Luc would simply wait outside the village until he could return unseen. Instead, he came to his feet and extended his hand. "Travel with God, sir."

The knight brushed his hand on his cloak before taking Faucon's. "And I wish you much good fortune in this new duty of yours, Sir Faucon."

Chapter Nine

As Sir Luc made his way to the kitchen door, he sent a quick look over his shoulder at his former nurse. It seemed Milla had been waiting for this sign. She put aside her bowl and followed the knight outside the kitchen.

Leaving the door open behind them, they stopped a few paces beyond the opening. The wind flattened Sir Luc's cloak against his back and set the cook's head-cloth to fluttering. Faucon watched their mouths move as they spoke. Although he could hear nothing of what they said, Milla looked as though she chided her former nursling. Then the cook rose on her toes and pressed a swift kiss to the knight's cheek.

As Sir Luc made his way toward Offord's gate, Milla the Cook returned into the kitchen. Panting against the cold, she stopped in the doorway. All the softness she'd shown Sir Luc was gone from her face. Instead, the lift of her brow invited her unwelcome guest to leave.

"I have questions for you regarding Sir Robert's death," Faucon said, in reply to her rude and unspoken demand.

"I think I can have nothing to offer in that regard, sir," she replied as she straightened her head covering, tucking her hair back beneath it.

"It will take but a moment," Faucon persisted.

She freed an impatient breath, then looked at Nobby. "Run you to the hall, boy," she said in her native tongue. "Ask one of the maids to come fetch the pot."

"I can carry it," the lad protested.

"Nay, it's too heavy for you and posset is too dear to spill. Rather, after you bear your message, stay in the hall and lay out the cups, claiming one for yourself as you do," she told him.

That put a smile on the lad's face and wings on his feet. He sprinted from the kitchen. Milla shut the door behind him, then stood with her back to it as she again aimed her sharp gaze at Faucon. "Ask your questions, sir, but swiftly so, if you please. I yet have work to do before I can call this day done."

"Perhaps you overheard my conversation with Sir Luc? Sir Robert's bell has gone missing. Would you have any idea who might have taken it?" Faucon asked with a smile, lifting his cup from the seat of the stool to see if there was anything left in it beyond dregs. There wasn't.

"How would I know who does what in the hall? This," the lift of the cook's hand indicated the kitchen, "is my home. Save for the occasional feast day, I spend little time outside this place."

"Were you in the hall for last night's feast?" Faucon asked.

"That was not a feast, only a celebration," Milla corrected him. "And I was in the hall, but only for a brief time during the meal."

"While you were there, did you notice anything unusual?" Faucon pressed, wondering if it was just her nature to be so tight-lipped or if there was purpose behind her defiance.

Her expression flattened. "The only thing unusual about last night's meal was how Sir Adam stole all the joy from an event meant to honor his daughter."

"I think you overestimate Sir Adam's effect on Lady Martha," Faucon told her. "The lady says she very much enjoyed that special dish you made for her and her grandsire."

An unreadable emotion dashed through Milla's blue eyes. Her mouth tightened slightly. "Ah, the quail. It is Sir Robert's favorite dish, however I believe Lady Martha's fondness for her 'little birds' is because it pleases her grandsire that she shares them with him. No one else likes the dish. The sauce is too tart. But that child would do anything to win Sir Robert's smile, and he feels the same for her.

"However, in honor of the little lady's special day, she was allowed her very own dish this time. Because the birds were hers alone, I also erred on the side of sweetness for her sauce."

Here, Milla allowed the corners of her mouth to rise into a narrow smile. "I vow, it was a waste of honey. We could have piled ashes on that platter and our little lady would have eaten them with relish, so overjoyed was she at having a dish she did not need to share with anyone, especially her sister."

That teased a laugh from Faucon. The rules of courtesy required the gently-born to eat in pairs, at least at the day's main meal and certainly on more formal occasions. Each couple shared one trencher and one cup between them, and served each other, bite by bite, sip by sip. There had been more than a few times in his youth when he'd begrudged Will every morsel of a dish he wanted all to himself.

Still smiling, Faucon asked, "What say you? Lady Bagot insists that her father but answered our Lord's call last night. Not so Sir Adam. He believes someone helped Sir Robert into heaven."

Every bit of emotion left Milla's handsome face. "I would know nothing of that," she offered swiftly. She crossed her arms before her. It was a drawbridge lifting to ward off besiegers.

Her reaction battered at Faucon's thus-far lackadaisical hunt. Yet, no matter how he turned those pieces of his, he could find no trail to follow. Every sign he saw said there was nothing to find in regard to Sir Robert's passing.

At last, all he could think to say was, "Lady Bagot says Sir Robert's final ailment was brought on by overeating and last night wasn't the first time he ailed after giving way to gluttony."

"What would I know of those spells of his? I'm no healer," Milla replied, with a dismissive lift of her brows.

In frustration Faucon shifted to follow the tracks Sir Adam had so diligently created for him. "Did you know Lady Offord was using the dairy as her hidey-hole?"

"I did," the cook replied. As she spoke both her expression and her arms relaxed although her tone remained flat. "All of us who serve at Offord know where the *lady*, if you can call her that, hides."

The corner of her mouth lifted into a sneer. "What use is it wedding a common man's daughter to a knight if she isn't willing to take on the duties that belong to her new position? Lady Offord's lack of liver shames those of us who are her peers."

"Some among Offord's servantry seem to support her," Faucon prodded. "This afternoon, your bailiff barred the hall door against Lady Bagot, holding it at Lady Offord's command."

Angry color washed over Milla's face. Her jaw tightened. "Regardless of how it may appear, you can be certain that our bailiff held that door for his own profit and no other reason."

"He has wronged you," Faucon said, leaping to exploit the first hint of weakness she'd revealed.

She considered him for a long moment then heat came to flickering life in her gaze. "You tell me, sir. A beloved brother sends his sister, a widow, whose husband squandered both her dowry and dower, and her dying babe to nurse a Bagot heir. She begs her brother's advice on how to safeguard the coins they pay her, only to later discover those coins are gone, spent without her knowledge. With no profit to show after years of work, she begs her brother to help her make right where wrong was done. Instead, he offers an even deeper injury."

She paused to draw a fiery breath. The twist of her lips was filled with wicked amusement. "Ah, but here I am, in the right place to watch as my brother finds himself made as poor as me. Now that Sir Robert is gone there's no one left to coddle that cowardly son of a worm, no one to excuse his errors and misjudgments."

Faucon frowned. "Why would Sir Robert protect his bailiff if the man is incompetent or worse?"

"For love's sake," Milla spat out. "Just as I nursed my poor dying Etta alongside Sir Luc, my brother sucked one of my mother's teats while Sir Robert had his mouth upon the other. Closer than blood they were and Sir Robert forgave my brother everything. That is, until this past summer. First, disease took almost all of our newly-castrated wethers. The next month the wool merchant's buyer came for our spring fleeces. But when he inspected them, he complained they had too many locks and only offered a tenth of what they should have been worth."

Again, she showed him that hard smile. "Pity poor foolish Sir Adam, who has so longed to own Offord that he forgets all caution. Now, Sir Robert departs this earthly vale at the very moment that there's not one coin in Offord's purse and Sir Adam's coveted second property may very well drag down his first.

"Having heard that, sir, do you think Offord's new master will keep the old master's bailiff?" She lifted her brows. There was vindictive pleasure in her gaze. "You cannot know how much I'll enjoy watching my brother lose all he holds dear, just as I did."

Her words hit Faucon like a blow. Hadn't he all too often heard that same hateful tone in Will's voice? Hadn't he seen that same nasty bend of lip on his brother's mouth? The destruction Milla wished upon her sibling was no different than the fate Will wished for his younger brother.

Unable to bear the woman's presence for another moment, Faucon set his cup on the seat of the stool and left the kitchen.

Chapter Ten

Head down, lost in dark thoughts, he crossed the yard and jogged up the porch steps. As he shoved open the hall door, he collided with Lady Helena. Sir Adam's elder daughter gave a quiet cry and stumbled back against the wooden screen. Her heel caught in the hem of her cloak and she began to fall.

Faucon grabbed her by the shoulders to steady her. At his touch, Helena's freckled face took fire. Beneath the faint red arch of her brows, her blue eyes widened in something that wasn't quite fear. He instantly released her. Yet pressed against the wooden panel behind her, she eased to the side, just out of arm's reach, her hands clasped as if in prayer. There she stood, staring up at him, the gusting wind toying with the tendrils of golden-red hair that had escaped her plaits.

"My pardon," Faucon said with a reassuring smile. "I wasn't paying heed as I walked."

"The fault is mine, sir," the child-woman replied, her voice strained and tight.

Sudden moisture filled her eyes as the color on her cheeks flared even brighter. Everything about her, from her stance to her clutched hands, suggested she would very much like to curl in a ball to hide. Instead, she held her ground, her gaze yet meeting his. "I was on my way to the kitchen to fetch the posset," she told him at a whisper.

Fetch the posset? If the pot was too heavy for that lad, it was certainly too heavy for Sir Adam's daughter.

But Nobby had been commanded to speak to a maid. How had Lady Joia even known to send her child instead?

Tears trembled on the girl's eyelashes but did not fall. Her mouth opened. Words tumbled from her lips so quickly that they almost collided with one another. "Your clerk tells us that only knights with an income of twenty pounds a year can serve as Coronarius."

Faucon's surprise tumbled into understanding. Lady Bagot had asked Edmund about him. Edmund, who saw every question as a simple quest for information, had no doubt answered truthfully, most likely including every detail he'd collected about his employer's family, marital status, and the particulars of Faucon's financial arrangements with his benefactors.

Satisfied by what she heard, Lady Bagot had used the posset as a pretense so her almost-eligible daughter might intercept a potential husband. From the look on Helena's face Faucon suspected she'd been most sternly commanded to engage her Crowner in conversation of some kind. Unfortunately, or perhaps fortunately for him, Helena was neither old enough nor sly enough to understand the subtlety required by her mother's command.

A tear started down the girl's cheek. Only then did Faucon realize he was glowering at her. That was worse than unfair. If there was blame to be had regarding this awkward moment, it belonged to him for not warning Edmund to guard his tongue. But as a second son with little inheritance, Faucon had never once expected a gentlewoman might scheme to present her daughter to him.

He arranged his mouth into a smile. "Brother Edmund speaks true," he told her. "Those knights who wish to hold this position must have such an income. As for the posset, I know it's ready, but I also know the pot will be too heavy for you. Race back into the hall and tell your lady mother to send a maidservant to fetch it. Best you insist that your servant makes all haste. I've already tasted the brew. It would be a terrible sin, were it to grow cold before you had your portion."

Looking like someone who had just been snatched back from a hell mouth, Helena gave a quick bend of her knees. "Thank you sir. I'll not tarry," she assured him, already racing back into the hall.

Faucon retreated to stand on the edge of the porch. Could this day get any worse? God forbid Will might learn what had just happened. His brother would only hate him all the more if their great-uncle's favor made it possible for Faucon to marry first. Because of Will's odd and unpredictable behavior since his injury, their father had had little luck finding a bride for his eldest son, despite Will's inheritance.

A lone man was making his way across the bailey, coming from the back pasture toward the gate. Head bowed, the man had his cloak hood pulled low over his brow. He held his outer garment closed with one hand as if shielding whatever he carried in his other arm. It was a moment before Faucon recognized the orange chausses and the fleece cross-gartered to his calves.

"Bailiff?" he called out.

Milla's despised brother raised his head. There was no doubting that Milla and Eustace were kin. They shared the same fair hair, long face, and fine features.

As Eustace recognized his new Crowner, he gave a lift of his chin. "Sir?" he called back.

Faucon jogged down the steps to meet Sir Robert's milk-brother. "I think I owe you thanks for seeing to my horse," he offered by way of greeting.

Eustace shook his head. "You owe me nothing. Offord has always been careful of its guests, and Sir Robert, a gracious host. I intend to maintain that tradition for as long as I can," his voice broke. Releasing his cloak, Eustace covered his face with his hand.

"My condolences," Faucon offered. "I think I regret never having met Sir Robert. From all I've heard thus far, he seems to have been a good man, beloved by both his servants and family."

Eustace lowered his hand. Tears glistened in his eyes. "He was, indeed," agreed the servant who had covertly defied his dear master last night by offering Sir Luc shelter.

"Speak with me," Faucon said. "I'd like to hear from you the tale of what happened last night. More to the point, I'm hoping you can tell me why Sir Adam believes Sir Robert's death was anything but natural."

Eustace blinked. All emotion drained from his expression, then his mouth tightened in refusal. This covert resistance was another trait he had in common with his sister. He again pulled his cloak around him, holding it shut with his hand.

"My pardon, sir, but I cannot tarry to speak at the moment. I'm for our far sheepfold and must reach it before darkness falls."

Faucon almost grinned. Anything that kept him out of Offord's hall and away from its womenfolk for a time was a boon. "Well and good! I'll walk with you and you can answer my questions as we go," he said.

Pivoting, he started toward Offord's unguarded gateway. He frowned as he once again eyed the unmanned opening. What was the point of a fine defensive wall if no one watched to see who came and went through its gateway? He had almost reached it before he realized Eustace hadn't joined him.

He glanced over his shoulder. The bailiff stood where he had been, staring after his better. Although his brow was creased and his eyes again red-rimmed, every line of the man's body suggested the last thing he wished to do was speak with his shire's new Keeper of the Pleas.

"Come, then. I thought you had a need for haste," Faucon prodded.

Once again, resistance flashed across Eustace's face. When it disappeared, all that was left was that blank expression every servant aimed at his better. Lifting his heels, the bailiff joined his Crowner.

Faucon held his peace as they started down the slope and into Offord Village. Whitewashed cottages capped in gentle brown thatch lined the track. Dogs barked, a pig squealed, and from a nearby cottage a girl with a reedy voice was singing a lullaby. Watching the smoke rising from each home bend sharply to the east, Faucon looked to the west. The thick layer of clouds gathered there said there'd be rain upon the morrow.

Boyish laughter heralded the pair of lads who burst through a gate in one of the toft fences. Dressed in green tunics with blankets for cloaks, their faces identical, they sprinted onto this track, punching and grabbing at each other as they ran. They pushed past him, then caromed into Eustace, who walked a little ahead. The bailiff snatched at them and missed.

"Pardon, Eustace!" the twins shouted in unison as they raced on without stopping.

"Slow down, you two, else I'll complain to your father," Eustace commanded in his native tongue. There was no bite to his threat.

"Aye, Eustace," one lad cried and slowed. His twin only laughed and raced on. "Come back here!" the first shouted then looked behind him at his bailiff. His face was alive with his longing to catch his brother.

"Take him if you can, Ned. Or are you Ed?" Eustace called with a laugh and the boy sprinted after his brother.

It was the sweetest moment Faucon had enjoyed

this day. Grinning still, he looked at Offord's bailiff. "I'm told that you and Sir Robert are milk-brothers, and that neither of you hail from Offord."

Eustace shot him a startled glance then fixed his gaze ahead of them. "True enough. Our birthplace was a manor some miles north of here, but yet within the bounds of the Forest of Arden. Sir Robert's sire fostered him with Lord Robert of Stafford. When Sir Umfrey, Lady Bagot's grandsire, chose to join our old king's Irish invasion, he petitioned Lord Stafford to lend him a squire for the adventure, as he had no fosterling of his own. Stafford gave him Sir Robert, then the eldest of his squires. Lord Robert's only condition was that Sir Umfrey should knight his squire before they returned to these shores, if Robert proved worthy."

That caught Faucon's attention. Sir Adam had said his father-by-marriage had taken treasure enough in Ireland to win him Offord. But as a squire, any plunder Robert might have collected would have belonged to Sir Umfrey, his to disperse among his retainers as he saw fit. "Then Sir Umfrey must have found Sir Robert worthy right quickly," he said.

Eustace nodded. "So Sir Robert always says— said. His tale was that Sir Umfrey knighted him shortly after they reached those barbarous shores. Later in their adventure, they came upon a wondrous rich treasure trove in some ancient cave.

"Even Robert's half of that cache would have been enough to win him the hand of Offord's heiress. But as it happened, just before they were to return home, Sir Umfrey fell ill. The knight knew immediately this would be his final illness. Upon his deathbed Sir Umfrey not only gave his portion of the treasure to his erstwhile squire, he commanded Sir Robert to wed his daughter. Indeed, the man was so set on the union that he even put his signet to parchment, so all would know this was his last wish."

Eustace shot him a sidelong glance as he continued. "This he did because Sir Adam and his sire had designs on the heiress of Offord, having pressed Sir Umfrey to promise her to Sir Adam before the knight left for Ireland. Once Sir Robert was married, he called me to Offord to serve him. I came, leaving home and family to honor the love he and I share."

Faucon's brows rose as those pieces of his shifted anew, although there was yet no pattern to be seen. Sir Adam had been wrong to claim Sir Robert cursed. It seemed the man had been uncannily fortunate, especially for an extra son. Well, except in his inability to produce a male heir and losing the last piece of his Irish treasure to theft.

"Did you know that Sir Robert's bell was stolen last night?" he asked the bailiff.

Eustace stopped abruptly, his eyes wide. "Last night?! But that's not possible!"

"It must have been possible. The bell is gone," Faucon replied.

The bailiff freed a ragged breath, shaking his head like a man stunned. "My pardon, sir, but it simply isn't possible. After I helped Sir Adam take Sir Robert to his bed, I stayed in the hall until Robert was no more, then joined the others in his chamber, praying for his soul until dawn. Nothing untoward happened over those hours."

"So you may say, but the bell is still gone," Faucon insisted. "Lady Offord and I discovered it missing from its box when I went to Sir Robert's chamber to view his body. I brought the empty coffer to Sir Adam and he rode off for Wootton Wawen to confront the prior."

"What?!" The bailiff gaped. "He accuses Prior Thierry? This is stranger still. While it's true that the prior was alone with Sir Robert for a time last night, the

Churchman couldn't have taken the bell, nor would he have taken it without its coffer. First and most importantly, Sir Robert would never have given him the key."

"I'm told that by the time the prior arrived, Sir Robert couldn't move or even speak. Lady Offord showed me where the key ring was kept on Sir Robert's bed post. Surely, the prior could have found those keys and opened the coffer while he was alone in Sir Robert's bedchamber," Faucon said.

"But why take the bell without the box?" Eustace insisted.

"Because he could not hide the box on his person?" Faucon suggested.

"Nor could he have hidden that bell under his clothing," Eustace retorted. "That piece is no small thing, being almost as long as my forearm," he said. "As I said, I came into Robert's chamber after he was gone to pray for my master's soul. It was Father Prior who led us, during which time he folded and unfolded his hands, knelt then rose, then knelt again. When the prayers were finished, he walked with the rest of us down the stairs. I saw no bulge beneath his garments. At no time did I hear so much as a 'tink' with all his shifting and moving. Nor did anyone else, for had they heard something, they would have commented on it, especially Lady Joia."

Eustace gave a firm shake of his head. "Arrogant and full of pride that Churchman is, but I cannot credit him with thievery."

"Lady Bagot suggests Prior Thierry was trying to force Sir Robert to make a gift of the bell to the priory," Faucon said. "Would Sir Robert have given the bell to the prior last night?"

"He would not have," Eustace replied instantly, "not last night, nor at any time since he married Lady Offord a few months ago. He'd made that bell part of Lady

Offord's dower. He would never have been forsworn."

Faucon studied the bailiff, wondering at the man's certainty. "Huh," he said with a shrug. "Well then, the bell has most definitely gone astray."

"Of all the things," the bailiff murmured, still sounding stunned, as he began again to walk along the path.

They continued in silence until they reached the sheepfold. The pen stood just beyond the farthest-flung cottage and shared a wall with the fence around that home's toft. As with the animal enclosures at Blacklea, this one was built of tall, woven withe panels that had been lashed together. It was large enough to hold a good number of sheep, and from the ovine cries coming from inside the walls, it did.

As he and Eustace drew near, a dog began to bark in vicious warning. "Hsst, you. It's only me," the bailiff called in his native tongue, announcing himself to the canine.

That won a far friendlier whine from the hidden watchdog. Eustace pulled a wrapped packet out from under his hidden arm. From that scrap of hempen sacking he produced a thick, meaty bone. This he tossed over the enclosing fence. As the dog settled into its meal, Eustace started around the pen, testing the lashing that held panel to panel.

"I'm told it's been a difficult year for Offord's flock," Faucon said, as he watched the man retie a knot.

Eustace shot him a frowning glance. "That's hardly true. This year has been better than some, but not been as good as others." His tone suggested that any discussion of Offord's business or its luck, or lack thereof, was none of his Crowner's concern.

"Then you did not lose lambs to disease and the wool buyer did not complain about the quality of your fleece?" Faucon countered.

Yet holding the bit of braided rope he was tying, Eustace eyed him for a moment. "You've spoken with my sister," he said at last, his tone defeated. "You may have noted she's not so fond of me."

"She told me you spent coins that belonged to her," Faucon replied.

The bailiff's expression hardened until he looked as angry as his sibling. "That is a lie," he retorted.

He gave his knot a final jerk, then put his back to the wall to face his new Keeper of the Pleas. "Or at least it offers but half the tale. I'll give you the other half and you can choose to believe what you will.

"I had only come to Offord when Sir Adam inherited Bagot upon his father's death. Shortly after that his stepmother died in childbirth, leaving Sir Adam in need of a nurse for Sir Luc, his newborn half-brother, a nurse who spoke the noble tongue as he doesn't tolerate any of his kin speaking my language. It so happened that my sister's husband had also just passed, leaving her with no dower and a child at her breast. She had learned her French well, having served in our lord's house before her marriage.

"Matching need to need, I brought her to Bagot and Sir Adam offered her a fine sum for her services. Being a stranger to this land and fearing theft because of it, Milla didn't wish to keep such riches with her at Bagot. She asked me to hold the purse safe. But I was also newly come, having only just arrived at Offord, and wasn't comfortable doing this for her. After much discussion she at last asked me to carry the purse to our father, believing she would one day return to our family home.

"I warned her against it," Eustace continued, "but in the end the choice was hers, and didn't our sire do just as I warned? He claimed what belonged to his daughter by his right as her father, she being widowed.

"Milla didn't discover this until she finally left Bagot years later. Didn't she come to me then, begging my aid? But what was there for me to do?" Eustace offered helplessly. "The coins were gone and there was no getting them back.

"In her rage at being cheated by those who should have been trustworthy, Milla let her anger spill over onto someone who had done no wrong. Who, in fact, did what he could by begging his master to find a place for her at Offord."

Eustace paused for a breath. When he continued, his expression was flat and his tone lifeless. "Now sir, having told you this tale in my own defense, I cannot see what it has to do with Sir Robert's death."

"Nor can I," Faucon agreed with a friendly smile. He kept his gaze fixed on the bailiff's face. "Then let me ask a more pertinent question. Why did you hold the hall door against Lady Bagot and her daughters today?"

The bailiff only shrugged. "Because Lady Offord begged me to do so. She is my master's widow. Offord is still her home, at least for the moment. She feared Lady Bagot meant to lock her out of doors. Earlier in the day Lady Bagot had said things in her grief that made me think she might do as she threatened, driven to it by her upset.

"To honor Robert, I protected Lady Offord, who knows nothing of the village. As for Lady Bagot, she knows very well she is always welcome in my home. She could have taken her daughters there to wait in comfort for Sir Adam's return."

Faucon eyed him, brows raised. "To your home, where Sir Luc was hiding?"

The bailiff blinked as if startled, then cocked his head and crossed his arms. In that moment he looked very much like his sister even though he was the weaker of the two. He said nothing.

"Why did you give succor to Sir Luc last night after Sir Robert banished him?" Faucon asked.

No emotion crossed the man's face. "Because Sir Robert commanded me to do so."

It took all Faucon's will not to gape. "How can you say that? Not only do both Sir Adam and Lady Bagot claim that Sir Robert banished Sir Luc from Offord, so does Sir Luc. Does the knight not bear the bruises laid upon him as Sir Robert beat him out of the hall?"

"All of that is true," Eustace agreed. "However, again it is but half the tale. After Sir Luc left the hall, Sir Robert instantly regretted what he had done. He stopped where I sat at the table and whispered to me that I should follow after the knight and offer sanctuary. This I did. You may ask Lady Bagot if she remembers me following Sir Luc from the hall. I know that she watched both of us leave."

The bailiff drew a breath and some of the harshness drained from his face and form. "Robert was angry at himself for allowing Sir Adam to provoke him to violence. He didn't want Luc leaving Offord before they made peace. Later that evening, after I told him Luc had agreed to stay in my home, Robert promised to come on the morrow so they could speak privately and out of the reach of Sir Adam's ears."

Here, he sighed. "Little did either of us know that his illness would take him before he could do so. In the end it cheated him of the opportunity to make right where he felt he had done wrong."

That had Faucon frowning. "Once he knew he was dying, why didn't Sir Robert call for Sir Luc to come to him?"

"Because Sir Adam refused to leave his side, save for when the prior was in Sir Robert's chamber. At that moment, Sir Luc's presence would only have driven Sir Adam deeper into his madness," Eustace said, then turned back to the fold to test the final knot.

As he completed his inspection, the bailiff drew his cloak around him again as he looked at his Crowner. "Thus ends my day, sir. I'm for home now. Best you make your way back to the hall before Lady Bagot commands the gate barred for the night."

"You have yet to answer my first question," Faucon replied. "What would make Sir Adam believe that human hands helped Sir Robert to Saint Peter's gate?"

"How can I know what Sir Adam believes?" Eustace said, his expression as flat as his voice. "All I can tell you is that most of the household was in the hall last night, and most of us for the whole of the celebration. Didn't we all notice that Sir Robert once again overindulged, just as he had done more than once these past months? And didn't we all watch as he grew steadily more ill over the course of the hours, just as he had done in the past? Now good night, sir." The man offered a nod of farewell, although he remained where he stood.

However unsatisfying Eustace's answers, Faucon could think of no more questions to ask. "To you as well," he replied, and started his walk back to the manor.

He reached the bailey of Offord Manor just before the same manservant who had rekindled the hall fire closed and barred the gates. Without a man at the gate overnight, and unless there was a postern door, Sir Adam and Will were locked out of Offord Manor until dawn.

Entering the hall, he stopped at the corner of the screen. With the fire now blazing and additional torches in place on the far wall, Offord's public room was warm and decently illuminated. The pot that held the posset sat on the hearthstone. It was close enough to the flames to keep it warm, however there was no sign of Nobby, nor did any cups remain on either of the lower tables. If the maids and manservants had also been allowed a taste of the treat, they'd already drunk up, and the manservants had departed. That left only four maids in the room. They were unrolling their bedding, hempen bags stuffed with hay or straw.

Idonea and Helena sat on their stools at the back of the hall. Having set their cups at their feet, they were playing a game that required a complicated pattern of hand movements timed to a chanted song. When one of them made the wrong motion or said the wrong word, they broke into giggles and started the game anew.

Lady Bagot had pulled a bench close to the fire and sat with Martha cradled in her lap. Her youngest daughter had tucked her cup into the crook of her elbow. The two were singing quietly to each other.

Although Brother Edmund's precisely arranged writing tools remained at the end of the high table, he was no longer there. Faucon found his clerk near the curtained bed in the room's far corner. Head bowed, the monk knelt at a prie-dieu, something that had appeared in Faucon's absence. That Edmund used the private prayer stool made Faucon wonder if the monk and Lady Bagot had parlayed, setting aside their differences as they discussed their Crowner and his life. Drawing a bracing breath, he stepped around the screen and started toward his hostess.

As if she'd been watching for him, Lady Helena noticed him first. Hot color stained her cheeks. Idonea followed her step-granddaughter's look, then leaned closed to Helena, her hand to her lips as if to hide her words. Helena's face flamed even brighter, then the two of them snickered.

Their laughter brought Lady Bagot out of her song.

She lifted her head. Exhaustion had carved hollows beneath her eyes while the fresh signs of grief had stained her cheeks. "Ah, there you are, Sir Faucon. We held aside a bit of posset for you if you wish to have some," she called.

"I've already enjoyed my cup and cannot take more than my portion, my lady," Faucon said as he came to a stop on the opposite side of the hearth from her. "Share what is left among you and yours."

Martha gave a happy gasp. Taking her cup in both hands, she looked up at her mother. "May I, Maman?"

"Be patient, my little love," Joia said to her youngest.

As Martha made a sound of dismay, her mother shifted on the bench toward Brother Edmund. "Brother, what of you? Have you changed your mind?"

Having heard his employer's voice, Edmund had stirred from his prayers and started toward the high table and his belongings. "As I told you earlier, I am fasting," the monk said, his tone flat and cold.

Faucon's brows rose. So no parlay. Perhaps Lady Bagot had offered the prie-dieu as a sop, using it as a way to thank the monk for the information she'd managed to sniggle out of him.

"Now may I have more, Maman?" Martha pleaded.

"Now," her mother agreed. "Idonea, you and Helena may also share what's left with Martha."

Both girls gave pleased cries and hurried to Lady Bagot's bench, their cups in hand. "I'll pour," Idonea offered. As the younger ladies portioned out the remainder of the brew, Edmund began to pack his tools into his basket.

"It appears that Sir Adam will not return this night," Lady Bagot said to Faucon, then sighed. "Would that I had been more clear-headed earlier this day. If I had, I would have asked Sir Luc to escort you and your clerk to Bagot. We are too many," she continued, the movement of her head indicating the girls she shepherded as well as her maidservants, "and we cannot sleep in my father's bedchamber, not with him in it. We must use the hall. The only decent space at Offord that can serve you and your clerk for your nightly rest is our kitchen."

Never had Faucon been more grateful that no woman, regardless of her status, slept near unrelated men without a kinsman to act as guard and chaperone. He offered her a tight smile. "My clerk and I are accustomed to rough conditions as part of our new duties. Having visited your kitchen, I can safely say that it offers better accommodation than I usually enjoy," he replied. That was no lie. In the last weeks, he had indeed slept in places far less welcoming than Milla's domain.

"Are we truly so far from Blacklea that we cannot ride for your home, sir?" Edmund asked swiftly as he rolled up his lengths of parchment.

"Farther than I care to ride in the cold and dark, and most certainly farther than your mount will tolerate," Faucon replied. "I promise, Brother. You'll find the kitchen adequate. The door has a bar. Your prayers won't be disturbed."

The monk glanced from his employer to the women. Resistance flared in his eyes. "Does Offord have no church or chapel I can use?" he almost pleaded.

It was Lady Bagot who answered. "We do not. The priory at Wootton Wawen, where my husband went, serves as our parish church. But there is also Saint Mary's at Haselor. Father Otto is a commoner, but a kind man. I'm certain he would welcome your company for a night."

Having to bear company with an English priest was almost as distasteful to Edmund as sleeping in close proximity to women. His resistance melted into reluctant acceptance. "Perhaps you are right, sir. It's too dark for riding. The kitchen will do."

Faucon again lifted his lips in that tight smile as he offered Lady Bagot a brief bow. "Many thanks for your hospitality, my lady. We'll bid you a good night, then."

Dismay drove the grief from Lady Joia's face. She shifted her daughter out of her lap and came to her feet. "But there is no need for you to leave the hall right this moment. Milla is not yet finished with her chores for the evening. Come and take your ease until she enters the hall. Brother Edmund tells us you were a crusader with our king. Perhaps you would share your adventures with us?" It was a reasonable request. Tales were the usual coin with which a guest paid for his bed and board.

"We like stories," said Martha as she sat on the bench. She swung her feet as she continued. "We also like songs, don't we, Maman."

"We do," Lady Bagot agreed.

Standing near the fire, Idonea covered her mouth with a hand to hide her laugh, then looked at Helena. "We all want Sir Faucon to sing for us, don't we?" she taunted her step-granddaughter.

That drove Faucon back a step as he scrambled for a polite way to excuse himself. He bumped into Edmund.

The monk leaned closer as he tucked the pouch containing his quills and ink into his basket and slammed the lid upon its top. "For the sake of your position, I have tolerated the lady's many questions," he muttered in complaint, proving he was oblivious to the hornet's nest he'd stirred. "I have also agreed to stay here rather than seeking out my brethren. I pray you, do not force me to listen while women sing."

Again, Faucon offered his hostess a brief bow. "Would that we could join you in your entertainment, my lady. Unfortunately, Brother Edmund and I have work to complete before our day is done."

That still wasn't enough to stop the lady. "Milla is an excellent cook but an unlikable woman, who especially dislikes strangers and allows no interference in her kitchen. Far better that you wait until she arrives in the hall." Lady Bagot's tone said she was certain of her snare this time.

Faucon almost sighed in relief. It was irony indeed that Lady Bagot had herself given him the key to her trap when she sent him after Sir Luc. "I didn't find Milla unlikable when I joined her in the kitchen earlier," he replied. "Indeed, she offered me both posset and food, then gave me a seat near the fire, out of her way as she worked. I cannot think she'll mind if my clerk and I do the same again while she completes her day."

Lady Joia frowned at that. Edmund dragged the strap of his basket over his shoulder. "Is there a proper place for me to work in the kitchen?" he asked.

"Very acceptable, considering the tasks that need your attention this evening," Faucon told his clerk. That was no lie since there was nothing for Edmund to do.

That spurred Edmund into motion. He turned toward the door. "When you are ready, sir," he said.

Faucon once again began to bend in preparation of offering his final farewell.

"But Maman, the sir cannot leave until he asks me about Grand-père," Martha cried to her mother in protest. "You promised me I could tell him what I know."

That had Faucon once again eying the forward child in dismay. If he had no other reason to reject an alliance with this family, Lady Martha would suffice.

"Hush, my love," Lady Bagot warned her youngest. "You may speak with him on the morrow, once your father has returned."

"But I don't wish to wait until the morrow," Martha

whined. "The sir should talk to me tonight."

Faucon hesitated no longer. "Good even to you all, my ladies," he said, then hurried to catch his clerk.

Edmund had stopped on the porch to wait for him. As Faucon stopped next to him, the monk looked at him. "What is it that needs doing this night?" his clerk asked.

"Nothing at all. I didn't wish to remain in the hall without Sir Adam present," Faucon replied, gathering his words as he prepared to chide Edmund over his wayward tongue.

"We most certainly should not remain in that hall!" his clerk said harshly. "That woman is beyond forward. It was bad enough that she refused to tell me the name of her confessor. Can you believe that after you left with that other knight she pressed me to explain all the particulars of the position of Coronarius? No response or refusal to answer on my part stopped her pestering. At last, for the sake of my sanity I gave her what she wanted, just to end her interrogation.

"Someone," Edmund added, looking pointedly at his employer, "should speak to her husband, reminding him that it is his honor his disrespectful wife besmirches with her behavior."

That teased a choked laugh from Faucon. He started down the porch stairs. "You have my permission to chide both husband and wife as sternly as you wish, as is your right, Brother," he called over his shoulder as he went. "Me, I intend to beg our Lord that the morrow brings the answers we crave so we might resolve both the matter of Sir Robert's death and the theft of the bell, and leave this place."

Edmund came abreast of him. "Amen," the monk breathed.

Chapter Eleven

Faucon catapulted out of his dreams, his hand already reaching for his sword. It wasn't at his side. His eyes flew open and he peered into a claustrophobic dimness scented with rosemary, garlic, and rain. Alarm melted away. This was Offord's kitchen.

From close by came a quiet but rhythmic whistling, louder on the exhale, wispy on the inhale. He smiled. This was Offord's kitchen and Brother Edmund was again snoring, having traded his earlier growling bear for this tiny squeaky bird.

As he relaxed, Faucon caught the raucous call of another, more distant bird. But ravens were day hunters. How could it be past dawn and neither he nor Edmund had awakened? He rolled up to sitting then blinked.

Lady Martha sat on the floor near his knees. Her lips were pursed as she whistled or rather, tried to whistle. She held her unfinished poppet in front of her, making the plaything dance to her breathy squeaking.

Concern shot through him. He glanced at Edmund. They'd chosen to take their rest in front of Milla's worktable, stretched out foot-to-foot. Curled on his side, his clerk had his cowl pulled down until it almost covered his face. Faucon gave thanks. He wasn't awake enough to deal with Edmund's certain hysteria, should the monk awaken and discover a girl-child had invaded their makeshift bed chamber.

"What are you doing here?" Faucon demanded quietly of the lass.

"Good! You are finally awake," Martha said as she smiled up at him.

Her voice set Edmund to muttering in his sleep. Faucon pressed a finger to his lips, warning the little lady to quiet.

"Ssh," Martha agreed at a whispery hiss, mimicking his gesture.

"How did you get in here? The door was barred," Faucon chided quietly, battling irritation. It didn't bode well that he must begin this day by complaining to his hostess over her wayward daughter.

"Nobby let me in when I knocked. I told him it was time for you to rise. He went to fetch water for washing," Martha replied, matching his quiet tone. "Milla will be here soon," she continued, "even though Maman told her that we should all wait to break our fast until you rose. Milla doesn't care that you are our guest. She told Maman that the kitchen is her home and she meant to rouse you."

Just then the kitchen door creaked open and the scent of rain flowed in with the wind. Faucon peered across the chamber. Rather than Milla, it was Nobby. The boy's fair hair was wet, his red tunic was dappled with moisture, and his well-worn leather shoes were thick with mud. The promise in yesterday's clouds had come to pass, and it had rained all night.

Both Faucon and Lady Martha watched as the lad carried his sloshing bucket to the hearth. After filling a small pot with water, Nobby went to the hearth and removed the clay cover that had protected the wooden kitchen from wayward sparks during the night. Setting the water pot directly into the yet-smoldering ashes, he tugged on the metal arm from which hung the cauldron filled with potage, repositioning it over the center of the hearth.

As the boy began to feed twiglets to yesterday's embers, Faucon rose to his knees. Martha was right. It was time to rise, if for no other reason than to return her to her mother.

He found his tunic on the top of Milla's table, right where he'd left it and right next to his sword and belt. By the time Nobby had shifted from twigs to branches, Faucon had his boots on.

Coming to his feet, he extended his hand to Sir Adam's indulged daughter. "Come with me, Lady Martha."

The child scowled at him. "But you have not asked me about Grand-père. Milla told Maman that you asked her about what happened to him. Now you must ask me." Her voice grew louder with every word.

Again Edmund muttered in his sleep. Faucon bent a chiding look on the little lady. "That is for me to decide, not you. For the now, you will return to the hall and your lady mother."

Faucon grabbed her hand and lifted her to her feet. Startled, she dropped her poppet as she rose. Rather than release her hand so she could reclaim her toy, Faucon caught it up for her. Its creators had done an admirable job packing it, for the plaything was heavier than he expected, its fabric skin stretched taut and smooth.

He gave it to Martha. She tucked it into the crook of her arm. Her eyes narrowed as she prepared to argue. Again, the kitchen door opened. This time Milla stepped inside.

The cook's eyes widened as she saw the child by Faucon's side. She put her hands on her hips and glared at her master's grandchild. "Hey! Your lady mother commanded you to remain in the hall. Get you hence, knowing I will complain to Lady Bagot that I found you among strange men," she scolded harshly.

"What?!" Edmund cried, coming upright with a start, fighting to push his cowl off his face. "What's happening?"

At the hearth Nobby freed a laugh as amusement filled his pale, round face. "Didn't I warn you Milla would be angry if she found you in here?" he said in English to the little lady.

Lady Martha stuck her tongue out at the lad, then looked up at her Crowner. "You may take me back to the hall, sir."

"Indeed I shall," Faucon promised, his tone as harsh as Milla's. He started toward the door, his hand tight around hers.

"Where are you going, sir?" Edmund called after him, sounding both dazed and frantic.

"I'm returning this missing object," Faucon replied as he exited the kitchen. "I'll be right back."

Outside, the day was dark and drear, made all the more miserable by a wind that turned gentle moisture into stinging rain and sent the clouds scudding across the sky. So dark a day explained how he had missed dawn's light, but not how he might have slept so late. With the next breath he realized it was Will's fault. He hadn't slept easily since his brother's arrival. With Will absent, he'd finally allowed himself to rest.

A horse snorted from behind them. Faucon glanced over his shoulder, then turned, dragging Martha around with him. Alf was guiding his big piebald nag into the bailey. All Faucon could see of the second man on the horse was a well-worn shoe and a bit of bare leg. The soldier had draped his cloak over his passenger's head and body to protect him from the wet.

"Alf! Is that Brother's Colin's shoe I see?" Faucon laughed.

"It is, indeed," the lay brother answered for himself, dragging off the cloak. The pull of woolen fabric across his head set the monk's pure white hair to floating around his tonsured head. His round face wreathed as he smiled, dark eyes gleaming with pleasure beneath snowy brows. Caught between the monk and Alf was a large traveling basket. No doubt it was whatever herbs, tinctures, or tonics that basket contained that Alf's cloak had really been meant to protect.

"It's good to see you again, Sir Crowner," the former apothecary called in greeting.

"You as well, Brother," Faucon replied, then looked back at Alf. "I know I overslept, but it cannot already be midday."

"You are correct, sir. It is not midday," his man-at-arms replied as he brought his mount to halt beside the porch so the monk would have an easier time dismounting. "God was good last night. Or perhaps it was just that our Lord knows how little I like squandering my prayers," he offered with a grin. "I met the brother on the road not too far outside Priors Holston. He was on his way to Alcester and agreed to spend the night with me at Blacklea rather than Saint Radegund's. We left at first light."

Faucon led Martha up the steps, then released her hand when they reached the porch. "Stay right here, my lady," he warned her as he turned to aid the elderly monk.

Colin handed him the basket. After setting it aside, Faucon caught the older man by the waist as the lay brother slipped off the broad-backed horse. The monk returned to earth with a grunt, and stumbled back a step when Faucon released him. He smiled as his Crowner caught him by the shoulder to steady him.

"Many thanks, sir," the healer said. "I fear the day

comes when I must accept that I'm too old to sit astride for even so short a ride. Although four legs make shorter work of any distance, my hips complain far more than my feet ever do," he said as he straightened his habit and cloak around him.

"Then I am all the more grateful that you agreed to make this ride on my behalf," Faucon told him.

Only then did he remember Martha. He glanced around him. The girl was gone.

"She disappeared inside the instant you turned your back," Alf said as he dismounted.

"Why, that sly little imp!" Faucon snapped.

"Do we need to fetch her back?" Brother Colin asked.

"Absolutely not," Faucon retorted irritably, then looked at Alf. "Take your mount to where you see Legate grazing. After that, join us in there," he pointed to the kitchen shed.

To Brother Colin, he said, "I beg your pardon, Brother. I not only overslept, I didn't expect you this early. I've yet to prepare for the day. Do you mind attending me while I wash?"

Faucon swiftly splashed the still-cold water on his face then scrubbed his skin dry with the bit of sacking Milla had provided. That the water wasn't warm was Edmund's fault. When the monk complained about washing in front of a woman, Milla had instantly demanded they remove themselves to the smithy. Unlike the cook, Offord's smith had been overjoyed to lend them his space, for it meant he could take his ease in the hall while he waited to break his fast.

Although the smithy was but a three-sided shed, it was dry and warm, what with coals already glowing red in the fire box. Faucon washed first because Edmund and Colin wished to pray. Heads bowed, the two monks knelt near the smith's workbench as they chanted. Alf leaned against one wall, his arms crossed over his chest and his head bowed. Although his pose suggested that he prayed with them, Faucon knew better. They both had a soldier's ability to sleep on their feet.

With his face washed, Faucon found his purse and took out the twig and bit of cloth he used to clean his teeth. Carving a new point on the end of the twig, he set to work. He had finished that chore by the time the brothers fell silent.

Edmund came immediately to his feet, turning his back on the older monk who struggled to rise. He joined his employer beside the worktable and began to pull his arms out of his habit to strip to the waist. "Are you finished, sir?"

"I am," Faucon replied, handing over the tiny pot of soap and sacking before going to aid Brother Colin back to his feet.

"Many thanks again," the lay brother said. "So sir, if we have a moment, will you tell me why I am here?"

"You didn't explain?" Faucon asked Alf in surprise.

Alf gave a startled jerk, then raised his head. He blinked.

"You didn't explain to Brother Colin why I needed him?" Faucon repeated.

"He didn't ask," Alf replied with a shrug. "The moment I said it was you who called for him, the brother agreed to come. Thinking you knew best what to say, I left the explanation for our arrival here."

That made Faucon grin. "I only hope the day never comes that you consider your trust in me misplaced,

Brother Colin," he said to the monk. "As to why you're here, the night before last, Sir Robert of Offord died of some strange malady after a celebratory meal. This illness started in his toes and progressed steadily upward over the hours, numbing his limbs and making his muscles ache. Just before he died, he could not even move his tongue."

Colin's eyes widened. "God have mercy on that poor knight's soul," he cried. "That was no illness! He was murdered, poisoned by hemlock."

Hemlock?! Faucon had not yet been five when his mother had taken him to where the poisonous plants grew in their pasture. She, who had once sickened herself almost to death by making a whistle from a hemlock stem, made him study all the parts of that plant. Then his mother had used a stick to beat him so he would never forget that there was death where he found stems spotted with purple.

"Have a care with your words, Brother Herbalist," Edmund chided his brother in Christ, his face dripping. "Only our Coronarius can pronounce a man murdered, and only when he addresses the inquest jury."

Colin bowed his head and tucked his hands into his wide sleeves. "Of course you are right, Brother," he said meekly. "I misspoke. The symptoms Sir Faucon de-scribes, including death, perfectly match the symptoms of ingesting a deadly dose of hemlock," he restated.

"A deadly dose?" Alf asked, winning a frown from Brother Edmund, who tolerated the soldier as little as he tolerated the lay brother. "Is there a dose of hemlock that is other than a deadly?"

"Of course," Brother Colin said. "Like many poisons, small doses offer help instead of hurt. I use hemlock for a number of ailments, such as congestion in the lungs or afflictions that cause the joints to swell."

That set one of Faucon's pieces to spinning. He didn't much like that he found himself facing a trail he'd yesterday believed fabricated to mislead him. "Would there be any telltale marks on the man's body to confirm it was this poison that ended his life?" he asked the monk.

Colin shook his head. "Hemlock leaves no such mark but the path to death is just as you related, with slow, steady paralysis. A man may also purge his stomach, or suffer from too much water in the mouth."

"And no other poison or illness works in this way?" Faucon pressed.

"As I said, the symptoms are distinctive," the healer replied, confidence radiating from him. "Should we find the remains of the concoction the knight ingested, we'd swiftly know beyond a doubt, for hemlock has a nasty odor—" Colin broke off. His brow furrowed as he thought for a moment.

"My pardon. Brother Edmund is correct," he said. "I should not have suggested murder. Hemlock has a strong, mousy smell and taste. That would make it difficult for any man to secretly poison another. No one would willingly drink so vile a brew, at least not without asking what was in it. That begs the question. Did your knight take the poison himself, intending to end his life?"

Edmund gasped and swiftly crossed himself. "Again Brother, you overstep!" he cried, this time in horror. "Sir Robert is your better and you are no priest. You have no right to accuse him of a mortal sin."

"I do not accuse, Brother," Colin replied, once again retreating into the humility expected of a lay brother. "I have simply lived too long, cared for too many, and seen too much to ignore what a man might do should his life's burdens grow too heavy. If our new Crowner is to discern what happened, I think he must consider all possibilities."

Again, Faucon's pieces shifted, and again he didn't much like the trail the new pattern revealed. Milla had said Sir Robert's purse was empty. Could the knight have chosen to exit life rather than face penury and ruin?

Everything in him rejected this. Suicide doomed a man's body to burial in unhallowed ground and his soul to eternal damnation. What trained knight would choose such a fate when, if he truly wished to court death, he need only make his way onto some battlefield and let God choose the moment of his passing?

That made Faucon sigh. Or was it only that he didn't wish to imagine Sir Robert could commit such an act? With that, his own life burdens came to rest all the more heavily upon him. He should never have come to Offord. Rather than hunting for the one who took Sir Robert's bell, as he should have been doing, he instead faced a trail that might lead to the destruction of a man's legacy.

Setting aside his regrets, Faucon looked at Edmund. "Brother, you know very well that I must consider all possibilities. But take heart. I see no proof that Sir Robert has committed such a heinous act," he said.

"God be praised for that," his clerk said on a relieved breath, then returned to his washing.

Just then, Nobby came around the corner of the smithy. He looked at Alf. "Speak for me if you please. Say to your master that Lady Bagot invites him and all his party to break your fast in the hall."

"His master hears you," Faucon replied in the lad's tongue, speaking for himself, "and thanks Lady Bagot for her kind invitation, Nobby."

That won a surprised grin from the scullery lad. "My

pardon, sir. I didn't think you would understand. Best that all of you come now. The potage is always good cold, but much better when it's warm," he advised his new Crowner.

Chapter Twelve

L ike the hungry lad he was, Nobby hurried ahead of them into the hall. By the time Faucon entered, the boy was seated at the lower end of one of the servants' tables. Faucon envied the lad. Would that he were as eager to find his place. All that awaited him here was another attempt by Lady Bagot to matchmake.

This morning, Idonea sat in the chair at the center of the high table, as was her right as Sir Robert's widow, at least until she was removed from Offord by Sir Robert's heir. Lady Bagot was at Idonea's right while Lady Helena was to her left. Lady Martha should have been at her elder sister's left, instead the place was empty. Faucon suspected that meant the child was paying for her earlier misdeed.

It was Idonea's duty to greet her guests and invite them to the meal. Instead, Lady Bagot came to her feet. Although it was clear she grieved, the exhausted shadows were gone from her pretty face. "Good morrow to you and yours, Sir Faucon," she called, then pointed to the head of one of the lower tables.

"Your man may sit there, on the bench with Eustace." As was true at many houses, Offord's bailiff had the right to dine at his employer's expense. As the position of bailiff was one of the highest ranking among those who served, Eustace sat at the head of his table, right in front of the household salt cellar. At Offord the salt was contained in a good-sized lidded wooden box.

"Brothers," Lady Joia said, nodding toward the monks, "if you please, you may join me on this side of the table. Sir Faucon, if you would sit next to Lady Helena?"

Faucon had expected nothing less. He stepped aside, allowing both Edmund and Colin to precede him, then waited at the edge of the high table as they took their places. Edmund went no farther than the end of the bench he'd used yesterday, which put him as far from Lady Bagot as possible. Brother Colin had no such hesitation. He easily slid onto the bench next to Sir Adam's wife.

"My ladies," Faucon said, addressing all the gentle-women at the table, "may I present Brother Colin, a lay brother and herbalist from the abbey of Saint Peter in Stanrudde. I requested he visit, hoping he might be able to identify the illness that took Sir Robert's life."

Colin shot Faucon a startled look. As well he might, since he had already identified the cause of the man's death. Faucon offered a tiny shake of his head, warning the monk to silence. With a lift of his brows and an equally tiny nod, Colin agreed.

Although the mention of her father's death made tears glisten briefly in Lady Bagot's eyes, her voice remained steady as she again spoke in Idonea's stead. "Well come to Offord, Brother," she said. "Would that you had might have visited two days ago. Perhaps you might have recognized what affected my sire on that night and known how to save him."

Colin gave a quick bend of his head. "My lady, your grief is mine," he replied. "I will add your father to my prayers." His offer won a trembling smile from Sir Robert's mourning daughter.

Unable to avoid his seat any longer, Faucon made his way behind Lady Offord's chair to where Lady Helena sat. As he went, he gave thanks that this was the morning meal, the one meal that didn't require him to play the swain. "Good morrow, Lady Helena," he said in greeting as he took his seat next to her.

Bright color stained the girl's face. When their gazes met, she gasped and swiftly bowed her head. "Good morrow to you, Sir Faucon," she whispered.

Faucon looked beyond her to Idonea. "And to you as well, Lady Offord."

Although her injured eye was yet swollen, Idonea was no longer the beaten child of yesterday. She offered him a quick smile, then stifled another giggle behind her hand as her one-sided gaze shifted from him to Helena. "And to you, sir," she replied, ever-so-politely.

Lady Bagot touched her stepmother's arm, drawing the girl's attention. "Ask if one of the brothers might lead us in prayer," she instructed at a whisper, and with that the meal began.

Served with fresh bread and the same soft cheese that Sir Luc had enjoyed, the potage proved to be as tasty as Faucon had hoped, and Helena as well-behaved as she had seemed yesterday. Although Lady Bagot more than once reminded her daughter to be a good seatmate, Helena managed to choke out only a few questions. Faucon suspected she was as relieved as he when the maids came to clear away all trace of their meal.

"It has been my pleasure to share this seat with you, my lady," Faucon said to her as he rose, offering the required phrase and bow.

This time, Helena's face lost all color. For an instant he worried she might swoon. She caught a deep breath and came back to herself. "As it has been my pleasure to share it with you, sir," she replied, reciting her own required rote phrase.

His duty as a guest complete, Faucon gratefully retreated to stand behind the monks. While Edmund, who had eaten sparingly and said nothing, sat hunched unhappily at the end of his bench, Brother Colin looked very much at ease. Colin's mastery of the Norman tongue and the way he balanced the conversation between the two gentlewomen suggested that the former apothecary had interacted frequently— and successfully— with his betters during his years as a tradesman.

"Thank you, my ladies," Colin said with a nod as he came to his feet. "Your company has brightened an old man's day. Now if you will excuse? It seems our new Crowner—" he used the English word— "has need of me."

"Crowner?" Lady Bagot said in surprise. "What is Crowner?"

"It is the word the commoners use for my title. They find it more pleasing to their tongues than Coronarius or Keeper of the Pleas," Faucon explained, then looked at Idonea. "Lady Offord, would you like Brother Colin to examine your bruises and your swollen hands while he is here?"

"If he pleases," Idonea replied, her voice more alive than Faucon had heard it since he arrived. But then, Colin had asked her to describe her life in the great town of London, something it seemed not even her husband had asked of her.

"Come into the light, so I can better see you," Colin said, leading Idonea to the fire. Both Faucon and Lady Bagot followed, Lady Joia moving close to her stepmother as if to chaperone. Turning the widow until she best caught the light from the shifting flames, Colin studied her face.

"I have a salve with me today that will serve for both the bruise and your eye," he said, then raised his hand to touch the tail of the sheer wimple that covered her shorn head. "Do you often fever?"

"Not of late. My mother has said that I may once again allow my hair to grow," Lady Offord replied shyly, repeating what she'd already told her Crowner.

The monk then took her hands into his and ran his thumbs gently over her swollen knuckles. That drew a pained gasp from her. He turned her hands palms up in his. The skin on her palms was flushed and red. He gave a 'tsk' and a shake of his head. "You ache all the time, poor thing," Colin said to her, speaking in English this time.

"I do," Idonea replied in the same tongue, her voice trembling. "But lately my belly swells and aches even worse than my fingers and knees."

"As would happen, given your affliction," the healer agreed with a nod. "You suffer from an excess of cold and wet humors, and too much water, hence your distended belly," Colin told her, then paused. "And so it will always be for you, I fear."

Idonea freed a little squeak at that, and pulled her hands from his to fold them anxiously in front of her. "That's what our apothecary in London told Mama, but she swore he was wrong. She promised that my health would improve once I gave birth to a child, because she said that was what happened to her."

"I pray that your mother is correct," Colin replied, regret still filling his voice, "but know that this is not what happens for most who suffer as you do, my lady. You should prepare yourself for the possibility this ailment will always be your cross to bear."

"What are you saying?" Lady Bagot almost de-manded, glancing from the English lay brother to the tradesman's daughter. "I cannot understand you."

"Please, Brother. You must be wrong," Idonea begged, speaking over her stepdaughter. She put one hand on her swollen abdomen. "Are you certain this is bloat? Perhaps I am with child?"

"Idonea," Lady Bagot said more forcefully. "In my tongue if you please. You as well, brother."

Colin nodded to Lady Joia. "When was the last time you had your woman's flow?" he asked Lady Offord in French.

Idonea gasped at the question, one more usually asked by a mother or a midwife, not a monk. Color flooded her face. She bowed her head, her hands again folded tightly in front of her. "It arrived four days ago," the widow whispered, still speaking English.

"And the last time you lay with your husband?" Colin even more boldly inquired.

"Not since we arrived at Offord," Sir Robert's wife again whispered in her native tongue.

Stunned, Faucon stared at the widow, wondering if she was lying. What man married a woman to get an heir then didn't bed her?

Colin glanced at his Crowner, then shook his head at Idonea. "If that's so, then you cannot be with child," he said told her gently.

Idonea freed a quiet moan. A tear escaped her uninjured eye. "But I so wanted to be! I want to be hale and whole. I am tired of always being ill," she whimpered, at last reverting to French.

"Take heart, my lady," Colin offered swiftly. "Who's to say what sweetness our Lord holds in store for your future? Although I cannot banish your ailment, I do know treatments that can offer relief. Do you use anything now, anything that works well for you?"

Everything about Idonea said she wanted to run, to be as far from this place and the fate Colin had laid upon her as she could get. Her lips still trembling, she said, "I do have something, but lately it helps only a little. I keep it in Sir Robert's chamber, in his chest. Shall I bring it for you to see?"

Colin offered a smile and a nod. "That would be helpful, my lady."

"I'll fetch it then," the widow said, already turning toward the tower wall.

Her stepdaughter caught her by the arm. "I've told you before, you mustn't do these things for yourself," Lady Bagot warned, her voice low. "Command a maid to go in your stead."

Idonea shook off her stepdaughter's restraining hand. "Leave me be, Joia. I have to get it because I keep it in Sir Robert's locked chest and they aren't allowed to open that," she cried, tears of disappointment already staining her face.

As she turned to limp as quickly as she could toward the tower door, Lady Bagot freed a frustrated breath. "Commoner!" she muttered after her father's widow.

"Lady Bagot!" a maid cried as she jogged around the screen, then trotted toward the hearth. "My lady, Sir Adam returns and has brought Prior Thierry with him. Take heed," she added breathlessly as she stopped across the fire from them. "All is not well with Sir Adam," she offered, her voice low.

Lady Bagot groaned at that. Faucon drew a bracing breath. All was not well with Sir Adam, and Will had returned.

An instant later Sir Adam, his cloak sodden and his rusty hair dripping where it escaped his brown cap, rounded the wooden panel. Everything about the knight suggested that he raged as hotly now as when he'd left Offord. Following him was a tall, broad-shouldered man who looked more baron than Churchman.

Rather than a habit, the prior wore a thick dark blue woolen cloak, its hood thrown back, atop a well-made short, green tunic and chausses of the same color. The hem of his tunic was decorated with a thick band of embroidery, from which silver and gold threads gleamed. His nose was narrow, his cheekbones high and his jaw clean-shaven. His only nod to his holy vows was the tonsure carved out of his thick steel-gray hair. And, just like Sir Adam, the prior's expression said he raged. His jaw was tight and his dark eyes narrowed beneath heavy, grayed brows.

Neither man carried a bell in his hands.

More shuffling than walking, Will brought up the rear of this discontented party. He moved slowly, his head lowered and his shoulders hunched. As he reached the bench closest to the door, he dropped to sit, then buried his face in his hands.

Faucon watched in horror. God help them both! Will's head ached.

"Where is our bell?" Lady Joia asked her husband as he stopped across the hearthstone from her.

Her worried question freed what little control Sir Adam exercised over his rage. "He claims he doesn't have it," he roared, venting what consumed him on all their ears. "We didn't believe him when he told us this, so we searched every corner and crevice of that place and found nothing! That's when I demanded that he," the jerk of his thumb indicated Prior Thierry, who came to a stop next to him, "put his hand on that reliquary of his and swear on the saint's bones that he didn't have our bell."

"He, he, he!" Prior Thierry snarled, glaring at the knight. "You speak as if I don't stand right here. Take heed! God will punish you for your effrontery!" His accent confirmed that he was from across the Channel. "How dare any of you accuse me, one of our Lord's servants, of theft! How dare you drag me here to speak

142

to—" The Churchman's gaze shifted from the knight and his lady, across the two monks until it came to rest on Faucon.

"You?" he demanded. "Are you this Coronarius, who goes about the countryside accusing innocent Churchmen of burglary?"

"Sir Faucon de Ramis, Keeper of the Pleas for this shire," Faucon offered in introduction. "You are mistaken; I have accused no Cchurchmen of burglary. However it is my duty to identify those in this shire who have committed burglary, murder, and rape. Have you?"

The prior frowned in confusion. "Have I what?"

"Committed burglary, murder, or rape?" Faucon asked without inflection or emotion.

Ruddy color stained the Churchman's lean cheeks as his eyes widened. "I have not," he spat out. "But even if I had taken that bell, I would have committed no crime, nor any sin. The bell belongs to Mother Church. It is blasphemy that it was ever in Sir Robert's hands! So I told Sir Robert when he first showed it to me and so I say to you now. Sir Robert understood. He vowed to return it to me. He confirmed that promise on his deathbed."

"With what tongue?" Lady Bagot shot back, as bold in addressing a Churchman as she was monks or her Crowner. "He could no longer speak by the time you arrived."

The prior turned his raging gaze on Lady Bagot. "Lying daughter of Eve," he accused. "You were there! You saw. He needed no tongue. He nodded when I asked him if he still wished to give me his bell."

"That's not what you asked him," Sir Adam shouted. "You asked if he wished to be alone with you! And he didn't nod, he but blinked his eyes."

"In agreement," the prior snapped back.

Lady Bagot spoke over him, her voice rising with every word. "And then you forced us to leave. You locked us out, separating me from my father, leaving him to suffer alone until his last breaths," she wailed, emptying her aching heart on the one who had done wrong.

Her grief had no effect on the prior. "If you do not make right where your sire has sinned, your father will burn for all eternity," he threatened. "What was taken from our Church must be returned to her!"

"Enough!" Faucon shouted, holding up his hands in a plea for peace. "Enough, all of you," he said more quietly when he had their attention.

"Sir Adam," he said, looking at the knight, "if Prior Thierry has sworn on holy relics that he doesn't have your bell, then he doesn't have your bell. Surely, you can see that."

"But—" Sir Adam started to argue.

"Let me speak," Faucon insisted, then looked at the Churchman. "Father Prior, I have not accused you of theft because I do not believe you took Sir Robert's bell. However I do believe you entered his chamber the night he died intending to take it. Now, tell me true. What did you see when you used the key to open the bell box?"

His jaw tight in refusal, the well-dressed Churchman said nothing.

Brother Edmund came to his feet. "Father Prior, you are a foreigner here and may not understand," Faucon's clerk said. "By royal decree, if Sir Faucon questions you, you must answer, and do so honestly."

"I am not bound by your laws or to your king," the Churchman retorted.

"And I am no Churchman to pronounce sin," Faucon replied just as sharply. "I deal in the law of our land. Our law does not find wrong when no wrong was done. You don't have the bell, so you couldn't have taken it. Now, tell me true. The coffer was empty when you opened it, wasn't it?"

The prior freed a harsh breath, then gave a single sharp nod. "When I opened the lock, I found the coffer empty."

Lady Bagot freed a horrified cry, the force of her reaction driving her back a step. When she collided with Brother Colin, she dropped to sit on the edge of the hearth, gasping for breath.

"That cannot be," Sir Adam cried in panic as his wife broke into noisy sobs. "This man has to have the bell. If he doesn't have it, that can only mean he's given it to another with a command to keep it hidden from us. Or he's already spirited it out of our land! Keeper, you must command him to tell us who has our bell!"

"Think about that night, Sir Adam," Faucon said, with little hope the knight could actually be brought to reasonable thought. "How could Prior Thierry have taken the bell out of Sir Robert's chamber without someone here at Offord noticing? Where could the prior have hidden it in Sir Robert's chamber that you couldn't have seen it while you and he knelt at the dying man's bedside?"

Sir Adam shook his head. "There could be places," he started.

Faucon spoke over him. "But how could you not notice him retrieve the bell when it came time for him to leave? How could he have taken it out of that hiding spot while you watched? You and your wife were both in Sir Robert's bedchamber with him."

The knight's jaw tightened at this. "Then he must have hidden the bell on his person while he was alone with Robert," he insisted stubbornly.

"Could he have?" Faucon asked, glancing at Eustace. Unlike the rest of Offord's servants who had swiftly and quietly disappeared upon Sir Adam's angry arrival, the bailiff had remained at the table next to Alf. Both men were watching what went forward with undisguised interest.

"I'm told that all of you prayed together for a goodly while after Sir Robert's demise," Faucon continued, watching Sir Adam. "Could the prior have hidden the bell in his clothing and you not notice a bulge? Could he have knelt, bent in prayer, arisen and walked, and that bell not have shifted to reveal itself or sounded as he moved?"

"But he has to have it," Sir Adam cried as if his heart were as broken as his wife's. He fell to sit on the edge of the hearthstone across the flames from Lady Joia. His head drooped and his shoulders slumped. "He has to have it," he repeated quietly, his tone pained.

"So Coronarius, since you're convinced I don't have the bell, who does?" Prior Thierry demanded.

"I don't know," Faucon admitted. "I'm not yet convinced that it was stolen. It was Sir Adam who believed you had the bell."

The prior sneered. "Of course he did. But now you have heard my tale and you also know how these—" His lips drew back from his teeth as he glanced from the defeated Sir Adam to the knight's grieving wife— "people have profaned a holy relic. As you search, you will remember that this bell belongs to our Church, not to them. And when you find it, you will return it to its true owner," the Churchman warned more than requested.

It was Edmund who replied. "Father Prior, Sir Faucon cannot declare in a matter of disputed ownership. His only powers are first to command the inquest jury to accuse the thief then to assess the accused man's estate on our king's behalf. If God is good, perhaps Sir Faucon will find this bell. But know this. If he does, he has no choice but to return it to the one who made the complaint of burglary. Did you make such a complaint?" the monk then asked, his tone making it clear the question was rhetorical.

Prior Thierry shifted the full force of his attention on Edmund. "Brother, this is a *sanctus bell*. Although ancient, it was anointed and blessed. A holy object does not belong in the hands of the impious. If you, an avowed monk, do not claim it on behalf of our Mother Church, if you allow the unholy to keep what belongs to our Lord, you betray your vow to God and his Church."

Brother Edmund did not flinch under the assault of a superior. "You are correct, Father Prior. A sacred artifact should not be held by anyone save those bound to our Lord. But Sir Faucon is not a representative of our Father in Rome. He is a servant of the English king. He cannot help you in this matter. Instead, if you have not already done so, you should make your complaint to your bishop or our papal emissary."

The corner of Prior Thierry's mouth curled. His gaze shifted from the monk to Faucon. "Not only impious, but heathens, all of you, with no respect for God's law," he spat out, then turned on his heel and strode from the hall.

Chapter Thirteen

The instant the prior's back turned, Faucon eased between Brother Colin and the seated, sobbing Lady Bagot. Around the hearth he went, passing Sir Adam, who now hung his head as if he also mourned. Will had his fists pressed to his temples. Dropping into a crouch in front of his brother, Faucon balanced on the balls of his feet, ready to fall back, should his brother strike out.

"Will?" he asked gently.

His brother's only reply was a feral sound. Someone touched Faucon's shoulder. He almost toppled as he looked up.

It was Colin. Questions filled the monk's eyes. As Faucon returned to his feet, Alf left his place at the table to join them. Eustace followed, stopping a respectful distance from Offord's guests.

"My brother, Sir William de Ramis," Faucon said quietly to the healer, fearing a louder voice would aggravate his brother's pain. "From time to time his head aches beyond all toleration."

That was the promise Faucon had made to their father, that they never told anyone outside the family more than Will's head ached from time to time. There was to be no mention of the fits of screaming rage that came from nowhere or that Will sometimes ran mad.

"Ah, I'll be right back," Colin said with a nod, already moving toward the hall door.

Alf stepped closer. "Is there aught I can to do help?" he asked.

Faucon looked from his man to Eustace, and hesitated. It was hard enough to keep Will's secret at home. It would be impossible here in this strange place, especially if Will did race from Offord Hall. His brother knew nothing of this locale nor any of the landmarks. He'd truly find himself lost once he returned to sanity. Better to ask for help to keep him here than to plead for assistance to search for him.

"When my brother's head hurts this much, he can react strangely. Be ready to help me hold him in the hall should he seek to leave. He's strong, especially when he's like this, and he will lash out," he explained, looking from Alf to the bailiff, including Eustace because it might take all three of them to hold Will.

But Will didn't rise or run. Instead, he kept his fists at his temple and rocked on the bench. A few moments later Colin returned with a small clay jug. Its glazed green exterior wore glistening dark streaks as if the monk had spilled as he filled the vessel.

Colin gently touched Will's shoulder and got a startled groan for his effort. "Sir William, if you can bear the taste, this potion will make you sleep deeply, although not for long. I've given it to others who suffer as you do. Most find relief after they awaken."

Perhaps it was a stranger's voice, or mayhap the promise of relief. Rather than ignore an offer of help, as Will was wont to do at home, he slowly extended his right hand as if to take the jug. It was something Faucon had never before seen him do when he was in this state.

Taking this as agreement, Colin knelt in front of Will and guided the knight's fingers until they closed around the neck of the jug. Then, with his own hand on the base of the jug, Colin steadied it as Faucon's brother sought to bring it to his lips. "I warn you. I usually mix this with something to cut the taste, for it is truly foul," Colin said, speaking quietly. "But if you can bear it, drink it all."

The jug tilted. Will struggled to raise his head high enough to swallow. Instead, the liquid trickled down his chin. He freed a muffled sound of frustration. "Pery," he gasped out.

Faucon stared at the sibling he had once adored, torn between astonishment and disbelief. For the first time since his accident, Will was asking him for help. Coming to stand next to Colin, he said, "Perhaps we can lift his head for him so he can swallow?"

Retrieving his jug from Will's control, concern creased Colin's face. "He's as bad as that?" he muttered, returning to his feet.

The monk studied the knight for a breath. "Rather than force him to raise his head, which could cause more pain, lean him back toward the table. I can then help him raise the jug." To Faucon's brother, Colin said, "Sir William, this will take longer, and you may still struggle to swallow."

Although Will made no move or noise to acknowledge what the monk had said, Faucon motioned to Alf and Eustace. With soldier and bailiff at either end of the bench and Faucon steadying his brother, they lifted man and bench away from the table. When Colin nodded his approval, Faucon took his brother by the shoulders and pulled Will back. Colin helped Will bring the jug to his lips. Will sputtered, gagged, but managed to swallow most of the dark, thick liquid.

When he was done, Faucon brought him back upright and retreated. Will sucked in a full breath, coughed, then groaned at the pain this caused him. After that, he again brought his fists back to his temples.

"How quickly will this help?" Faucon asked on Will's behalf. Then he wondered if Will could even think to wonder such things while he was in this state.

"If it works, he should grow drowsy soon enough that we must swiftly find him a place to rest," Colin said.

Faucon looked at Eustace. "Is it possible for my brother to take his rest on a pallet here in the hall?"

"I'll see to it, Eustace," Lady Helena answered. She yet sat on the bench they'd shared at breakfast. This time, when Faucon looked at her, she neither blushed nor blanched as their gazes met. She left the table for the hearth and her mother. Lady Bagot's noisy sobs had ebbed into quieter gasping breaths.

Helena took her mother's hands. "Come, Maman. You should rest as well," she said gently, leaning down to press a quick kiss to her mother's brow.

Her head bowed, Lady Bagot came obediently to her feet. As Helena put an arm around her, turning her toward the bed in the far corner, she looked over her shoulder at Faucon. "You should follow me with Sir William," she told him.

As if his daughter's voice had stirred him to it, Sir Adam lifted his head. "He awoke this morn, complaining about his head aching," he said flatly.

The knight's expression was as lifeless as his voice. At the moment, he seemed a smaller man. It was as if, having spent his rage for no gain, he had folded in on himself.

As Faucon met his gaze, Sir Adam added in the same flat tone, "Your brother told me the changing weather makes it happen."

"That is so," Faucon agreed, ignoring the uncomfortable twist deep within him that always happened when he lied on Will's behalf. But with it came surprise that his brother had bothered to excuse his behavior to a stranger. That wasn't something Will had ever done while Faucon yet lived in their home. Nor, to Faucon's knowledge, had Will ever repeated any of the standard explanations their sire had concocted to disguise his eldest son's weakness.

Turning, ready to help his brother to his pallet, Faucon came face-to-face with Colin. The monk aimed a narrow-eyed look at him. "This is no ache brought on by a change in the weather," he whispered. "How was your brother injured that he suffers so?"

"He took a blow to his head while practicing the joust as a squire," Faucon replied, almost as quietly.

"Did he fall unconscious?" the healer wanted to know.

Faucon nodded. "For three days. We thought he would die." Perhaps Will had died during those days of unnatural sleep, for the man who returned to them wasn't the boy who had taken the injury.

"Such are the hazards of the warrior's trade," Colin said, speaking more normally, then shook his head. "That's two incurable ailments you've shown me this day. For your sake and your brother's, Sir Crowner, I pray forced sleep relieves his pain. Come, I'll help you get him settled on his pallet. After that, we should seek out Lady Offord. I thought she was bringing that cure of hers to me."

Will allowed them to remove his cloak and boots, but couldn't bear to lift his arms so they could remove his tunic. They left him fully dressed, stretched out on his back so he could keep his hands at the sides of his head. Alf went to sit with his back against the wall near

Will's pallet, having offered to watch over the knight until he was safely asleep.

As Faucon started toward the tower door with Colin, Edmund tucked his basket of supplies under his bench and joined them, unwilling to be shut out of the tower a second time. It was only as they reached the tower door that Faucon realized his opportunity. He looked back at Sir Adam. The knight remained seated on the edge of the hearthstone while Eustace had returned to his bench at the head of the servants' table.

"Sir Adam, I'd like to search Sir Robert's chamber and the storeroom below it for the bell, in case it's only been misplaced. Will you join us?" Faucon called. "Eustace, you should come as well."

Nodding, Eustace came immediately to his feet and started toward them. Sir Adam stayed where he sat. His head turned as Offord's bailiff walked past him. It was only after Eustace was around the hearth that the knight rose, doing so with an aching slowness, as if the movement required all his energy.

Faucon waited until both men reached the doorway, then started up the stairs. Their footstep echoed in the narrow stairwell until they sounded like an invading troop. If Lady Offord had lingered in the bedchamber, she was well warned of their approach.

Stinging moisture, driven by the wailing wind, spattered Faucon's face as he stepped onto the landing. The shutters on the wide window across the room stood wide. The ashy sludge that dripped from the brass pan in the brazier beneath the opening suggested they'd been left open all the night.

Idonea sat in the half-barrel chair, having turned it to face the stormy world outside the tower. A length of red fabric was pulled over her like a blanket. The rain had dampened her fine wimple until that wispy bit of silk clung to her shorn head.

Faucon crossed the room, passing the curtained bed and the corpse hidden within it, to stop next to the widow. Idonea glanced up at him. Her cheeks were wet, but not with rain. As their gazes met, she drew up the fabric until it hid her face.

Giving her a moment to collect herself, Faucon pulled his cloak around him and considered the view. From this prospect he could see almost all the cottages in Offord's village, as well as a goodly swath of pasture-land. That made him reconsider the unguarded opening. Although it was a terrible defensive decision, the pleasure it must have given Sir Robert had surely been beyond tallying.

Colin, his cowl pulled up over his head, made his way past Lady Offord's chair. Being a more sensible man than his Crowner, he closed the shutters. The chamber fell into an instant and rank dimness, making it even more drear in here than it was outside.

Then the monk retreated to stand at the opposite side of Idonea's chair. "Sitting in the cold and wet cannot help your joints," he said. There was no judgment in his tone.

The widow made a sad sound, raising her head out of that fabric. Her mouth trembled. "Should I care?" she asked.

"I think you should," Colin replied, "but then, I am an old man and have learned to cherish even the bad that has been in my life. Come now. You don't strike me as a coward. Gird your loins, my lady. Take up your sword! You may never defeat your enemy, but I guarantee you'll win more than a few battles before all is said and done." Then, having done his best to thrust his unwilling patient back into the current of her own life, he offered her a smile.

She met his effort with a quivering bend of her own lips. "You are wrong, Brother. I am very much a coward," she told him in English.

"Lady Offord," Faucon said. "We've come to search the room and the storeroom below for the missing bell. As it turns out, the prior did not take it on the night your husband died."

"Oh," she said on a sigh, "then I suppose I must move." As she came to her feet the red cloth spilled out of her lap. Only then did Faucon recognize it as the tunic Lady Bagot had chosen for her father to wear into eternity.

"While they search, I'd like to see that potion of yours. Were you able to find it?" Colin asked her, in another, more subtle attempt to drive her out of self-pity.

The new widow made a face at that, looking for that moment as young as Martha. Lady Bagot was right. Idonea was still a child, one who had been coddled as completely as Sir Adam's youngest daughter. But then Faucon expected it was easy to make a pet of a frail and ailing child.

"As you will," the widow said, her tone more agreeable than he'd expected, given the face she'd pulled. She pointed to the locked chest pushed against the wall on the other side of the chair. "Sir Robert allowed me to keep my coffer in his chest. Let me fetch the key," she said, starting for the bed.

After Colin stepped off the trap door, Faucon moved the chair then used the rope handle to open it. Once the door rested on the floorboards, he peered down into the storeroom. There wasn't light enough in the chamber to to show him the nearest chests, much less allow for a search.

Faucon turned toward the stairs. Edmund and Sir

Adam stood on the landing with Eustace yet in the stairwell, a few steps below them. The bailiff peered into his master's bedchamber from around the turn of the wall.

"We're going to need a few lamps, bailiff," Faucon said.

Eustace nodded and stared back down the steps. That stirred Sir Adam into movement. He crossed the room to stand at the edge of the opening. Edmund stayed where he was. The monk's expression said his curiosity had been satisfied by climbing the stairs, and he wasn't certain he wanted to be a party to whatever else might go forward in this chamber.

Carrying the ring of keys, Idonea knelt before Sir Robert's chest. It took her two tries before she found the right key, then metal scraped on metal and the lock fell open. As she lifted the lid, Colin moved closer to her.

Faucon followed, driven by curiosity. Just as he expected, Sir Robert's sheathed sword lay atop two thick linen sacks, the same sort of sacking that Faucon used for his own armor. Reaching down, he ran his fingers along a curve of metal that showed at the head of the chest. It was a spur. Pushing his hand down, he found its twin. These had no doubt been given to him by Sir Umfrey on the day that Robert the Squire had become Sir Robert.

Idonea reached across the width of the chest and dug out a small wooden coffer. Even in the dimness Faucon could see it was a cheerful thing, with top and bottom painted green and blue in a checkerboard pattern. That it was neither bound nor locked said it contained nothing of great value, save perhaps to its owner.

Setting it on the edge of the open chest, she lifted

the lid. The spicy scent of violets wafted from it. Beyond the dried flowers, it contained a string of prayer beads, a small knife, its hilt wound with brass thread, a simple fabric necklet decorated with embroidered flowers, and four small jars. Three of the jars were empty, their mouths left uncovered while the fourth had a waxed cloth tied around its neck to protect what it contained.

This was the jar Idonea handed to Colin. "This is the last one and it's nearly empty," she said, closing and setting aside her little coffer. "Mayhap it's a good thing you came to visit, Brother. I wasn't certain what I would do after I took the last dose."

Colin untied the thong and removed the cloth, then put his nose close to the mouth. After breathing in the scent, he dipped the tip of his little finger into the belly of the jar and touched it to his tongue. An instant later he winked at Idonea. "Now, that's an apothecary who knows how to make a cure anyone would take."

His jest won a quick smile from the kneeling widow. "So he does. I like honey," she admitted. "Mama always paid him extra to add the sweetness because she wanted to be certain I would take every drop."

Colin handed the jar to Faucon. "Taste this, Sir Crowner. Just a little bit on your finger as I did."

Faucon did as bidden, carrying a small amount of dark syrup to his tongue. He grimaced. The heavy sweetness of the honey was marred by a musty dark flavor that was both decidedly unpleasant and unfamiliar to him.

"Sweet as it is, I think I wouldn't want to drink much of this," he said, handing the jar back to Colin as he offered Idonea a nod. "You're wrong, my lady. You're no coward. I think you're far braver than I."

That made her lift her hand to her mouth to hide another laugh.

"Now imagine that taste trebled," Colin said, replacing the waxed cloth, "then treble it again, for that would be the dose we discussed earlier."

"This taste is hemlock?" Faucon replied in surprise.

"Hemlock?" Sir Adam echoed faintly from where he stood at the edge of the door in the floor. Something stirred in his expression. He blinked, then his eyes narrowed as if he strove to shake off his strange stupor.

"Hemlock?" he repeated. "There is hemlock in her potion?" he said, his voice gaining strength with every word.

Then, as swiftly as rage had emptied from him, it returned. Sir Adam's shoulders tensed. He straightened to his tallest. His hands curled into fists as he gaze locked on the new widow.

"Poison is a woman's weapon," he roared. "Murderess! You killed Robert!"

Her mouth open in terror, Idonea fell back to sitting. She scrabbled onto her hands and knees, but when she sought to rise, she slipped on the wet floor. Faucon caught her by the arm and lifted her to her feet. Holding her by the wrist, he pushed her behind him. Much to his relief, Idonea didn't fight to escape. Instead, she cowered into the middle of his back.

"Did I not tell you she killed Robert," Sir Adam charged, stepping closer than Faucon liked, then leaned closer still, as if he meant to tear through his Crowner to reach the lady.

Swift footsteps sounded from behind Faucon then Edmund came to a rustling stop next to his left elbow. Together, they formed a wall between raging knight and terrified lady.

"Murderess! Foul little blouze! You'll hang, I'll see to it!" Adam promised at the top of his lungs.

"Cease, Sir Adam," Faucon shouted back. "Lady

Offord's syrup didn't kill Sir Robert. The amount of hemlock in her cure isn't strong enough to cause death."

"Not even if someone consumed every drop that jar could hold," Colin added quietly, still standing next to the chest.

Rather than soothe the knight, Sir Adam's triumph and certainty dissolved into something darker. "What is this?" he snarled. "What has this little whore given you to purchase your protection? The bell!" he answered himself, his eyes flying wide as if all was suddenly clear to him.

He raised a fist in threat. "She took the bell after she killed Robert, and now she's offered it to you so you look the other way! No man takes what should be mine!"

The insult rolled over Faucon. Rage tore through him, the emotion was far colder than the air in this chamber. With every fiber of his being he wanted to deliver a deadly retort to the man for his slur. Had his right hand not been around Idonea's wrist, he would have drawn his sword.

"Have a care with your accusations, Sir Adam, unless you intend that we should meet upon the field," Faucon warned, his words chipped from ice.

Edmund touched a finger to his employer's left fist. "Sir," was all the monk said.

It was exactly what was needed for Faucon to regain control. As rage ebbed, disbelief followed. What sort of fool spouted so lethal and impossible an insult to a man he barely knew? Sir Luc and Lady Bagot were right. Sir Robert's marriage had driven Adam of Bagot completely mad, and the knight was all the more dangerous for it.

"What say you, Sir Adam?" Faucon demanded, his voice still cold. "Do I put your insult up to momentary madness on your part and help you search the store-room? Or do we repair to Offord's bailey and settle the question of my honor between us as men are wont to do?"

Sir Adam's brows rose slowly. His mouth half-opened and confusion filled his gaze, as if he struggled to understand what his Crowner had just said.

Footsteps rang out from behind Faucon. Head down as he balanced the four clay lamps and an unlit torch in his arms, Eustace came to a stop beside Faucon. "This should be enough—" he started to say as he raised his head. His words died as he glanced uneasily between the two knights.

"But she killed Robert. There is hemlock in her potion," Adam insisted weakly, sounding as confused as he looked.

"What will it be?" Faucon spoke over him, pitying Lady Bagot and forgiving Sir Luc for his dishonorable behavior. Sir Adam's younger brother was right. Someone had to protect Lady Offord from this madman.

"Choose now, and choose wisely," Faucon warned.

"Nothing in this last sack, save walnuts," Eustace reported. The tiny circle of light cast by his lamp marked his progress from the back corner of the store-room toward the ladder. Bags of nuts and grains crunched as he moved.

While the bailiff had offered to search the darkest corner of the storeroom, Colin had explored the area around the barrels containing brined foods. As that had been the easier chore, he now sat on the chest Lady Bagot had left open yesterday, the one that Faucon had once again opened and closed today. Brother Colin held his lamp in his lap, its flame just bright enough to show Faucon the weave of the monk's well-worn habit.

"Then we are finished," Faucon replied to the bailiff. He stood beside the ladder guarding their burning torch. They'd jammed it in between the rungs, but it kept tilting.

They were the only searchers. Edmund had returned to the hall on the excuse that he needed to note that Prior Thierry had been cleared of the charge of theft. Faucon's clerk had taken with him his employer's request that Alf include Lady Offord in his protection. Idonea had fled the chamber the instant Faucon released her wrist, which he'd only done after she vowed not to stray from the hall, not even to her dairy hidey-hole.

As for Sir Adam, almost from the instant his Crowner has asked him to choose, he'd once more begun his descent into that strange stupor of his. When it came time to begin the search, he had instead knelt at the side of Sir Robert's bed and begun to offer up prayers for the soul of his father-by-marriage.

"So, sir," Eustace said, as he came to stand near the ladder, "what now?"

What now, indeed. Once again, Faucon shuffled those pieces of his. For the first time since he'd arrived at Offord, a pattern began to form.

"Eustace, now that you know Prior Thierry was able to breach this door," Faucon lifted his hand to indicate the open square above their heads, "and attempt to take the bell, are you still certain it couldn't have been spirited away from Offord's walls?"

"I am, with all my heart," the bailiff replied. "Last night was a desperate moment, what with Sir Robert dying. Only a man as powerful as the prior could ever have locked us out of Robert's chamber, and only that locked door could have given him enough time to find the key, open the coffer, and take the bell unwitnessed. But even that would have exposed him, since all of us at Offord would have known he was the thief once the bell's absence was discovered."

Faucon nodded at that. "And do you also still maintain that Prior Thierry couldn't have taken the bell from the coffer and left Offord with it hidden on his person?"

"I do," Eustace said in complete certainty. Then he added, "And, before you ask, Offord has had no other powerful visitors who could have breached Sir Robert's bedchamber, certainly not since we all last saw the bell. The little ladies had it out to make merry at midsummer."

"So I was hoping you might say," Faucon told the man with a smile. "Now tell me that Sir Robert journeyed away from Offord at least once since his return with Lady Offord from the Michaelmas court."

"How could you know to ask that?" Eustace cried, the torchlight bright enough to reveal astonishment on his face. "He did indeed leave us for a time. It was more than a fortnight ago, just after he recovered from his second ailment. He went without a word as to where, and returned just before Sir Adam and his family moved in for the winter. They stay at Offord throughout the season to avoid depleting all of Bagot's stores before spring, then Robert moves to Bagot with them until we at Offord begin to collect summer's bounty," he offered in explanation.

"How did Sir Robert seem, both before he left and after he returned?" Faucon wanted to know.

Creases formed on the bailiff's brow as he thought. "Sir Robert has not been himself since his marriage, perhaps even before then. However, I would say his heart was lighter when he left than when he returned," the knight's milk-brother replied at last. "I remember asking him what weighed so heavily, but he told me he couldn't yet say, and I didn't press."

Faucon grinned as Eustace confirmed the tale those pieces of his were beginning to reveal."Sir Robert removed the bell from its box and took it with him on that journey," he said.

"It's not possible that you can know that," Eustace protested. "More to the point, where would he have taken his bell without that box, and for what reason?"

"He took it to a place where he thought he might trade it for coins," Colin answered for his Crowner. As he spoke, his lamp shifted in his lap and its tiny flame set to dancing. "Am I right, Sir Faucon?"

"You are," Faucon agreed.

"But this cannot be," Eustace said in vehement denial. "Sir Robert would never have sold the bell. I told you, he had promised it to Lady Offord as her dower. He would never have been forsworn."

"I don't believe Sir Robert intended to cheat Lady Offord," Faucon said quickly. "Instead, he meant to sell the bell so he could leave her its value in coins. Perhaps he feared Prior Thierry would succeed in claiming it, leaving Lady Offord with no dower at all."

But if that had been his intention, then Sir Robert must have expected to die before his sickly wife. With that, a different possibility unfolded. Idonea was right— her father was a canny tradesman. He'd married off a defective daughter, a girl that others had rejected, at next to no cost, and lifted his line into the gentry. Even without bearing a child, Idonea returned to her family as Lady Offord, having added her title to her dowry and increased her worth. All this her father had done to help a knight keep his prized possession out of the reach of another knight.

Sir Robert's only reason for marrying had been to punish Sir Adam for trying to bully his way into control of Offord.

Indeed, Robert had chosen Idonea precisely because she was a sickly girl unlikely to bear children or live to an old age. That was why he'd made his bell her dower. For as long as Idonea lived Adam couldn't touch the bell, and neither could the Church. Nor could Idonea's family, a widow's dower must remain intact for it returned to her husband's family upon her death.

That was also why Robert had exploded on the night of his death, beating both his wife and Sir Luc. He knew he hadn't planted a child in Idonea's belly. But any child by her, whether his or another man's, would have ruined all, and stolen his grandson's inheritance.

"But why leave the coffer? The box is worth at least half as much as the bell," Eustace asked, looking baffled.

"Because Sir Robert didn't want anyone to know the bell was gone. As long as the locked coffer remained in the storeroom, everyone would assume the bell was still inside it," Faucon told him, and yet another piece fell into place.

Thus had Sir Robert called for the prior when he knew he was dying, and why he'd agreed to be alone with Prior Thierry. He'd wanted the Churchman to open that coffer and see it was empty. No doubt he hoped the Churchman would believe the bell was forever out of his reach. Perhaps he also hoped that the prior would reveal it was missing to Sir Adam for the same reason.

"That Sir Robert returned disappointed from his journey means one of two things," Faucon continued. "The first would be that he sold the bell and suffered over giving up a beloved object. If that were so, wouldn't we have found a purse containing coins to match the bell's value in one of these?" he asked the bailiff, the sweep of his hand indicating the two chests near the ladder.

Eustace's resistance began to ebb. "If there were such a purse, it would have been stored here. But we found no purse," the bailiff added quietly.

"Which brings us to the other possibility for Sir Robert's disappointment," Faucon continued, " and it is two-pronged. Either he found he couldn't bear to part with the bell, or he discovered that no honest man would give him the coins he wanted for it because it is what Prior Thierry described, a sacred object." And a dishonest man wasn't likely to offer the full worth of the bell for just that reason. "Either way, it means Sir Robert returned with the bell yet in his possession."

"But why didn't he return it to its box?" Colin asked.

Eustace caught a startled breath at the question."Because he knew the prior meant to take it from him."

"Not the prior," Faucon said with a shake of his head. "It was someone else, someone he had once trusted deeply and no longer did. You were right, Eustace. There could never have been a theft, and there never was. The bell is still at Offord, hidden in some place known only to Sir Robert, a location he took with him to his grave."

That had Faucon sighing. Sir Robert had been a fool not to give his bell to the priory the moment it was identified as a holy object. Instead, the knight had kept his precious bell and it had cost him his life.

Chapter Fourteen

Extinguishing their lamps and smothering the torch, they returned up the ladder to the bed-chamber. Sir Adam yet knelt at the side of Sir Robert's bed. If the knight prayed, he was doing so while staring vacantly at the draperies that enclosed Sir Robert's body. Faucon left the man to his shattered thoughts and returned with his fellow searchers to the hall.

Will slept on his pallet, rolled onto his side, his legs bent and his arms relaxed. That said Colin's brew had delivered on its promise. Faucon's brother suffered no more, at least for the moment.

Alf had returned to the bench he'd used at the morning meal. Not far from him, Idonea and Lady Helena sat on the rush-strewn tile floor, facing the hall door, their backs against the warm hearthstone. Both girls had their heads bent as if concentrating on something in their laps.

Just then Martha's poppet rose into view above the leaping flames. Martha followed, holding her plaything high as she came to her feet. The child leaned over her sister to give the toy to her step-grandmother. Apparently the little lady's term of punishment had come to an end.

More than ready to be done with this place, Faucon stopped beside Edmund at the end of the high table. Both Colin and Eustace stopped with him. Edmund once again had his writing tools spread out before him.

"All is well?" Faucon's clerk asked, his gaze shifting

166

briefly in the direction of the tower door.

"All is well," Faucon assured him, and was suddenly anxious for a private moment with his clerk. Edmund deserved more than the simple thanks Faucon had already shared with him. As for Faucon, the better he came to know this man, the more he liked him, in spite of the complications he ever seemed to create.

"All is well for me," Faucon amended with a smile. "As for you, I fear you'll be making free with your knife. The bell was not stolen," he said.

"Not by the prior," Brother Edmund agreed.

"Not by anyone," Faucon told him. "I believe that for his own reasons Sir Robert hid the bell here at Offord. It may never be found."

As he spoke, he caught a sharp movement from the corner of his eye. It was the little lady. Martha had snatched her toy back out of the widow's hands.

"Hey!" Idonea cried in surprise. "If she's to wear a gown, I have to fit it to her," she chided her step-grand-daughter. "I promise I won't poke her with the needle."

Clutching her poppet close, Martha shared her frown with her sister and her stepgrandmother, as well as the men behind her.

"Do you want her to be dressed or not?" Idonea demanded.

Martha relented. "She wants a gown," she said, giving the plaything back to Idonea.

"You're certain?" Edmund asked at the same time, looking aggrieved over the idea of scraping ink off his precious parchment.

"As certain as we'll ever be if we don't find the bell," Faucon told him.

His clerk gave an irritable sigh. "Then off it comes," he grumbled. He picked up his knife, then hesitated, still watching his employer. "What should I include

167

regarding the manner of Sir Robert's death?"

"Nothing as of yet," Faucon replied with a sigh. No matter how he rearranged those pieces of his, the tale they were supposed to tell remained as scrambled as ever.

"Perhaps you'll never know," the monk said quietly, as if avoiding a declaration of suicide was the same as declaring that a man had not taken his own life. Such an earthly deflection would hardly save a soul from suffering its rightful punishment for the ultimate sin.

That left Faucon gnawing on the conundrum of Sir Robert's passing. It was certain that the man's life had ended at a ruinous moment, when his treasury was bare, and as his son-by-marriage sought to steal his independence, and just as he discovered that someone he'd once trusted dearly intended to steal a precious artifact. Those were certainly reasons for a man to contemplate his own death. But by consuming hemlock?

Faucon twisted and turned this in his mind, and still couldn't make suicide fit. Sir Adam said he had sparred frequently with Sir Robert. A hesitant step, a weak wrist, turning an instant too late. These were all possible avenues to certain death, one that didn't cheat a man of his heavenly reward.

"Come with me," he said to Colin and Eustace as he started toward Alf.

At Faucon's suggestion, Eustace brought a bench around to the inside of the table so he and Colin could sit across from the soldier and their Crowner as they talked. While the girls at the nearby hearthstone chatted quietly and sewed, Faucon said to Eustace, "Tell Brother Colin about Sir Robert's recent illnesses."

Nodding his agreement, Eustace looked at the monk. "Two times since Sir Robert returned after

Michaelmas court, he overindulged at his meat and became ill. Each time he complained that his stomach was afire and his legs ached. These illnesses caught him, and those of us who serve him, by surprise. Sir Robert has been hale and hearty these past years."

Colin's snowy brows lifted. "How long before your master arose from his bed, free from his complaint?" he asked the bailiff.

"Truth be, I was startled that he even agreed to take to his bed," Eustace said, with a wry twist of his mouth. "Sir Robert wasn't the sort to allow any illness to lay him low. But Lady Bagot pleaded to care for him, and because I knew she loved him, I added my voice to hers. He agreed. She even got him to take that tonic she makes. To both of our pleasure, his pains began rapidly to ebb and he didn't once complain over her ministrations," the bailiff said on an amused breath. "As for how long, I don't think he stayed abed for more than a day or two each time. And when he arose, it was in complete health."

"You're certain he didn't complain of lingering effects or permanent deficits?" the monk pressed.

"If there were any, Sir Robert never mentioned them to me," Eustace replied.

Colin grinned. "Hemlock," he pronounced again.

"What?" Eustace cried in surprise. "Are you saying Sir Robert was poisoned as Sir Adam charged?"

The ladies at the hearth fell into an instant silence. Faucon glanced at them. All three were staring boldly at the men seated around the end of the table.

Moisture filled Idonea's eyes. "There was poison?" she whispered, then lowered her gaze back to her lap where it belonged, doing so only to hide the fact that her tears were falling.

A frowning Martha looked at her sister. "What is

'poisoned' and why is Idonea crying?" she whispered loudly.

Lady Helena shot a swift glance at Faucon, blushed, then turned to her sister. "Hush, Martha. It's none of our concern, that's what it is. Now lower your gaze as you know you must," she chided softly, sounding like her mother. As Martha did as she was told, Helena put a reassuring arm around her step-grandmother.

Faucon looked back at the bailiff. "That's what I'm beginning to believe, but belief is useless to me. Help me, Brother Colin," he begged the monk. "Tell me how that taste could have been disguised so thoroughly that Sir Robert might have drunk enough of it to end his life."

"I cannot," Colin said with a shake of his head. "You know that, having tasted it. Hemlock would never be a poisoner's first choice."

"Then, if not drink, could it have been added to his food?" Faucon demanded on a frustrated breath.

"I cannot say as I've ever once tried mixing it with food," the monk replied with a sorry smile. "I fear I haven't had much experience killing men."

Faucon pushed back on his bench, his hands resting on the table. "And yet, the way Sir Robert ailed in these instances tells us that the hemlock was there, hidden in something he consumed. If not drink, then it must be the food. Bailiff, tell me everything you can remember about those meals. You say he overate. What was it he ate most of?"

Frowning, his blue eyes narrowed, Eustace rubbed a hand over his bearded chin. "Two meals, so far apart, and me thinking nothing about them, not even after Robert grew ill," he muttered. "I mean, we were all at these tables with him and the food was all cooked in the same pots. If the meal were poisoned, wouldn't we have ailed as well?"

"Then can you remember who was at the table with him each time he fell ill?" Faucon asked.

"Lady Offord, of course," Eustace told him. "And Lady Bagot as well, along with the little ladies."

That startled Faucon. "Lady Bagot, but not Sir Adam?"

Eustace nodded. "Over this past year, Lady Bagot has often ridden over from Bagot to enjoy a meal with her father. She and her daughters were present at both of those meals. And for Lady Martha's saint day celebration, of course, as was everyone else."

Then Eustace blinked. Something flashed across his face and his eyes widened. "But you cannot think Lady Bagot would ever have done aught to hurt her sire," he cried in protest. "I've known her from the moment of her birth. Never has there been a more loving daughter nor a more adoring father, especially over these last months. You've seen how distraught she's been since Robert's death."

"Eustace, you're trying to leap the stream before we even know where it is," Faucon assured him. "Calm yourself. Tell me whatever you can about the meals themselves."

Instead, the bailiff's expression shuttered. Just as Milla had done yesterday, Eustace had closed the drawbridge and manned the ramparts. "Sir, you're asking the wrong person. Two meals so far apart, and we who serve don't always eat the same dishes as the family," he said, contradicting himself.

Faucon watched him closely. "Perhaps I should ask Milla instead?"

"Perhaps that would be more helpful," the man agreed flatly. "As for me, it's time I got on with my own chores. If you'll excuse, sir?"

"Many thanks for your help this morn, Eustace," Faucon said with a smile.

"For the sake of my dead master, I am glad to do my duty," the bailiff replied politely, then turned to stride from the hall.

"That is a frightened man," Alf said quietly, as they watched Eustace round the screen.

Faucon nodded. "So I was thinking as well." But whatever frightened Eustace, it wasn't something he thought his sister knew. "I think it's time I returned to the kitchen to talk with the cook."

Just then Idonea rose, offered the poppet to Martha, then came to stand next to Brother Colin on his bench. Her eyes were wet and she'd knotted her hands at her waist.

"Sir Faucon, I pray you. Don't believe Sir Adam. I did nothing wrong, and I would never have harmed my husband," she cried. "I wouldn't even know how, so I vow!"

It was Colin who answered. "But of course you didn't, my lady," he said, seeking to soothe even though no one yet knew if what the monk said was true.

Rather than challenge Colin's assumption, Faucon leapt to grab the opportunity Idonea offered. Although Lady Offord was barely older than Helena, as Sir Robert's wife, she could serve as chaperone. That made it possible for him to speak directly to Lady Helena without treading into worrisome territory.

"Will you come join Lady Offord, Lady Helena?" Faucon asked Sir Adam's older daughter. "Perhaps between the two of you, you can recall the meals that caused your Grand-père to ail."

Being a biddable girl, Helena did as he asked. As she came to stand at Idonea's right, Martha followed, tucking her poppet under her arm. The plaything now wore a sleeveless shift. She pressed herself between her older sister and Idonea, then forced her free hand through Idonea's clenched fingers until the widow relented.

"I'm not certain what we ate," Idonea said on a ragged breath. "All I remember is that Sir Robert began to complain about his stomach before we began the second dish." She looked at Helena. "Do you remember that?"

Her head modestly lowered, Helena glanced up at Faucon before she spoke. "I remember only that Grand-père drank too much wine on each of those nights. When Maman warned him that he should drink no more, he told her he had to have more wine because his stomach ached so."

"I remember what Grand-père ate," Martha said, her tone serious. She stared directly at her Crowner. "Grand-père ate his little birds on each of those nights."

Helena raised her head far enough to frown at her younger sister. "Martha!" she chided. "Have a care with your words. Don't you recall what Brother Edmund told us yesterday? Sir Faucon is the king's servant. If he asks you a question, you must be certain the answer you give is the truth. If I cannot remember what any of us ate, how can you possibly remember so well that you could swear what you say is true?"

"But I do remember and it is the truth," Martha insisted, her voice rising. "He ate his little birds," she told her sister.

Then she looked directly at her Crowner. Her gaze was steady and her chin firm. Everything about her said she took her obligation to speak the truth very seriously. "I do remember and I can swear it, sir," she told him.

Faucon eyed her narrowly. "But did you not say

yesterday that your grandsire always shared his birds with you? That is, until you had your own portion for your saint day?" he asked.

"He always did, except on those nights," she replied, nodding to affirm this was what she recalled. "That's why I remember what he ate. I wasn't allowed to share his meal."

"Why were you not allowed?" Faucon asked, a little startled.

A shameless glint took fire in Martha's pretty green eyes. She lifted a dismissive shoulder, then the corners of her mouth twisted into a wicked smile. "I am not always Maman's good girl. On those nights, I had to stay on the bench with Helena and eat stew, instead of sharing the birds with Grand-père."

The huntsman in Faucon stirred sharply at that. Although the spoor he saw on the trail ahead of him was faint and confused, and still felt improbable, the trail he must follow was appearing at last.

Then Martha's golden-red brows flattened in question. "Sir, what is 'poisoned'?"

Curious, Faucon replied in English. "It's when someone eats something that makes them ill."

"Like when Grandpapa took ill on my saint day after he again ate his own little birds?" she asked in the same tongue, making the transition with ease and speaking without accent.

"For shame, Martha," her sister scolded. "You know very well both Papa and Maman have forbidden you to use the commoner's tongue."

The child slanted an impatient look at her sister. "My Anie spoke it. The sir speaks it, and so does Idonea," she said, moving without hesitation back into her parents' native tongue. "Besides Papa isn't here and Maman is sleeping. They can't hear me," she said, now lifting her chin to an imperious angle, looking very much like her mother as she did so.

Faucon eyed the little lady. Helpful, beautiful, but disobedient, disrespectful, and as spoiled as rotten meat. It was a good thing for Sir Adam that Martha was his second daughter, not his first. Where Lady Helena would someday make a good wife, no man in his right mind would have Martha, not even if Sir Adam could afford to give her a dowry, or chose to divide what was Helena's between his two girls, thereby diminishing both their chances for advancement. Instead, Faucon wagered Martha would spend her life in barren service to her family, at least for as long as her family could tolerate her.

Chapter Fifteen

Leaving Alf to watch over Idonea and the little ladies, Faucon and Colin made their way through the spattering rain, heads down and picking their way around mud puddles, to the kitchen. Once inside, Faucon basked in the welcome heat of the fire at the same time that he caught his breath at the stink of fish and blood. He glanced at the barrel that had last night contained swimming eels, only to find it now empty of water and filled with their entrails.

Across the room it was Nobby, not Milla, hard at work at the table. The lad stood on a short stool so he could reach the tabletop. Spread out in front of him was an array of vegetables— turnips, onions, parsnips, cabbages, along with a great pile of greenery. Faucon watched the boy take a delicate stalk from that green mound, strip what he thought parsley into a bowl then toss aside the stem. This was hardly a scullery lad's usual duty. That had Faucon grinning. Nobby, it seemed, had ambitions.

"Nobby," Faucon called to announce himself.

So completely was the boy immersed in his task that he started and almost tumbled off his stool. Catching the edge of the table to steady himself, he turned to face them. Under his thatch of fair hair, his brown eyes were wide and his face colorless. He held his free hand to his chest as if seeking to restore his heart to its rightful place.

"Sir!" he cried breathlessly.

"My pardon," Faucon offered, still smiling as he and

176

Colin rounded the hearth to join him at the worktable. "What's this?" he teased gently. "Have you become cook in Milla's stead?"

That steadied the boy's heart better than his hand ever could. He grinned proudly. "Perhaps some day. It's eel pie we'll have for our meal today, with stewed fish as the second dish. I'm preparing the vegetables for the stew while Milla is at the ovens baking the pies. If you want to speak with her, you should go there. Do you know where the ovens are?"

"In the garden, I believe," Faucon replied and got a nod from the lad. He started to turn, then caught himself and considered the boy for an instant. "Nobby, do you remember the meals where Sir Robert overate and became ill?"

"It wasn't my fault," the boy said instantly, his expression pinched.

"Why would you say such a thing?" Faucon retorted in surprise. "How could it be your fault?"

The lad looked at his Crowner, stricken. "Milla says the betters will always blame the cook if one of them ails after a meal," he whispered.

"Does that happen often here? Did Sir Robert blame Milla for making him ill?" Colin asked gently.

Nobby gave a quick shake of his head. "Not Sir Robert. He is always kind. It's Lady Bagot. She thinks everything is Milla's fault. Too much salt, too little salt. Too bland, too bland, always too bland, even though all the rest of us like how Milla seasons our meals." The boy frowned in disapproval. "The lady blames Milla despite that she knows very well Sir Robert won't spend coins on spices save for very special occasions."

"But how can Milla be blamed for anything when her meals are so tasty that her employer is tempted to eat more than he should?" Faucon asked with a reassuring smile. "That's what Lady Bagot told me, that Sir Robert enjoyed his meals too well, and overeating caused his illnesses."

"The lady said that?" Nobby replied, looking truly shocked. "But I was here when she came after that first meal when Sir Robert took ill. She was crying and Milla doing her best to comfort her. When I asked Milla why the lady was so upset, she told me that Lady Bagot said the birds had made Sir Robert ill. This, even though Sir Robert had eaten the same dish the week before with no untoward consequences," he added, his choice of words suggesting he quoted his mistress. As well he might, given that he had no French and Lady Bagot no English.

"Well, Milla was so distraught over the lady saying the birds made Sir Robert sick that she sent me to fetch another bird. She wanted to cook it and have the lady taste it, so she would know the flesh wasn't bad."

"An intelligent test," Faucon said, enjoying the storyteller as much as the tale. "So did the lady taste it and was she convinced the birds weren't at fault for Sir Robert's illness?"

Nobby shook his head. "Milla ate it instead. Oh, she offered it to the lady, but the lady refused to take a bite. Instead, she watched Milla consume it. And did Milla grow ill? Nay, not even a little bit." The boy's shrug said he had expected no less. "Of course not. How could she when all those birds come from the same flock? If one was bad, all would be bad," he said, sounding again as if he were repeating what he'd been told.

"But these are wild birds," Faucon said, frowning. "How can anyone know if they all come from the same flock?"

"They aren't wild," Nobby replied, stripping another parsley stem of its leaves. "We raise them here at Offord especially for Sir Robert's table."

The thought of raising a bird that men usually netted in their fields startled Faucon. Then he was surprised at his surprise. If a man loved the taste of a particular bird and could find a way to make them breed while cooped or caged, why not keep a flock for himself?

"Could I see Sir Robert's flock of wild birds?" Faucon asked.

That teased a shrug out of Nobby. "I'm sure you can, if you don't mind walking in the rain. They're not here at the manor. It's Eustace who raises them. Keeps them at his home, he does. When we want them, he brings them here alive in a special cage. It's my job to wring their necks and pluck or skin them."

Brother Colin glanced sidelong at Faucon. Faucon's brows rose. Eustace, the frightened man. The man who must have suddenly remembered what Sir Robert had eaten each time he ailed, as well as on the night of his death.

"Nobby, tell me this. Did everyone at the high table eat quail on Lady Martha's saint day?" Faucon asked.

"Nay, no one had it but Sir Robert," the boy replied, stripping another stem. "No one else likes them, mostly because of that sauce the master prefers. Everyone else, both high and low, ate dove with the sauce we all do like."

"Everyone?" Faucon stared at him in surprise.

"Everyone," Nobby told him with a firm nod. "We all had dove."

"But how can that be true? Milla told me yesterday that she'd made the quail for Lady Martha as a gift for her special day."

The lad frowned, his head cocked. "Are you certain that's what she said?"

"I am," Faucon replied.

179

"But that cannot be," the boy protested. "It's true that Milla intended to make quail for the little lady. Hadn't Sir Robert come to the kitchen the day before and told Milla to be sure to have six quail instead of four for the next night? Our master had promised Martha— the little lady," Nobby corrected himself, "that on her special day they would dine together. He would have four birds and she would have two of her own.

"Then early the next morn, the lady came to the kitchen. After the lady left, Milla told me that she'd complained that the quail were far too small, much smaller than our usual, when of course they weren't."

He paused, his expression tight as he thought, then he shrugged. "Well, they might have been a little smaller. I was the one to pluck them that day, and they were different than the ones of the previous week. But they weren't that small.

"Anyway, Milla said that the lady thought it wasn't enough food for her father if he was to share with her daughter. She wanted us to go to Eustace for two more quail. She said because it was a special celebration, her father should have the six small birds while Lady Martha would have her own two."

Here, the boy scoffed and shook his head as if astonished at the idiocy of the lady's request. "We couldn't just ask Eustace to bring us two more and have them ready to serve for that night's meal. They have to be killed, plucked, gutted, then brined, don't they? Else they'll break your teeth. There was no time for all that. That's when Milla decided to give the little lady doves. It's not as if anyone at the high table would ever know the difference. Birds all look the same, legs, and wings and such, don't they?" Nobby said, his brows lifted to peaks over his eyes.

"So we chose two of the smaller doves, left them

whole, just like the quail, and made a separate dish meant for the little lady alone. Sure enough, no one at the high table noticed that anything was different. I know. I was watching."

"And did Milla serve Sir Robert all of six of the quail?" Faucon asked.

Nobby nodded as he ran his fingers down another stem of parsley. "Of course she did. Hadn't that been what the lady said she should do?"

There was only one place to go after that. "Nobby, how do I find Eustace's home?" Faucon asked.

The track through the center of the village was crowded despite the persistent storm. Rain or not, folk were out and about on their daily business. Faucon and the monk parted to go around a man balancing a wide yoke across his neck and shoulders. The buckets that hung from his yoke were filled with stones. Then they shifted together to one side to pass an old woman. The goodwife had her head bowed and her bright blue hood pulled down to her eyebrows while she balanced a large bundle of faggots on her dripping back.

Ahead of her was a man wrestling an empty hand cart through the mud. His cap was pulled so low that he only saw them at the last moment. "Pardon," he muttered breathlessly as he yanked his cart to the side so they could pass, and got a nod of thanks from his Crowner in response.

As they reached the expanse of the village green, Brother Colin looked up at him. "I yet struggle with the idea that hemlock could have somehow been infused into the flesh of these birds and leave no taste." He sounded both puzzled and frustrated.

"As do I," Faucon agreed. Together, they turned at the far edge of the green as Nobby had instructed. "But no matter what we struggle with, this is where the trail leads. You say that hemlock killed the man, and you've ruled out drink. We asked what the knight ate and discovered that each time he ailed he'd dined on these birds."

Faucon rubbed at his brow. "Perhaps we should try boiling quail meat in a deadly dose of hemlock and see if the taste remains?" he offered with a wicked grin.

That made the monk laugh. "My pardon, but I think I'll refuse any invitation to dine at your table."

That won him a quick wink."Have no fear," Faucon told him. "Lady Marian would never allow me any control over my kitchen."

Just then the wind gusted. Tucked into its folds was a stench Faucon recognized. His head came up with a jerk. He scanned the line of cottages ahead of him. Two faint streams of smoke bent over a fence behind the house where the track curved. By Nobby's description, this was the bailiff's house.

"Hie, Brother," Faucon said, already sprinting toward Eustace's cottage. Rounding the structure, he followed the line of woven toft fence, eyes on the smoke.

"Stop, Eustace! Stop, I say!" a woman shouted from inside the toft. "Have you gone mad? You cannot kill them all! We have to keep some for next year."

Reaching the gate, Faucon threw himself at it, expecting it to be barred. Instead, it flew wide, the leather hinges tearing through the weave of the panel on which they hung. He stumbled inside the long expanse of the toft.

A single straight path cut this space in twain, with half the land given over to the household garden while the other half was cluttered with sheds, folds for livestock, and a small pasture area in which stood a tall gray horse. Although no courser like Legate, this animal was too fine to belong to a village bailiff. Sir Luc had not left Offord as he suggested.

His back to the gate, Eustace trotted ever farther down the dividing path. Trailing him by an expanding distance was a heavyset woman wearing a white head-cloth and a dark woolen shawl over her bright blue gown. Her hems flew and her brown braids swung as she strove to catch the bailiff.

Faucon made his way to where those struggling columns of smoke rose from a wide hole in the earth. The closer he came to them, the stronger the stench of burning feathers. He caught back a cough as he reached the edge of the hole, then grimaced. Twelve small carcasses lay upon a pile of smoldering twigs and branches. Hissing and spitting, the flames battled the rain, the fire steadily gaining as it burned away feathers to char the flesh below them. The birds were too far gone for him to make use of them.

As Colin came to a panting stop beside him, Faucon again scanned the toft, squinting into the rain. Eustace had stopped in front of what looked like a sheepfold, but the fence was shorter than that used to enclose a flock. That allowed Faucon to see the curved roofs of the structures it guarded. These were the same sort of small houses the villagers at Blacklea used for their fowl.

The moment Offord's bailiff stepped into the pen, at least a dozen chickens and ducks exited around his legs, as if they'd been plotting their escape on the other side of the door. The birds headed at top speed for the garden. That had the woman following Eustace shriek-ing again. She tore off her shawl and flapped it at the birds.

"Hie, hie, hie," she cried, trying to frighten them back into their own yard. Instead, the escapees scattered in all directions. Giving up on her chase, the woman hurried to follow Eustace, her shawl once more around her. Standing in the opening, she spread her arms wide as if to block it. "Please, husband. Don't do this," she cried.

Eustace pushed past his wife with enough force that she dropped to sit on the ground. He carried with him four more small mottled-brown birds, two in each hand. All were dead, or so said the way their wings fell loosely from their sides.

He'd walked halfway back to the toft fence before he lifted his head. As he saw the knight and monk standing next to his fire pit, Eustace froze, his mouth agape. The bailiff's body tensed. Faucon rose to the balls of his feet, ready to give chase.

Instead, in the next instant the bailiff's shoulders drooped. His fingers opened. The dead quail dropped to the mucky ground. Eustace fell to his knees. "It was me," he keened. "I killed Robert." Sitting back on his heels, he buried his face in his hands.

"Nay! That's not true. You did nothing wrong!" his wife screamed in terror from where she still sat. As she fought to rise, she began to weep noisily.

Faucon strode to where Eustace knelt and snatched up the dead birds. Holding them up in display, he turned to Colin. "What say you, brother? I intend to skin and skewer these birds, then roast them over those flames for my midday meal. Will you join me?"

Confusion blossomed on the monk's face. Reluctance followed. Faucon laughed out loud. Then, still holding tight to his little birds, he went to help both the bailiff and his wife to their feet.

Chapter Sixteen

"**Y**ou mustn't eat them, sir," Eustace said yet one more time, speaking in his native tongue. He now sat on a bench at his table across from Faucon and Brother Colin. The bailiff didn't look at either of them as he spoke. Instead he aimed his words and his gaze at the scarred wooden boards of his tabletop.

"Enough, husband," chided his wife. Seated on a stool at the end of the table, knife in hand, Nell took up the fourth quail. Cutting a slit in its skin, she caught one edge and stripped off its feathery hide as if it were a tunic. "Our Crowner believes these birds didn't kill Sir Robert, else he wouldn't be wanting to eat them. He knows there's nothing amiss with our birds," she asserted firmly.

Save for her tongue, there was nothing hard about Eustace's wife. Her face and body were round and soft. Her nose was a button, her lips plump. Even her clear blue eyes were more round than ovals.

Once Nell had understood that her new Crowner didn't believe her husband's confession of murder, she set about making her guests comfortable. That included draping their cloaks over stools near the hearth so they might dry, and serving them warm cider before she set about cleaning the four freshly-killed quail.

"But he cannot know that, Nell. The day before yesterday, six of our quail killed Sir Robert," Eustace insisted, his voice breaking.

"Our quail could never kill anyone," Nell replied

sharply.

As he listened to them quibble Faucon raised the household's only wooden cup and savored another sip of the housewife's best cider. It was barely fermented and tasted of sweet summer apple. Eustace's wife had insisted on warming it for them, stating that warm cider was better for their health on such a cold, wet day. Colin hadn't disagreed with her. Rather he was enjoying his own cider, although his had been served in a small wooden bowl.

Nobby had said the bailiff's house was the biggest dwelling in the village, and so it was. But Faucon guessed it was also the most quiet. Eustace and Nell had no children. With the four of them sitting in silence at the table, the only sounds were the snap and crackle of the fire on the central hearthstone and the occasional moan of the wind.

And the movements of the man hiding in the loft over Faucon's head.

That platform stretched about halfway across the width of the cottage, with two posts holding up its leading edge. Had there been children, Nell and Eustace might have used that raised space as a private sleeping area. Instead, a length of raw linen fabric stretched like a curtain beneath the overhang, suggesting that was where husband and wife spent their nights.

Having skinned the birds, Nell rose and went to the wall behind her. Although the usual barrels and bags of supplies cluttered the beaten earth floor at the wall, above those supplies were lines of wooden shelving spaced at regular intervals. This was where she kept her cookware, including a large metal spoon amid a pile of wooden ones, a stack of wooden bowls in various sizes, a sieve, and several small iron pots. Displayed upright on a wooden stand at the very center of the wall was a large, green, glazed platter, surely one of Nell's prized possessions.

The rest of the couple's furnishings circled around the hearthstone. There was this table, about as big as his table at Blacklea, and a half-barrel chair, its tall back turned to the door to protect the occupant from the draft. A single long chest was pushed against one wall. Although it had no lock, this would be where they stored their clothing as well anything else that needed protection from vermin, such as the seeds they saved for next year's garden.

Returning to the table with a slender iron rod and a wooden handle, Nell stripped the breast meat from the carcasses and threaded the small pieces of flesh onto her spit. After fitting the handle onto one end, she rested the spit into the Y-shaped braces that stood at either side of her hearth and began to turn it.

Yet again, the man hidden in the loft moved. As the straw rustled, Nell freed an impatient sound and sent a narrow-eyed glance above her.

"Will you come down and join us, Sir Luc?" Faucon called in the commoner's tongue.

Colin glanced at Faucon in surprise. Nell gasped, then shot a worried look at her husband. Eustace only grew all the more ashen.

"You really should come down," Faucon called again. There was still no answer from above.

This time, he spoke in French. "You should join us, Sir Luc. The goodwife's cider is truly excellent, although you may already know this, having stayed here these past two nights."

That got the reaction Faucon intended. Dressed only in his shirt and chausses, Sir Luc climbed down the ladder. Without a word of greeting or explanation to his fellow knight, he sat next to Eustace on his bench, his jaw tight and his mouth held in a narrow line.

"You didn't leave last night as Lady Bagot re-quested," Faucon said by way of greeting.

The knight gave a lift of his shoulders but said nothing. There was nothing for him to say, not after his lie and dishonorable behavior had been exposed.

Faucon smiled. "Sir Luc of Bagot, this is Brother Colin, herbalist and healer for the abbey of Saint Peter in Stanrudde," he offered politely, looking from knight to monk. To Colin he said, "Sir Luc is Sir Adam's half-brother, and steward for Bagot Manor."

Taking another sip of cider, Faucon once again addressed Luc. "I, for one, am glad you stayed. It turns out that I have more questions for you. And for Eustace as well," he said, glancing at the bailiff. Eustace only blinked.

"Milla was your nurse," Faucon said to Luc, "but she remained at Bagot long after you were weaned, did she not?"

Caution and confusion filled Luc's face. Guarding both his expression and his tongue for once, he studied Faucon for a long moment. At last, he said, "That is true."

As that was no answer at all, Faucon tried again. "How many years was it after your weaning before your brother no longer wanted her?"

Again, the red-headed knight's jaw tightened, but he didn't defend his beloved nurse. Eustace again studied the tabletop. Nell steadily turned her spit, the fire crackling as the meat wept and charred. Faucon sipped more cider, content to wait. To his surprise, it was Nell who finally broke the silence, doing so in the Norman tongue.

"Milla served Sir Adam as his cook," she said, her words heavily accented. Nell kept her gaze focused on her task as she spoke. "She took the position even before he," the jerk of her head indicated Sir Luc, "could walk. As Sir Adam had offered to wed Lady Joia on the day of her birth, he knew he'd have no wife to run his household until she came of age. It seemed only natural that Milla, who was already managing his household's food, might step into the role of chatelaine." It was a stilted explanation, as if Nell couldn't bear to admit that her sister-by-marriage had taken on all the duties of wife to the knight.

"Did she remain Bagot's housekeeper even after Sir Adam wed Lady Joia?" Faucon asked.

That stirred Sir Luc to speech. "Lady Joia was only twelve when she and my brother wed," he said, his words clipped and harsh. Again his expression was strictly schooled. "She wasn't ready to shoulder the duties of both wife and housekeeper. By then I was gone from Bagot for my fostering, not to return for more than the occasional visit until my twenty-first year. Joia was glad for Milla's presence, and Milla was pleased to serve as her teacher. And just as she had done for me, orphan that I am, Milla opened her heart to Lady Bagot."

"How long ago did Milla come to Offord?" Faucon wanted to know.

"Six years past now," Eustace said with a weary sigh.

"And haven't we rued every day since that one?" his wife said sharply, speaking in English again. She pulled the spit from its braces to check the meat. "They're cooked through," she announced.

"Good enough," Faucon said, answering in French for Sir Luc's benefit. "No need for a bowl or trencher, goodwife. They are but bites. Just pull them off for me if you will."

"Are you certain you wish to do this, Sir Faucon?"

Colin asked, his voice low.

"What is he doing?" Sir Luc glanced from the monk to his Crowner, sounding more like the man Faucon had met in Milla's kitchen. "What is that meat?" he asked Faucon.

"Sir Robert's quail," Faucon replied. "I'm curious as to how it tastes."

"I can tell you that it tastes like nothing special when cooked like that," Luc said.

Faucon took the first little breast from Nell. It really was no more than a bite. He chewed and swallowed, then gave an approving nod. "I say it tastes almost like duck. The next?" he said to Nell, who slipped off another piece and gave it to him.

"Sir," Colin warned quietly.

Faucon ignored him. "Do any of you know how long Milla has been making her special quail dish for Sir Robert?" he asked as he held out his hand for the next piece of breast.

"Long before she ever came to Offord," Sir Luc said, his voice warmer, although he looked confused. "These birds nest in our wasteland and our folk have always netted them during the summer months. Milla usually made them into pies for the household until one day, while Sir Robert was visiting, she decided to use whole birds. That's when she created that sauce of hers. Adam didn't care for it, but Sir Robert found it very much to his liking. I say it was that dish that caused Sir Robert to offer her a place at Offord."

"As cook?" Faucon asked, taking the next piece of meat from Nell.

"As housekeeper," her husband replied quietly. "Sir Robert's second wife had just died. It seemed a profitable situation for them both." As Eustace said this, he glanced at Faucon. It was a reminder of Milla's stolen coins.

That startled Faucon. The position of chatelaine, when occupied by a woman who wasn't the master's wife, was equal in prestige to the position Eustace held. Yet Milla had chosen instead to live in the kitchen as a cook. "Milla did not wish to keep Offord's hall?" he asked.

Luc gave a half-hearted shrug. Eustace again studied the table top. Nell concentrated on removing the remaining bits of breast from the spit.

Faucon's brows rose. Thus did Milla hate her brother. Had Eustace known when he brought his sister to Sir Robert that the position the knight offered included the same bedding arrangement Sir Adam had enjoyed?

As Faucon took up the next piece of breast, Colin caught his hand. "Sir, I cannot allow this. What if Eustace is right and the meat is poison?" he asked quietly in English.

Faucon only shook his hand free of Colin's grasp and put the breast in his mouth.

"Poison?" Nell cried in response to the monk. She sounded truly shocked. "Why would anyone think there's poison in these birds?"

"What did she say?" Sir Luc asked, glancing from Nell to Eustace.

"Brother Colin recognized that Sir Robert met his end two nights ago by way of poison hemlock," Eustace told him quietly, his voice quivering. His hands rested on the table. They began to tremble. He curled his fingers into his palms.

"That's not possible," Luc protested strongly. "How could he have been poisoned?"

"It was the quail," Faucon replied.

"What?!" Sir Luc protested. "No one can be poisoned by eating a bird."

"Oh, but they can be," Nell replied evenly, winning startled looks from all the men at her table. Offering a knowing nod, she glanced across the faces of her guests. "Didn't my own uncle and his family die from eating poison birds?"

"How so?" Colin demanded in sharp interest.

"These birds can eat hemlock seed with no ill effect," Nell told him, pointing her spit at the carcasses littering the end of the table. "Although none of us in my family knew that on the late summer's day when my uncle brought his family a net full of them. How he loved these birds in a pie! We all did." She sighed, the expression on her face saying she revisited a distant memory.

"My aunt used only half the birds that night to make her meal. The next day we found them and their little ones all dead. Cleaned and plucked, the remaining birds were yet on the table. Being filled with grief for our kin and knowing the birds were now rigid in death and would need brining to be edible, we left them where they were. While we were washing our kinsmen, a village stray crept in and stole a few of the birds. We were winding the bodies when he began to slaver and howl. Recognizing hemlock, my father finished the poor creature, then burned the remaining birds."

She looked boldly at the men listening to her tale. "That dog saved our lives. We wouldn't have known the birds were poison, and would have taken them home for our own pie."

"Poison birds?!" Colin cried in astonishment. "I cannot fathom it. What animal chooses to eat hemlock?"

Nell considered him for a moment. "You must be town born, Brother," she said with just a hint of condescension in her voice. "There's no herdsman or shepherd who doesn't know to keep their animals away from that poison weed."

"You've found me out, goodwife," Colin laughed. "I have indeed lived all of my life enclosed by stone walls of one kind or another. However, I did know that cows and sheep will mistakenly nibble on the plant, just as folk will die from time to time after eating the hemlock root in error. What I didn't know was that any animal could eat the seed and survive to poison whatever then ate them."

The monk bent his neck to her. "I bow to your wisdom, Nell. As old as I am, you've just taught me something new this day."

Nell's laugh was a cheerful sound as round as she. The spread of her lips revealed both dimples and that she'd been a pretty thing in her day. Then she looked at her husband.

"But shame on you, Eustace," she chided with a pointed finger, shifting back into English to address her husband, "for thinking there could ever be poison in any of our birds! What was the first thing I did when I came here after we wed?"

Color crept slowly back into Eustace's face. "You checked every rod of our land, looking for hemlock," he said weakly, replying in that same tongue.

"Indeed I did," she said firmly. "After what happened to my family, I won't have so much as a stray seed of that foul plant near me. For the same reason I won't allow our birds to wander freely outside the toft. I cut their wing feathers so they can't fly, just as my father taught me."

"I thought as much," Faucon replied with a smile.

Colin frowned at him. "Then why did we come here?"

"I wanted to repeat Milla's test," Faucon told him,

then looked at Nell. "Goodwife, I'm curious. Did you ever tell this tale to Milla?"

That had the housewife frowning in thought. "If I did, I don't recall."

With that, Faucon shifted back into French for his own purpose. He looked at Sir Luc. "Milla cooked and ate one of Eustace's quail in front of Lady Bagot after Sir Robert first ailed. She did it to prove that there was nothing wrong with Eustace's quail." Luc's expression grew hollow as he listened.

"But if not our birds—" Eustace started, then drew a sudden sharp breath. He looked at Sir Luc. "Earlier this year, I took a few dozen quail chicks to Bagot, didn't I, Sir Luc?" he said, his tone urgent.

"Did you?" Luc replied flatly.

Eustace nodded. "I did," he insisted. "You don't recall?" The bailiff caught himself. "Ah, that's right. It was Lady Bagot who came to me at Sir Adam's request. She said your brother had decided to raise a flock so Sir Robert could enjoy his favorite meal while he resided at Bagot."

Horror dashed through Luc's gaze. He instantly turned his attention to the tabletop. "God help you, Adam. What have you done?" he said quietly, shaking his head.

That had Faucon draining the last drop of cider from his cup. He rose to his feet. "Many thanks, good-wife," he told Nell with a smile, still speaking French, "for both the meat and the instruction. You've been more help than you can know. Now it's time we made our way back to the hall.

"Are you ready, Brother Colin?" he prodded the monk. He needed to reach Milla and the kitchen before Sir Luc. Colin held up a finger on his free hand as he brought his bowl to his lips to empty it.

Sir Luc rose from his bench. "Give me a moment to dress, Sir Faucon, and I'll accompany you," the knight said swiftly.

As Luc started for the ladder and the loft, Colin set down his bowl and freed a small belch. "And we're off, Sir Crowner," he said, then smiled at Nell. "Goodwife, that is excellent cider. If I ever return this way, would you be willing to share a few branches of your apple tree so my brothers may add them to our abbey orchard? Our cider isn't nearly as fine."

"It would be our pleasure. I'll start some treelets for you this winter if you'd like," Nell said happily, as she retrieved their outer garments from her stools and offered them to her guests.

Faucon threw his cloak over his shoulders. It was pleasantly warm if not dry. He took a step toward the door, but Colin looked prepared to chat comfortably for a few more moments. Leaning down, Faucon said quietly in English, "Hie, Brother. We need to leave immediately."

Colin looked up at him in surprise. "Without the knight?" he responded in the same tongue.

Faucon touched his finger to his lips, then glanced at the housewife and her husband. "Eustace, you saw," he said, his voice held low. "Sir Adam isn't himself just now. There could be deadly trouble if Sir Luc enters Offord with me. Anything you can do to delay him would be appreciated."

That had Nell hurrying to her door. She snatched up a pair of soft leather shoes from near the entry, then disappeared behind the curtain. When she reappeared, she opened her door so her guests could depart.

"Thank you again," she whispered as they passed her, "and I'll have saplings for you next spring, Brother."

Chapter Seventeen

Outside, the wind moaned but the rain had ended. Head down, Faucon shuffled and reshuffled his pieces as he and Colin slogged through the cold mud toward the manor house. When they once more came to rest, he found himself again agreeing wholeheartedly with Brother Edmund. They should never have come to Offord. He still had nothing but belief and guesses to offer his jurors, and he doubted speaking with Milla would change that.

As they reached Offord's gateway, he looked at Brother Colin. "I'm for the kitchen. There's no need to join me if you'd rather go to the hall and take your ease."

"I think not," Colin said stoutly. "I left the abbey two days ago, expecting no more than a long cold walk to distribute winter potions to our nearest daughter houses. Instead, here I am, swept into a grand adventure. And look how I've learned about birds that can eat hemlock, then poison those who eat them! I'm with you for as long as you'll have me at your side, Sir Crowner."

"Then come along," Faucon replied, happy to have the monk's company during what was sure to be a frustrating exchange.

Scraping what mud he could from his shoes, Faucon opened the kitchen door. As it had earlier, the warmth of the fire reached out to embrace him, but this time the air was redolent with mellow turnip, sharp fish, sweet raisins, and almond milk. Milla stood at the hearth, stirring the contents of a pot about half as large as the cauldron she'd used for this morn's potage. Nobby was nowhere in sight.

The work table across the chamber was cluttered with what would become the day's main meal. A dozen or so flat square loaves of bread filled one end. Once cut in half lengthwise, they would serve as trenchers, edible plates. Tall round eel pies, their crusts golden, filled the center of the table while at the table's far end were three large earthenware pitchers, one for each table.

As Colin entered behind him, a gust of cold air blew past them. Milla looked over her shoulder. When she saw them, she straightened, spoon in hand. Some emotion danced through her gaze, only to disappear under that hard expression she and her brother both employed to protect themselves.

"Milla, I must speak with you about your brother's quail," Faucon said, winding his way through the bags and barrels to join her at the fire.

She kept her back to him as she began again to stir her stew. "Speak as you must, knowing that I cannot stop or I'll lose the day's second dish."

"Do you or Nobby kill the birds yourselves or do they come to you with their necks wrung?" he asked, choosing a question to which he knew the answer and circling the hearth so he could face her.

She lifted her head far enough for him to see the sharp intelligence that filled her eyes. Bringing her spoon to her mouth, she tasted her stew, then reached down into the bowl at her feet. It was the parsley Nobby had prepared for her. Tossing a few handfuls into the pot, she stirred again.

"The birds come to us alive in a cage. One of us finishes them here. Why does it matter?" she asked, peering up at him.

"I wondered if there was any difference between the

birds that came to you from Offord, and those that came from Bagot," he said, hoping a quick jab might throw her off balance.

"No birds came to me from Bagot," she replied easily. "Bagot does not supply our quail."

"On the contrary, birds did come into your kitchen from Bagot, and their flesh was poisoned with hemlock," he told her, trying yet another jab.

Neither shock nor panic touched her expression. She lowered her gaze to her pot. "A poison bird?" she scoffed. "What animal eats hemlock and survives?"

"Quail," Faucon replied.

She barked a disbelieving laugh. "Well, if that is what you believe, then you must immediately seek out Eustace. And if my brother raised poisoned birds to kill his master, then he should hang. However," she continued, "should you accuse Eustace, know that I will testify on his behalf. There is nothing amiss with his birds. After what I told you yesterday, you well know that I'd be the first to pronounce against my kinsman if he'd done as you say."

She raised her head as she said this. Her face could have been carved from stone. She'd spoken the truth yesterday. She didn't need Eustace to hang. It was vengeance enough for her that her brother would lose his position as bailiff. Just then the stew bubbled. Searing liquid spattered. One droplet hit her hand and she returned her attention to the pot, moving her spoon 'round and 'round.

However insignificant, Faucon hurried to exploit the opportunity she'd just offered. "It seems you told me but half that story yesterday. Eustace convinced Sir Robert to offer you the position of chatelaine at Offord after you left Bagot. Did he know when he brought you to Sir Robert that the knight expected you to play the role of leman, just as Sir Adam had required of you?" As he said this, he wondered if it had been kindness or Sir Robert's love for Milla's cooking that resulted in Milla living in his kitchen instead of sleeping in his bed.

Her flinch suggested he'd surprised her. Despite that, she neither looked at him nor stopped the steady motion of her hand. Nor did she speak, using silence as her shield.

"If I ride to Bagot, what will the servants tell me about why and how you left their manor and their master six years past?" he pressed. "You know how it is with servants and villagers, everyone always whispering about everyone else. There's sure to be one among them who knows at least a part of your tale. Will that one tell me you lied to your master to protect the child you'd made your own? Will he tell me your purse was full when you left Bagot, or that Sir Adam sent you away without a penny to your name? Your father wasn't the only man to cheat you of your rightful earnings, was he?

"As for me," Faucon continued, "I'm wondering what Sir Adam believed you'd done that caused him to punish you so. More to the point, I'm wondering what Sir Luc had done that resulted in your punishment. Had he done then the same as he had on the night Sir Robert died, and stepped between a man and his wife?"

Having strung together his best guesses, Faucon waited. She said nothing. He tried a new angle.

"Milla, your brother is a well-liked bailiff, known for loving his milk-brother. Who will believe that he would poison a man he loves? However, if even one man knows how Sir Robert insulted you with his lewd invitation, he would think you do have reason. Nor will any man or woman in Offord ever believe that poison birds could enter your kitchen without your knowledge. But come into your kitchen they did. It won't be Eustace who hangs for poisoning his master— it will be you."

This time when she raised her head, confidence radiated from her. It formed a wall as thick and impenetrable as that of any keep tower. Nothing he'd said had even chipped her defenses.

"There were no poison birds," she said. "How could there have been? Ask Offord's maids or Nobby. I've prepared that dish for my master at least a dozen times since his return from the Michaelmas court with Lady Offord. If any poisoned birds existed, would Sir Robert not have died sooner or at least ailed more often? And what of Lady Martha, who often shared that dish with him? Why has she never ailed?" she asked, wielding an unexpected weapon, one that sent her opponent's blade flying from his fingers.

Faucon sighed. He had expected no less. "You truly do love them enough to spend your life on their behalf."

Her brows rose slowly. Her eyes gleamed. It said he had just given her an advantage to exploit, when Faucon hadn't known he had it to offer.

"Spend my life for whom?" she asked.

It was in her face. No matter what name Faucon gave her, Milla would correct him, offering the name of another man, the one who had misused her. Faucon had no doubt her lie would be convincing, and that she'd go happily to the gallows if she thought she could take that man along with her.

He watched her for a long moment, then shook his head, refusing to be used by her. "I am finished here, Brother Colin. Shall we return to the hall and see how my brother fares?"

As the kitchen door closed behind them, Colin asked, "So, did Milla poison her master?"

"If by that you mean did she carry cooked birds she

knew to be poisonous to her master, then yes," Faucon replied. "But she raised no poison birds and had no true reason to kill her employer."

Colin frowned up at him. "So who will you accuse when you call the jury?"

"I can't call the jury," Faucon said sourly, stepping around a puddle. "No matter what name I offer, the moment I tell the jurors that poisoned quail killed Sir Robert, every man among them will look at Eustace. Both Milla and little Nobby will affirm that the only quail in their kitchen came from Offord's bailiff." Because as far as Nobby knew, they had, even if it wasn't always Eustace's quail on Sir Robert's trencher.

"The poison birds!" Colin cried, brows lifted. "We must ride for Bagot for them."

"What birds?" Faucon shot back. "I wager if we rode to Bagot right now, we'd find all those birds dead, or, if they still live, they'll prove to be as clean as the birds Eustace raises."

Colin freed a slow breath as he understood. "Pity poor Eustace," he said.

"Pity him, indeed," Faucon replied, "but not because he was ever intended to carry the blame for this. He wasn't. Eustace is only endangered because Sir Adam's mad need to destroy Lady Offord led him to me, something beyond the scope of this plot.

"Now here I am, having discovered Sir Robert's death was anything but natural, but also having discovered that I cannot declare the knight poisoned without endangering an innocent man," he finished with a sigh.

"Do you know why Sir Robert was poisoned?" Colin asked.

Faucon nodded. "It was his bell. Without it, Sir Robert's treasury is empty. I suspect Sir Adam demanded Robert cede him his bell as collateral, to protect what Bagot had invested in Offord. But if Sir Robert had agreed, he would have been forever after under the control of his son-by-marriage, something he couldn't bear and which drove him to show the bell to Prior Thierry, and make an insincere offer to give it to the priory upon his death. Although I again but guess, I think Sir Robert saw that bell as nothing more than an exotic and ancient curiosity. Thus he was startled when he suddenly had two men in a frenzy to take the bell from him. That's why Sir Robert married Idonea and made the bell her dower, to put it beyond the reach of both of them, at least until Idonea's death."

What a strange family this was, all of them dancing to the tune of Sir Robert's bell. Sir Adam consumed by greed, Lady Joia, the girl who had made that bell into a precious plaything with Luc, her dearest childhood friend. Luc, the boy Sir Robert loved as if he were his own son, yet believed capable of betraying him by lying with his new wife. Was that because Luc had already lain with Robert's daughter, giving him the grandchild he loved beyond all others? And Milla, who had been willing to risk all for children who weren't her own because she believed she yet had riches in store, only to discover she'd been betrayed, just as she betrayed another.

"Then there will be no justice for Sir Robert," Colin said sadly as they reached the porch before the hall door.

"Hardly so," Faucon replied with a quick smile as they paused to kick mud from their shoes yet again. "Sir Robert saw to his own justice when he hid that bell."

Had Sir Robert hidden the bell because he realized he was meant to die? If he'd known that much, he must have also known both who and why. That meant that two nights ago he would have counted the number of the birds on his trencher and known it was his time. Was it suicide if a man allowed what he most loved to kill him?

Faucon and the monk stopped at the corner of the hall screen to shake the moisture from their sodden cloaks. In the hall, the little ladies were still at the hearth, Alf watching over them, as they created a gown for Martha's poppet. The plaything would match her owner, wearing the same red fabric that made up Martha's gown.

Sir Adam sat in his father-by-marriage's chair, staring at the fire. He looked as if he'd again collapsed into himself. Lady Joia must yet be sleeping, for she was nowhere to be seen. Edmund once more knelt at the prie-dieu near the bed. His head bowed, his lips moved as he chanted quietly. Seated on stools near the monk were Offord's three maids. Each of them held a spear-like distaff clamped between her knees. Fingers twisting, weighted spindles spinning, they drew fibers from the clumps of fleece impaled atop their distaffs and turned it into yarn.

Faucon's gaze shifted to the pallet where Will had rested. It was empty. Panic welled. Had his brother run?

Just then, Alf turned to look at his employer and Will leaned forward to peer around the soldier. Although painful hollows lingered on Will's face, his gaze was alert and his expression blessedly sane. Relief over not having to search the shire for his brother dissolved into astonishment. Why had Will chosen to sit with a commoner instead of the knight?

With Colin at his side, Faucon made his way toward

Alf and his brother, choosing to walk on the inside of the table so his brother wouldn't have to turn to see him. "Are you restored, Will?" he asked carefully when he stopped across the table from his brother.

"I am, many thanks to your monk," Will replied, offering Brother Colin a friendly nod. For the first time since his arrival in Warwickshire, the sarcastic edge was gone from his voice. "Brother, do you have more of that potion? If so, may I purchase some for my own use?"

"I do and you may indeed have some," Colin replied with a smile. "But I think it wiser if you and I speak. The more I know of your injury and how it pains you, the better I'll know how to treat it."

Will instantly tensed. So did Faucon. He cursed himself for not having warned Colin that even the slightest mention of Will's injury— even the barest hint that there might be something amiss with him— could send Will into a screaming fit.

Again his brother surprised Faucon as Will forced himself to relax. "Perhaps over there?" he said, lifting his hand to indicate the back of the hall, a place well beyond the hearing of those presently in this big chamber. As he spoke, he sent a sidelong look at his younger brother. The gratitude in his gaze sent another wave of surprise over Faucon.

"Of course," Colin agreed and turned.

Just then, Sir Luc stepped around the screen and strode into the hall. Sir Adam's younger brother wore a mummer's expression of outrage. Faucon's hand fell to his sword hilt, certain the coming show would be directed at him. Instead, Luc kept his gaze fixed on his brother as he made his way toward the high table.

Idonea gave a frightened squeal as she saw her tormentor striding toward her. Lunging to her feet, she looked in panic at her Crowner. The lift of Faucon's hand bid her to him. As she ran, Helena glanced up at her uncle. Her face paled until her freckles stood out like pox. She was on her feet almost as quickly as Idonea, following with the poppet's half-made gown in one hand while pulling her younger sister along behind her. While Helena joined Idonea behind Faucon, Martha pulled free of her sister's grasp to press herself to his side. Yet clutching her poppet, she tangled her free hand in his cloak.

As the ladies fled the hearth, both Alf and Will left their bench to join Faucon. Alf stopped beside Martha, his hand on her shoulder. Will took a stance at Faucon's right. His brother shot him a swift smile and a cock of his brows. Faucon's lips curled. Here was his adored brother, come to visit at last.

"What did you do, Adam?" Luc demanded, as he circled the hearth and took a warrior's stance on the other side of the table from his brother. His voice was raised so that all were sure to hear.

Startled from his prayers, Edmund came to his feet to look at the knights. The maids stopped their turning spindles and watched. At the bed, the curtains shifted.

Adam stirred in Sir Robert's chair, slowly lifting his head. "Luc, what are you doing here?" he asked, sounding more like an awakening sleeper than the blindly raging knight of this morn.

"Not four days ago you said to me that you prayed daily for Sir Robert's death. Now he's gone. What did you do?" Sir Luc accused.

Faucon breathed out in glorious disbelief. For all her careful planning and cautious craft, Milla had made a crucial error. She had trusted a fool, and she wasn't the only one.

"Luc!" Lady Bagot cried from inside the curtained bed. The draperies billowed and swung as she sought to open them.

Her call brought life back to Sir Adam's blue eyes. He glanced at the bed, then back to his brother. "What are you talking about?" the older knight asked, his voice gaining power with every word.

"You!" Again, Luc spoke at almost a shout. "You took quail from Eustace and fed them hemlock." As he made his charge, he glanced over his shoulder at the man he was truly addressing, the shire's new Crowner, the man he expected to now step forward and accuse his brother of murder.

"What are you doing, Luc?" Joia shrieked as she thrust through the curtains, her hair loose around her.

Tumbling from the bed, she collided with Edmund. The monk gave a wordless shriek of his own and pushed her away from him with the heels of his hands. She careened to the side, struggling to catch her footing in the shifting rushes.

"Hemlock?" Sir Adam growled. As it had this morning, the mention of that poison fed his depleted spirit. "No man kills with poison! That is a woman's weapon!" he roared.

"Luc!" Lady Bagot wailed this time as she raced toward the high table.

The younger knight paid her no heed. "Only because that was how you crafted it to appear. But no woman killed Robert. You wanted him dead and so he is, made so by your hand," Luc accused at the top of his lungs, again glancing at his Crowner.

When Faucon still said nothing, the younger Bagot knight turned to face him. "Sir Faucon, I accuse Adam of Bagot of murdering Robert of Offord."

Adam threw back his head and roared. Fists clenched he thrust to his feet. "If hemlock killed Robert, it was by his wife's design. She has hemlock in her possession!" he roared.

"Stop, both of you!" Joia screamed, her voice piercing as she came to a gasping halt at the end of the table next to where Edmund had laid out his tools. "No one killed my father. There is no poison. It was just his time!"

Luc pivoted to face her. "But there is poison and it's at Bagot," he insisted, a note of panic in his voice. "Eustace says the healing monk with Sir Faucon recognized hemlock in the manner of Sir Robert's death. But Eustace's birds have no poison in them. Sir Faucon ate them to prove that to himself." He was cajoling now. "But there were quail in our garden, brought to Bagot by Eustace at Adam's request. Not four days ago didn't one of our hounds break into the garden and ravage those birds, only to die later?"

Eyes wide and her face ashen, Lady Bagot stared in horror at her brother-by-marriage. Sir Adam's fists opened. He glanced from his brother to his wife, then his lips lifted. Vicious triumph and unexpected intelligence gleamed in his eyes.

"I never asked for quail from Eustace. But such birds did arrive at Bagot," he said, then looked at his wife, his head tilted slightly. "It was you who said you wanted a flock so your father could have his favorite dish while he lived with us."

Lady Bagot moaned. She dropped to sit on Edmund's bench. Although she made no sound, her shoulders began to heave as if she sobbed.

Sir Adam turned toward Faucon. "If there were poisoned birds as my brother maintains, it was my wife who raised them and used them to kill her father."

Luc howled at that. Faucon sent a prayer of thanksgiving heavenward for what was surely divine intervention.

"Brother Edmund," he called to his clerk, who yet stood near the prie-dieu, "please note on your roll that I will be accusing Milla the Cook and Lady Joia of Bagot for the murder of Sir Robert of Offord when we call the jurors."

"Are you certain you wish to do that, sir?" Edmund asked, starting toward the table.

"Of course he is, monk," Sir Adam almost shouted, then dropped back to sit in Sir Robert's chair. "He has no choice. My wife killed her father!"

Gone was the defeated man. Instead, he spread his hands on the table in front of him, pressing his fingers against the wood in ownership. Every line of his body said he no longer cared that Offord's treasury was depleted or that the bell remained missing. Nor did it matter that his Crowner would appraise Offord's worth so the king could take his fee for murder from Lady Bagot's dowry.

Why should he care? Not only would Sir Adam's son now inherit Offord and one day wed an heiress to restore its treasury, but after Joia of Offord was hanged for murder, Adam of Bagot would be free to replace her with another heiress, adding even more to what he had just gained.

Chapter Eighteen

"Sir Faucon! But the jury cannot have come and gone as swiftly as this," Nell said in surprise as she opened her door. She shot a quick look at the sky to judge the time, which was nearing the hour of None. "I thought the last man only arrived at midday."

Brother Edmund and Alf stood behind Faucon outside the bailiff's door. Two days ago, Brother Colin had bid them farewell and left Offord in Will's company. Will had gone both to protect the monk and retrieve a potion Colin wanted for him. Faucon's brother promised to return to Offord if he didn't find him already at Blacklea.

"Come and gone already," Faucon said with a brief nod, stifling his sigh. Although a number among the hundred now greeted him by name, by the time they dispersed, he wondered if all of them weren't cursing him.

"I also bring you word from your husband," he continued. "He asks me to tell you that what you both feared most has come to pass. He says he'll remain with the other men of the village as they discuss what happens next."

Dismay filled Nell's face. "Well, if God wills it, then I must accept it," she quietly. "For today this is still my home. Come in."

Only when she stepped back from the door did Faucon see Lady Joia. She sat at Nell's table just as Eustace had done three days ago. And just like the bailiff, her head was bowed as if she studied the table top. The lady's hair was braided but she wore no head covering.

Seated across from her on the bench Faucon had shared with Colin were Idonea and Helena. Both girls had turned to watch the men enter. Worry and not a little fear touched their expressions.

Sir Adam had banished all of them from Offord Hall in the name of Lady Joia's son only moments after Faucon made his charge of murder. Idonea's dowry chest, including the fine draperies from Sir Robert's bed, had swiftly followed them here; even Adam knew better than to try to claim what wasn't his. As for Lady Joia, she hadn't been allowed to gather any of her or her daughters' personal possessions, and her pleas to tend to her father's remains and visit with her son who would attend the funeral had been roundly refused.

Faucon didn't find Martha until he reached the hearth. The child sat on the floor near her mother's feet. She had one hand curled into Joia's gown while she clutched her poppet close with the other arm. Martha turned her face to the side as he looked at her.

Although Alf lingered near the doorway, Edmund followed him to the hearth. "If I'm to complete my record, I'll need to use the table there," he said, the movement of his head indicating the area in front of the younger ladies.

"Lady Offord, perhaps you'll take Lady Helena and Lady Martha to the loft?" Faucon asked.

Idonea drew a deep breath, as if she had to muster the strength to rise. "Come, Helena," she said quietly.

Helena followed her step-grandmother to her feet, her gaze now focused on her folded hands. As Sir Adam's eldest made her way to the ladder, Idonea stopped at the end of the table and bent to address his younger daughter. "Come, Martha," the widow whispered.

Martha whined wordlessly and pushed herself deeper beneath the table. When Idonea tried to pull her out, the little lady grunted and kicked at her. Her daughter's rude, disobedient behavior won no response from Lady Joia.

The widow retreated, shaking her head. "We've tried to take her outside for air more than once," she said, still whispering, "but she won't leave her mother. Can she not stay where she is?"

It had been foolish to think he could protect any of these children from what he must say to Lady Bagot, especially here in Eustace's home. "Leave her be," Faucon told Idonea.

As Idonea followed Helena up into the loft, he looked at Nell. It should be Joia's choice to share what came next with those outside her family. "Will you give us a few moments?"

The housewife cringed at that, then hurried around the table to put a hand on Lady Bagot's back. "I'm off to do my chores, my little love. I'll be back soon." Again Lady Joia neither moved nor spoke.

Faucon looked at Alf. The soldier gave a responding lift of his brows. "Could you use a helping hand, good-wife?" he asked Nell in their native tongue.

"Always, thank you," the housewife replied, sounding grateful for the company.

Once the door closed behind them, Faucon drew a stool to the end of the table, knowing Edmund wouldn't tolerate sharing a bench with him and not wishing to sit with the gentlewoman. As he watched Edmund lay out his tools in his usual precise line above his parchment, Faucon struggled to find the right words only to decide there was no way to say what he must save plainly.

"Lady Bagot, we asked the jury to affirm that you

fed poison quail to Sir Robert of Offord, thereby causing his death, and that Milla the Cook did aid you in your plot," he said.

That won a tiny flinch from Sir Adam's wife. "I didn't kill my father," she said softly. This had been her constant refrain from the moment her husband had revealed that she kept poisoned quail.

"The process was tainted," Brother Edmund complained over her, his words instant and harsh. It wasn't the first time he'd said this. Eyes narrowed, a single spot of outrage staining each of his cheeks, the monk looked at his employer.

"I warned you," he chided. "There can be no certainty of guilt when you lack both a hue and cry and a tangible weapon. As long as the lady continues to insist on her innocence, as she has done more than once these past days, all you have is supposition. Thus did the jurors show us when they first refused to affirm. Then, instead of dismissing them, you allowed them to be bludgeoned with threats into affirmation."

Lady Joia had proved as well-known and well-liked as her father among those who lived near Offord and Bagot. Despite their Crowner's description of the crime, almost all the local men insisted that Joia of Offord would never have killed her father. As for those from a farther distance, none could believe either that birds could be poisonous or that anyone would raise poison birds to use as a weapon. Once Eustace testified that Lady Joia had tenderly nursed her father back to health the two times he'd ailed, not even men from farther afield would name her a murderess. That's when Sir Adam dismissed Offord's bailiff and threatened retribution against any other man who refused to accuse his wife of killing her father.

After that, nothing Faucon said, nor Brother

Edmund's promises of royal protection, changed matters. Having heard such threats from their sheriff in the past, the jurors voted as the knight required and swiftly departed.

"Again, you're right to chastise me, Brother Edmund," Faucon replied, struggling to tame his own outrage over how Sir Adam had perverted what seemed to him an almost sacred process. "Know that I have learned my lesson. That said, how can I not declare that murder has been done when I am certain that it has? But also know that today's jury was but the first skirmish in a wider war," he then reminded Edmund. "It's on us to see that the knight is punished for his interference."

Edmund sniffed. "As if fines and coins can set right what went wrong? I tell you now. Unless you directly command me, the only affirmation of murder I'll note is the one against the cook who fled, thus proving her guilt."

Lady Bagot drew a quavering breath and lifted her head. Her eyes looked raw. "Milla is gone?" she whispered, her face paling until it seemed she might swoon.

"Sir Luc as well," Faucon told her gently.

He suspected Milla made her escape from Offord the moment Sir Luc left the kitchen for the hall. As for Adam, he'd banished his brother immediately after driving off his wife. Faucon wondered if the exiled Luc now rode with the woman he thought of as his mother.

"They've left me?" she cried, sounding lost and as young as Martha. "Who will protect me now?"

When she received no response, Joia continued, her voice barely louder than a whisper. "Sir, know that Luc did no wrong at all. It was Milla who helped me. But nothing we did harmed my father."

"How can you say you did no wrong when you fed

your father poisoned quail?" Faucon demanded.

"Not to kill him," the lady almost pleaded. "Those birds were only meant to make my father ill. I just wanted the chance to show him that I still loved him, despite what I'd said to him and despite what he had done to me and to Martha," she finished at almost a whisper.

Her trembling words won a startled gasp from Brother Edmund. "You truly did raise poisoned birds?!" the monk cried in shock. "What madness is this?"

"To Martha?" Faucon asked over him. "What had your father done to Martha?"

At that, the shadow of the bold lady he'd first met reappeared in Joia's pretty face. "He showed our bell to the prior," she said. "He did it even though I warned him Prior Thierry would take it from him. He did it knowing he'd already promised the bell to Martha as her dowry."

That had Faucon frowning. "When did he make that promise?"

"Two years ago." Then, as if the effort of holding onto her previous self cost her too dearly, her arrogance drained from her. She again bowed her head. "He made his promise on the night that Adam demanded my father give him the bell to hold at Bagot. There, with both Luc and me to witness, my father told my husband that rather than cede his treasure to Adam, he would make it Martha's dowry."

Faucon stared at her in startled disbelief. "And your husband agreed to this?"

That the lady offered him a nod left Faucon as shocked as Sir Robert must have been when Sir Adam had agreed two years ago. Where Sir Robert had expected his offer to set his son-by-marriage's knees to knocking, he instead learned that Joia's husband hadn't known, and may not even now know, that Martha wasn't his child.

"I was overjoyed," Lady Bagot told him. "My father had just given both my daughters full futures. Although I assured my sire his word was enough for me, Sir Adam wasn't content with that. He wanted my father to hire a clerk to draft a will that included the disposition of the bell. For months he nagged, but my father always had an excuse for why it wasn't done. When my husband could no longer bear the delay, he hired the clerk himself. That's when my father went to the priory."

She glanced at him. "When my father told me what he'd done, I was beside myself. I reminded him of his promise to Martha. Do you know what he did then?

"He laughed at me," she cried, her voice tight. "He said his offer had been all in jest. He said that I, of all people, should have known that, as many times as we'd played the game where he pretended to make the bell mine, then took back his word. He said the bell was his treasure, his to do with as he pleased and it no longer pleased him to give it to Martha.

"I was hurt and angry beyond all thought. How could a man I trusted above all others, a man I honored and loved, break my heart and destroy my daughter's future? I called him an oath breaker and a dishonorable knight. He named me greedy and faithless, and said he'd destroy the bell before I or any of my children ever benefitted from it." Pain radiated from her. Her voice was low and hoarse.

"He said," she caught a gasping breath, "that I was no longer a daughter to him."

"Is that when your sire started seeking a new wife to get an heir of his own?" Faucon asked.

Joia nodded. "And in doing so, he drove my husband mad, and in his madness Sir Adam showed me how much I needed my father and his protection. I came back to Offord time and again, seeking my sire's forgiveness, but he wouldn't hear my pleas. Instead, he married Idonea and everything became impossibly worse. I just wanted to show him I was still the daughter he loved and that I still loved him—" her voice died away into a sigh.

Pausing, she raised her head and looked toward the cottage door, lost for the moment in the past. When she stirred from her memories, her face was twisted in grief. "That's when Milla said she knew a way to make my father ill using his quail. She said he'd never know and he wouldn't be harmed. She assured me his illness would last only a short while. All I had to do was feed hemlock seed to quail."

"But hemlock?!" Faucon protested. "To think you could control that poison is folly!"

"No, it was desperation," she replied, asking him to understand the incomprehensible. "Do you think I didn't ask Milla how she was certain my father wouldn't be harmed? She told me that once long ago, before I came to Bagot, she'd unknowingly baked a poison bird into one of the pies she'd made for the household. She and a few others ate from that pie. She said they all felt terrible for less than a day, then swiftly returned to health.

"Suspecting the bird was the cause of their illness, she asked the man who'd netted them if she was right. He said she was, telling her that quail sometimes ate hemlock seed and could make folk sick. But he assured her he'd never heard tell of anyone dying from eating them.

"How could I not believe Milla, especially when we ate quail pie so often during my time at Bagot? No one had ever once so much as grown ill. By then, I'd already brought Eustace's chicks to Bagot to raise on my father's behalf, still seeking to win back his heart. There was hemlock aplenty in our hedgerows and pastures. I collected the seed and greens and fed them to the birds," she finished with a tiny shrug.

Faucon stared at her, struggling to find sense in what she'd done. "But how could you know that the birds you gave your father weren't more poisonous than the one that Milla ate?"

That had her frowning at him as if his question were ridiculous. "Because I ate two of them first," she said, then shrugged at his shocked expression. "As if my life matters in any of this? If I die, nothing changes, not then and not now. My son yet inherits Offord, Helena still has her dowry, and Martha is just as bereft. Milla was right. I was only a little ill and I recovered quickly.

"I brought Milla two quail, and she replaced them for two of my father's usual four. It worked," she said, almost smiling. "He was affected no more than I had been. I begged him to take to his bed and allow me to tend him. At first it seemed that he would refuse, but Eustace added his voice to mine, and I was allowed to stay. While my father remained quarrelsome and short, he let me care for him. I told him how wrong I had been to chide, and that I knew the bell was his alone to do with as he willed. Although he didn't offer forgiveness, he listened.

"Now hopeful that he and I could regain what we'd lost, I waited a few weeks and again brought Milla two more quail."

The corners of her mouth lifted. "This time it was everything I wanted. He heard me and forgave, then asked me to forgive him. I hadn't been so happy since leaving my father's house for my husband's. We remembered how much we loved each other. I stayed with him even after he rose from his bed. We laughed, told tales, and played games, and let Martha and Helena, and even Idonea, entertain us."

Faucon shook his head at that. Lady Joia had been more successful than she knew. After their reconciliation, Sir Robert had ridden out to sell the bell. Eustace was wrong. His master had every intention of cheating Idonea of her dower. But then, Idonea's father had achieved everything he wanted from his daughter's marriage. Idonea would return to him with her dowry intact and a new title, making her far more valuable to her family.

Joia's smile faded. "Even now, despite all that has happened, I'm grateful for what I did. I think I might have died alongside my father had he passed without forgiving me," she added, then sighed again. "But our new peace only made matters worse. The moment Sir Adam realized I had regained my father's heart and trust, my husband began accusing me of plotting against him with my sire and Idonea. Then he accused my father of the same. After that, every day was miserable. They sparred constantly, beating each other bloody."

That caught Faucon's attention. "Do you mean on the practice field?"

Startled, Joia again met his gaze. "Sword to sword? Never," she told him with a swift shake of her head. "They've never met on the practice field, at least that I know, choosing instead to fight their battles with words. They certainly haven't drawn weapons since my father wed Idonea. I think if they had, my husband would have found a way to kill my father."

Her words shattered Faucon's carefully joined pieces, and everything he thought he knew crumbled. "Why didn't you destroy your quail after you no longer

218

needed them?" he demanded.

His forceful question drove her back on her bench. "I—I—" she stuttered, then tamed her tongue. "Because my father loved that dish, and quail are easy birds to keep, what with needing to be ever caged. I thought with enough time and proper food, the poison might clear from them. If it didn't, I'd still have their chicks to raise the next year."

The depth of his own idiocy ate at Faucon. "Did Sir Adam leave for Bagot after your family came to live at Offord?"

That startled Lady Joia. "He did. He rode home every day, departing after we broke our fast and returning before our midday meal," she said. "One of his horses had gone lame the previous month. He wasn't content to leave him in the hands of Luc and his groom."

Faucon leaned back on the stool, disgusted with himself. Almost from the moment he'd met Sir Adam, he'd allowed his own judgment and dislike to blind him. "Nobby says you came to see Milla on the morning before Martha's celebration. He says you and Milla argued over the number and quality of the quail being served to your father. Is that true?" he asked the lady.

"Argue with Milla?" Joia replied with a shake of her head. "Hardly so. I went to ask if she needed my help in preparing for Martha's celebration. She said she didn't. Then she told me Eustace's quail were undersized and she didn't think six would be enough meat for my father and daughter to share. She asked if she might give all six to my sire and instead make a special dish just for Martha, as a gift for my daughter's saint day."

Again, Faucon damned himself for an idiot. In the kitchen, Milla had offered him the truth he should have been seeking. But he, being already fixed in his judgment, had dismissed her for trying to manipulate him. Had he let her speak, clever Milla would have found a way to tell him about a knight who had discovered the truth of the quail being raised in his garden, who had found a way to see that Sir Robert ate enough poisoned birds to kill him. That left Faucon wondering whether Sir Adam had plied the cook with threats of hanging, or offered Milla the coins he had years before denied her. He suspected the latter.

"You did not kill your father," Faucon told Lady Bagot.

Joia drew a ragged, startled breath as she met his gaze, wide-eyed. "You believe me?"

"I not only believe you, I know it was your husband who brought those poison quail to Milla and forced her to feed them to your father," Faucon said. "I don't believe he intended to place the blame on you. It was Lady Offord he was intent on destroying, needing the lady to hang so the bell would return to him. But when Luc revealed the presence of the quail at Bagot, he released Adam from having to protect himself. That's when your husband saw how much more he could achieve from your father's death."

Edmund straightened on his bench. "Sir, you cannot recall the jury and now ask them to affirm against the knight," he commanded. "That can only serve to confuse them and further muddle the process."

"I most certainly will not ask them to return, Brother Edmund," Faucon replied. "I've taken enough of a beating today. I have no wish to repeat the experience. However, I have every intention of making right what I set wrong."

He offered the monk a quick smile, then shifting on his stool, he looked at Lady Bagot. "My lady, I give you my word. You will not hang for your father's death.

Listen to me now.

"Today, the men of the jury did not believe you capable of killing your father and instead argued in your defense. More than one spoke of your good character and your love for your sire. Between now and the day you're called to appear before the noble justices, I will assure each and every one of these men that they were correct in their judgment. I will inform them that I will call them to court when it is your time, to repeat what they said today. Brother Edmund and I will also stand with you to tell the tale of how Sir Adam misused the jurors. If our God is just, and I believe He is, then the barons and bishops who hear us will proclaim your innocence."

He looked at his clerk. "What say you, Brother Edmund? Am I right to assure her of this?"

The monk offered a firm and satisfied nod. "You are. Thus is justice assured when men seek to misuse the process."

Joia glanced at the men across from her. Tears filled her eyes. "Thank you," she breathed.

"I only hope you can one day forgive me for mis-judging—" The rest of what Faucon intended to say dissolved on his tongue.

Lady Joia and Milla weren't the only daughters of Eve he had weighed by their behavior rather than heeding their words. One more time, Faucon's pieces assembled, this time showing him one he'd dismissed as rotten meat. He looked beneath the edge of the table at Martha. The child yet sat at her mother's feet, her poppet held hard against her. Fear and upset filled her pretty face.

Faucon slipped from the stool and crouched to bring them eye to eye. "Lady Martha, the other day you wanted to tell me about your grandsire. The time wasn't right then. It is now. Speak to me, remembering that what you say must be the truth," he warned her.

"Grand-père made me swear not to tell anyone in my family," Martha said in quiet reply.

Her mother made an aching sound. She shifted on the bench until she could see beneath the table's edge. "Martha?" she whispered.

The child continued without looking at her mother. "Grand-père said when I gave him my oath it meant I couldn't break my word or I would burn forever. But you are not my family."

"I am not," Faucon agreed.

"I love Idonea," she told him, keeping her gaze locked on him as if she feared to look elsewhere. "But Grand-père said it didn't belong to Idonea anymore. He said he changed his mind and said it had always been mine," she told him. "But when the prior came, he said it was his. Papa called him a thief. If I keep it, will I be a thief?"

"What do you have?" Joia asked her daughter, her words strained.

Martha shook her head, refusing to look at her mother. "Grand-père said I could never give it to you, Maman, or Papa would take it from me."

Instead, she handed her poppet to her Crowner. "I don't want to be a thief. Don't hurt her too much when you open her," she pleaded.

Faucon came to his feet holding the plaything. He squeezed the poppet's torso, feeling for any hint of a hard edge. She was packed solid and there was nothing to suggest anything but wool under her fabric skin. Removing her gown and shift, he turned her until he found the seam that closed her. There were two layers of stitching, one atop the other. The first set was wide and uneven, and loose. The second line was tighter and closer.

"Who sewed her shut?" he asked Martha.

The child slid forward until she was directly below the edge of the table. "I did it the first time, but Grand-père said she needed more. He helped me the second time. He said he was proud of my sewing."

Faucon reached for the small knife Edmund used to scrape ink from his sheepskin. The monk's hand shot out as if to prevent his employer from touching it. The movement was so swift and unthinking that Faucon took no insult.

"Brother, may I borrow your knife?" he asked.

Heated color filled the monk's face. Without comment, he handed the tool to his employer.

Martha crawled out from under the table, then caught the hem of Faucon's tunic to pull herself to her feet. Her mother reached out an arm to her, but the child instead pressed herself against his leg. There was a rustling from the loft above them. Both Idonea and Helena had shifted to watch what happened below them.

As Faucon cut away the stitching, the toy nearly exploded, so tightly was she packed. Bits of fleece rained from her. He dug into the shredded wool, sending even more cascading down upon the table. His finger touched a slender length of metal. Yanking, he wrenched the bell from the poppet. As what had muffled its cavity dropped away, the clapper shifted and the bell sang out a clear silvery note.

"Papa!" Lady Joia cried, then buried her face in her hands.

Faucon examined the bell. Just as Idonea had described, there was a pretty stone at the top of its long silver handle, which had been wrought to look like ivy curling around itself. A circle of crosses in the Irish fashion decorated the top of the bell where the handle met the cup. Beneath that was another decorative circle, this one made up of figures. Time and tarnish had worn off all but the outlines of their faces and garments. He tilted the bell again, liking the sound of it.

"Sir," Edmund warned. "Prior Thierry is right. This is a holy object, not a plaything. Its voice is meant to call the angels."

Properly chastised, Faucon set the bell down upon the table.

"Am I no longer a thief?" Martha asked, still leaning against his leg.

That stirred Joia from her grief. "You were never a thief, my little love. The bell was and is yours," she insisted, her voice broken. She reached to claim the bell on her daughter's behalf.

"My lady!" Edmund chastised, slapping her hand away. "You of all people should not touch this bell after the game you played! If not for you and your ploy, your father would yet live."

Joia snatched her hand to her chest. Faucon watched-ed as grief and guilt tangled in her expression. She shifted on the bench, turning her back to them, seeking privacy in which to indulge her emotions.

"Brother, was that fair?" Faucon asked gently.

"The truth is not always fair, it is just the truth," the monk replied, then aimed his unforgiving gaze on Martha. "Nor should you touch it, my lady. Your grand-sire was wrong to keep this bell from its true home. However, know this. If your lady mother speaks true, and your grandsire did promise it to you before he promised it to Lady Offord, then his second promise is false. It never belonged to Lady Offord, and is instead your rightful possession. But I advise you for the good of your soul to make a gift of it to our Church."

"If it's mine, then I could choose to keep it?" Martha asked Edmund, her tone suggesting she sought clarification rather than ownership.

Although Edmund's lips curled ever so slightly as he eyed the forward child, there was no impatience in his gaze nor in his voice as he spoke. "You could keep it, but if you do, know that you cannot keep it for long. The bell must one day return to its rightful home," he told her.

Martha's lower lip extended a bit as she thought about that. "Does the bell miss its home?"

Edmund blinked as if startled by the idea of a metal object, even a blessed one, feeling lost. "Our Lord misses His bell," he replied, crafting an answer that made better sense to him.

"I will miss the bell if it goes home," Martha told him.

"But if you return it, the angels will be so thankful that they will all sing *Te Deum*," the monk replied.

Martha looked up at Faucon. "What is te deum?" she asked of the man who had previously defined a word for her.

"He means the angels will be happy," Faucon told her.

"So they shall be," Edmund assured the child. "After you return the bell, you must attend the ceremony that welcomes it home." His expression softened. He raised his gaze skyward as if he were seeking out those happy angels. "It is a magnificent spectacle. No less than a bishop will officiate. Dressed in his grandest vestments, he'll recite psalms, imploring divine assistance, then send up prayers to ward off the evils of the air, such as phantoms, storms, and lightning. After washing and drying the bell, he will anoint it, then fill its cavity with the smoke of incense and myrrh."

With that, Brother Edmund brought his gaze back to the child he sought to persuade. "After that the bishop will read a passage from the Gospel, the one that tells a tale of Mary and Martha."

Martha gasped in astonishment. "Martha is my name," she cried. "The bell will hear my name?"

Edmund nodded. "The bell will hear your name, but only if you allow it to go home."

Martha offered a single firm nod. "The bell wants to go home."

"Then so it shall," the monk replied, almost smiling. He looked up at his employer.

"Although this is not exactly the business of the Coronarius, because the ownership of the bell is disputed, I feel I must add its tale to our roll. It seems to me that it should be written somewhere. Will that suit you?"

"As you see fit, Brother Edmund," Faucon said in surprise. Edmund had never before asked his permission about what he added or didn't add to their record.

"Then this is what I shall note. I will say that the bell, which had been thought stolen, had instead been given by Sir Robert of Offord to his granddaughter Lady Martha of Bagot," Edmund said, speaking as much to himself as to his employer. "I will write that Lady Bagot once of Offord swears that two years ago Sir Robert promised the bell to his granddaughter as her dowry. I will add that Lady Martha affirms that Sir Robert repeated that same to her when he put the bell into her possession." He paused, his brow creased in thought. "However, I feel I must at the same time note that in the interim, Sir Robert had falsely promised the bell as dower to Lady Offord."

"If you like, you may add that it's my opinion Sir Robert knew he had wrongly made the bell Lady Offord's dower, and swiftly regretted his decision," Faucon said.

"That could help." Edmund again paused. His eyes narrowed as he tapped a finger to his chin. "It cannot be important to include that the bell was sewn inside the lady's plaything. After that, I'll inscribe that Lady Martha expresses the desire to make a gift of the bell to Prior Thierry of the Priory of Saint Peter ad Vincula in Wootton Wawen, doing so in honor of Sir Robert."

As he took up a new quill and reclaimed his knife from his employer, Edmund again hesitated. "Do you think that will be enough to protect the bell from Sir Adam? I feel certain the knight will try to claim it, perhaps even once again going to the priory to take it, as he has already once done. As he is Lady Martha's father, that is his right," he warned his employer.

"But only if he is truly Lady Martha's father," Faucon replied.

From the loft above, Idonea gave a startled gasp. He glanced up to see a wide-eyed Helena retreat from the loft's edge and out of his view. Although Lady Bagot didn't turn to look at them, her posture said she now listened closely.

Faucon addressed her back. "My lady, you'll never have what you or your father wanted for Lady Martha from this bell. The only question that remains is whether you allow Sir Adam to steal all hope of any future for either you or your daughter."

"If Sir Adam takes the bell," he continued, "I suspect he'll swiftly reduce it to the precious metal from which it's made."

"But that would doom him to hell," Edmund interrupted in shock.

Faucon slanted a look at him. "Where he already goes for murdering his father-by-marriage," he pointed out. "Such a man cares for nothing but the comfortable weight that silver will add to his purse, especially when no one save God is the wiser."

Again, he shifted to speak to Lady Joia. The lady now had her head turned to the side as if she sought to see him. "But if you allow Brother Edmund to note the truth of Lady Martha's parentage, the bell will be forever safe from your husband."

The lady drew a deep breath. Her shoulders lifted. "The bell will be safe, but what of me and my daughter, both of my daughters? Sir Adam has already murdered once to get what he wants," she warned quietly.

"Brother Edmund," Faucon said to his clerk as he continued to watch the lady's back, "add this to your scribbling. Say that Lady Martha makes a gift of the bell to the priory, in return for a pension for herself and her lady mother in a convent."

"Is that the desire of the ladies?" Edmund replied, glancing from his employer to Lady Bagot's back.

"Tell me, Brother," Faucon asked his clerk before the lady could respond, "how long must a husband wait before he's free to remarry after his wife retires to a convent?"

"Seven years," the monk replied swiftly. "That is, unless the man wishes to sue for an annulment, which will take almost as long and cost him dearly. Most men find it more practical to wait the full term."

Her back still turned, the lady freed a quiet breathy sound, then another and then repeated the sound yet again. It was a moment before Faucon recognized her laughter.

Chapter Nineteen

I t took Edmund much longer to complete his scribbling than he expected. That was because he decided
to create two chirographs— one for Lady Bagot, the
other for Prior Thierry— that included the terms for the
return of the bell. After that, he wrote a letter for Lady
Offord, informing her father that his daughter was now
a widow, which Faucon agreed to see made its way to
Londontown. By then, Eustace had returned home,
bringing news that Sir Adam had departed Offord,
taking with him all the horses belonging to Offord and
Bagot.

With Eustace came one Medwyn, one of the Offord's
villagers. He'd been among the jurors to protest Lady
Joia's innocence. Medwyn wanted his Crowner to know
that Sir Adam was sending him to Killingworth to
demand the sheriff arrest Lady Bagot for her father's
murder. That ploy resulted in Faucon hiring Eustace
and an oxcart to carry all the ladies to Pinley Priory, a
nearby Cistercian convent, for their safety.

It wasn't until mid-morning the next day before
they departed Offord. Alf parted ways with them
outside the village bounds, turning for Wootton Wawen
to bring Prior Thierry to the convent. After he led his
party across the Alne and found the track that led north
toward both the convent and Blacklea, Faucon lost
himself to the journey.

Sunlight gleamed on hill and pasture, and found
blue-black in the ravens soaring overhead. The gale of
a few days ago had left the trees dressed in the tattered

229

remains of their rusty fall finery. Riding directly behind him, Brother Edmund chanted his prayers in a low voice. Faucon savored air spiced with that scent particular to autumn, then sighed out tension. The hours passed to the steady huff of oxen, the creak of wooden cart wheels, and the jingle of the metal rings on Legate's harness.

As they drew near the fork that would take them to the convent, Faucon squinted into the distance. Two mounted men waited along the path. It was Alf on his piebald and a man mounted on a tall gray horse. If that was Prior Thierry, then the churchman once again wore the tunic and cloak of a nobleman.

Faucon kicked Legate into a canter, his gaze locked on the gray steed. As he drew nearer, he recognized the destrier. The horse was an old man for sure, but he wore his battle scars proudly, his face and form pronouncing his great worth. What sin had that Continental nobleman, one who could afford such a horse, committed that resulted in his banishment to a foreign and rural priory?

"Did you bring the bell?" Prior Thierry demanded before Faucon brought Legate to a halt a little distance from the warhorse.

"It comes with our party," Faucon replied.

"So there was no thief?" the prior wanted to know.

"There was not," Faucon agreed. "Instead, Sir Robert had hidden it with Lady Martha, the daughter of Lady Bagot, telling his granddaughter it was her dowry. The little lady chooses instead to return it to you and her Church, doing so to honor the man who loved her dearly. In return for her gift, she begs you to aid her and her mother in securing a pension for them at a convent."

"With the Cistercians?" the prior asked in surprise,

the jerk of his head indicating the path that led to Pinley. His sneer was filled with Benedictine snobbery.

Faucon shook his head. "Not necessarily. We travel to Pinley Priory for Lady Bagot's safety. Sir Adam banished her from her home and hearth after her father's death," he added carefully, not wishing to reveal much of Lady Joia's tale or Sir Adam's crime.

"That's hardly surprising," the Churchman replied, sneering still.

"What say you to the lady's request?" Faucon pressed. His tone was intense enough that it set the big gray to fretting.

Although his knees and hands barely moved, Prior Thierry brought the dangerous beast back to a calm stance. "I would first ask what right this daughter of Bagot has to make such a gift without her father's consent." The Churchman's brows lifted. "I'm guessing he cannot know she has it, for that man would never allow it out of his possession if he did."

Faucon smiled. "Martha of Bagot is not Sir Adam's child. He has no right to control what is hers, and this Sir Robert knew when he gave the bell to his grand-daughter."

That teased a quick and not unappreciative laugh from the prior. "Lady Bagot admits to her sin? Does she name the father?"

"Sir Luc of Bagot, who is also banished by his older brother," Faucon replied.

"Huh," the foreign Churchman offered on a harsh breath. "How is it that you, Coronarius, should become the advocate for another man's wife and her bastard?"

Faucon met the noble prior's dark gaze. "I erred, Father Prior," he replied simply.

Again the prior's brows lifted. He studied Faucon for a moment, then nodded. "And now you seek to make right what you set wrong. Here's a path I know well enough. You have my word. Once I know the bell is the one Sir Robert showed me and I have it in my possession, all will be arranged as the ladies require."

"There is one other request. Lady Martha begs that she might be allowed to attend the rededication ceremony for the bell," Faucon told him.

That won him a quizzical look from the former nobleman. "Why would a child make such a request?"

"She has formed an attachment to the bell," Faucon told him. "She wishes to see for herself that it is happily and safely home."

Much to his surprise, Prior Thierry's expression softened. He nodded. "A perceptive child, I think. All of this is acceptable to me, once I see the bell for myself."

Not wanting to startle the destrier, Faucon turned Legate and rode a short distance back toward his party. He put his fingers to his lips and freed a sharp whistle to catch their attention. "Hie, Brother Edmund," he called to the monk with a wave.

As Edmund raised his arm in acknowledgment, another man's distant, piercing whistle echoed from the path in the direction of Blacklea. It was followed by a second shorter whistle, then a third longer one.

"Will?" Faucon whispered in abject surprise.

He roweled Legate around and stared ahead on the track. At first, there was only haze. Then Legate's brother appeared, racing full out. A few breaths later and four more horses appeared out of the haze. God take them, the sheriff's men had mistaken Will for him!

"Stand ready here, Alf. My brother brings men to us," he called to the soldier, then again turned Legate toward his party.

Edmund's donkey had barely started away from the oxcart. "We are attacked! Protect the ladies any way you can," Faucon shouted, then started Legate back toward Alf.

Will was now only yards away. He rode crouched in the saddle, his head almost pressed against Nuncio's neck. As Faucon and Alf drew their swords, Prior Thierry brought his destrier alongside Legate.

As Nuncio carried Will past them, the Churchman pulled a stout wooden staff from the back of his saddle where once his shield would have hung. "Stay mounted or die under his hooves," the prior commanded. There was aught in his tone that won him their instant compliance.

Then almost as one, nobleman, knight, and soldier put their heels to their mounts and rode at the oncoming soldiers. Faucon aimed Legate at the man in the lead. His horse was exhausted, running with sides heaving and mouth open. Shouting, the soldier raised his sword high. Keeping his own weapon close, Faucon slowed Legate the instant before they met. Startled, the soldier caught back his blow and took a blow to his thigh for his trouble. Screaming, the man dropped his weapon. Free from control, his panicked horse circled and sent his rider flying as Faucon rode past.

Swords clashed to Faucon's left as Alf engaged his man. To his right, the prior swung his staff into the head of the third man. His skull cracked like an egg. Knight and nobleman rode toward the last man.

"To me!" the fourth soldier shouted as he turned his mount to race back the way he'd come.

"Mine," Prior Thierry roared at Faucon.

Faucon instantly turned Legate back toward Alf, his sword raised high. The sheriff's man shoved at Alf's sword and kicked at the piebald, trying to break free to protect his back from this new threat. He wasn't fast enough. Faucon buried his sword into the man's ex-

233

posed neck.

Roweling Legate around, ready to aid the prior, he was in time to watch the former nobleman bring his gray alongside the escaping soldier, then drive his staff like a lance into the man's back. As the soldier arched in his saddle Prior Thierry rode past, bringing his staff around for a backhanded blow that sent the man flying from his horse. Then he turned the big gray and drove him toward the fallen man.

As the soldier rolled and scrabbled in the mud to escape, the destrier rose with a scream and lunged at the fallen man, slamming his front hooves down upon the man's chest. When he had killed that one, the prior allowed the destrier to seek out the rest.

"We are forever bonded, he and I," Prior Thierry said to Faucon and Will, stroking the nose of his dangerous horse.

The prior hadn't allowed the knights or Alf to dismount until the bloodlust had left his destrier. Now, the deadly animal acted the part of pet, snorting and pushing his head closer to his master as if begging for more pats. Behind them, Brother Edmund was praying over the four mangled corpses that Alf and Eustace had laid along the path. The two commoners were gathering up their horses. As for the ladies, they had been content to remain in the cart, keeping their distance from the fork.

"But you are avowed. How is it that you can keep him?" Will asked, once again brushing at his face and beard. His wild ride had left him befouled with mud and sweat.

Prior Thierry smiled at that. "I argued that he had

not long to live and it was unsafe to deny him his beloved master." Then he winked. "There were those determined that I should end my life cloistered. When they realized he," he again rubbed the horse's nose, "was all that kept me tied to your world, my former world, I had my dispensation."

Then the Churchman looked at Faucon. "So, tell me, Coronarius. Whose souls have we just sent to meet heavenly justice?"

Faucon hesitated. More than anything, he didn't want to expose these soldiers as Sir Alain's men. Nor did he wish to lie to either Will or the Churchman. That left only a dodge. "What say you, Will? Who were these men, and how did they come to be chasing you?"

His brother frowned at him. "How am I to know who they are? This is your shire, not mine. Nor did I think to ask them what they wanted when we noticed each other along the road. Instead I assumed they were outlaws intent on murdering a lone traveler, for they took up the chase immediately."

Then Will smiled. The spread of his lips was untouched by any emotion save relief. It was his beloved brother, the boy who had almost perished in that accident, who looked at Faucon. "You cannot know how glad I was to hear your whistle, Pery."

Faucon grinned. "And you cannot know how surprised I was to hear yours," he replied.

"So now what?" the prior asked, glancing between the brothers.

Still smiling, Faucon looked at the Churchman. "Now, I call Brother Edmund to join us, then we walk to the cart where he left his basket. There, Lady Martha will present you with her bell."

saint eucherius of lyon's day

"**S**ister?"

The single whispered word startles me out of my inner silence. Today, on the day that celebrates the saintly bishop, Eucherius of Lyon, I have been contemplating the martyrdom of the Theban Legion. Six thousand, six hundred sixty-six Christian soldiers gave up their lives rather than enter battle against fellow Christians. I chose the lesson of Saint Eucherius to battle the despair that eats at me, that has eaten at me since I was confined to the infirmary.

I feel it. My time is at hand. But I cannot leave, not while we are only eleven. I promised them perfect paradise for eternity. But without the twelfth, do I doom us all to damnation or only myself?

As I return to consciousness, I gaze upon angelic perfection. The child's thick dark hair, caught in a braid that spills over one shoulder, frames her oval face. Her dark brows curve gently over clear blue almond-shaped eyes. Her nose is narrow, her cheekbones high. She is the image of our Lord's blessed mother as a child.

She notices that I watch her. Her lips spread into a smile so sweet, so completely filled with innocence, that I cannot help but smile in return.

"I wanted to come sooner," she tells me. By her careful, toneless voice, I know she is one of our students, a girl sent by her parents to learn wifely skills. This voice is their first lesson. "But Mother Superior bid

236

me wait. She said you were yet too ill for visitors."

Her comment confuses me for a moment. Then a memory rises. This is the child who breached my privacy. She is the reason I am trapped in the infirmary.

She is the reason I have not yet died.

The instant that thought rises out of my quiet center, the place where He lives in me, holy light bursts forth from her eyes. The illumination given to angels expands until her face and then her body is alight in glorious radiance.

Then the holy flame reaches out to me. I am overcome by the ecstasy of His touch. This is the one. She is why my flesh did not give way to the despair of my soul.

"Who are you?" I breathe in humble question to this unearthly creature.

Given the heat of the light that pulses from her, I expect the deafening voice of an archangel. Instead, she speaks with the voice of a bell, each crystalline syllable so exquisite that I am overcome by wave after wave of heavenly joy.

"I am Marianne, daughter of Sir John and Lady Marian of Blacklea."

A Note From Denise

Thank you for reading my fourth mystery novel and the hardest book I've ever had the displeasure to write. There are no words to express how lost I got in my own plot and how hard it was to find my way out of that morass. Here is the quote that led me astray and had me caught for all those months:

"I love the old ways, the simple way of poison where we too are as strong as men." *Medea,* Euripides

This goes to show that even when you think you've figured out this writing thing, something unusual pops up to make you humble all over again. However, I'm still loving Faucon and his mysteries, and this little hiccup/hiccough isn't going to make me quit now. So, on I go into my nineteenth book (if you're counting, I have one ghostwritten book which has never been published), bruised, battered and better for the experience.

As I wrote this book, I once again found myself writing about mistreated women. I swear I'm not on a crusade. It's just a fact of life for women in the Twelfth Century. But as you may have noticed at the end of the book, there was always a way to get even.

And, of course, if you liked the book, or I suppose even if you didn't, please consider leaving a review. If you've found any formatting or typographical errors, please let me know by email at:

denise@denisedomning.com.

I appreciate the chance to correct my mistakes.

Glossary

This book includes of number of Medieval terms. I've defined the ones I think might be unfamiliar. If you find others you'd like defined, let me know at denise @denisedomning.com and I'll add them to the list.

Chausses   Stockings made of cloth (not knitted). Each leg ties onto the waist cord of the braies.

Chirograph
            A written duplicate of something scribed into the official record. Often noted on a scrap of parchment, the chirograph usually includes a signet imprint of the issuing party and serves as proof of a promise or other legal agreement.

Courser   A swift, strong horse, used as a war-horse among those knights unable to afford the fabulously expensive and war-trained destrier.

Crowner   From the Latin *Coronarius,* meaning Servant of the Crown. The word eventually evolves into 'Coroner.'

Destrier   Usually stallions, bred specifically for war, with powerful hindquarters and the ability to coil and spring stop, spin, turn or sprint forward. They were as much a weapon as the knight's sword.

Dower   The bridegroom's offering to his bride. Generally dower should be one-third the value of the bride's dowry. Dower is an annuity for the wife, meant to support her after her husband's death. She holds her dower until death, and can accrue dower over the course of multiple marriages. Upon her death, her dower returns to the heirs of the original owner.

Dowry   What the bride brings to her husband upon marriage. Depending on her class, this can be a throne, estates, a skill (such as needlework), or in the case of peasant brides, pots and pans and other household goods.

Hauberk   A heavy leather or padded vest, sometimes sewn with steel rings. Usually worn in place of a chain mail tunic by common soldiers.

Hemp   A soft, strong fiber plant with edible seeds. Hemp can be twisted into rope or woven for use in making everything from storage bags to mattress covers.

Hundred   A geographic division of a county or shire. It once likely referred to an area capable of providing a hundred men at arms, or containing a hundred homes.

By the 12th Century it is often a far
larger area.

Inland   Land ineligible to be taxed by the
            Crown.

 Pleas of the Crown
            The list of pleas made to the king or his
            representative for justice. Not unlike
            the list of crimes and complaints filed
            at your local police station.

Toft & Croft
            A toft is the area of land on which a
            peasant's house sits. The croft, gener-
            ally measuring seven hundred feet in
            length and forty in width. It was in the
            croft that a serf would grow their per-
            sonal food staples, such as onions, gar-
            lic, turnips and other root crops, le-
            gumes and some grains.

Withe   A thin, supple willow (but also hazel or
            ash) branch